7 STEPS DOWN

A Novel of World War II Anzio

by

John Sears Barker

PublishAmerica
Baltimore

First printing

ISBN: 1-4241-7163-6 (softcover)
ISBN: 978-1-61582-512-7 (hardcover)
PUBLISHED BY PUBLISHAMERICA, LLLP
www.publishamerica.com
Baltimore

Printed in the United States of America

For
Jeshua

Carry on!

CHAPTER ONE

Sandy took a stance at the intersection where the *strada* leading in from the bay met the boundary road that defined the eastern edge of the deserted town. He turned slowly, studying the gaping black windows in the vacated buildings on his west and the almost flat but scrubby countryside to the east. He lifted his hands to the sky, his right hand flourishing his rifle, and as if beseeching the heavens, cried: "Where the Hell is everybody?"

Fortunately no one answered. If there had been any snipers hidden in the town, they would certainly have had Sandy in their sights by now. We had so far passed an uneventful morning and would just as soon keep it that way. The seven of us had jumped from the first launch in the two o'clock morning blackness, high-stepped through the lengthy stretch of shallow waters, crouched and crept along the fish-odored waterfront, waddled up and down sidestreets, and leap-frogged door-to-door up the littered boulevard that bisected the town—all without firing a single shot.

We had sprawled behind a low block wall that enclosed someone's corner patio, waiting for Company D to catch up with us. Our job had been to flush out, or smoke-mark for navy shelling, any pockets of possible ambush. But there were none. We had crawled through a lonely morning.

A few shots to our south suggested that the Ranger patrol might have found some pockets of resistance near Nettuno, but the shots could have been target practice with foraging rats, just to relieve the boredom. Our sector was free of even gutter rats.

We stretched out behind a low stone wall that edged a tile patio fronting a two-level dirty-white shop with black letters near the roof line, reading: *Vino Formaggio d' Antonio*. Regrettably, not open for business, partly because it was just about daybreak, too early for either connoisseurs or winos, but mainly because there was no Antonio, or anyone else, as far as we could tell, left in Anzio.

Sarge was helping Mouse unload the forty-pound radio that he had been backpacking since midnight. Sarge turned slowly toward the intersection where Sandy was continuing his slow pirouettes. Not quite a scream but more that a stage whisper, Sarge called: "Sandy, get your rear in here before someone shoots it off!"

Sandy was traveling on a morningful of adrenaline, as were we all, but basic training had taught most of us how to "take ten" and go limp. A soldier can drop anywhere, in any posture, at the magic words "take ten." He's not unconscious—just appears that way. He is still alert for the hacking introduction of a non-com clearing his throat to bark out the next order, the whine of an incoming shell, or even the footfall of an approaching officer's oxford.

So we were all stretched out in various forms of stupor, while Sandy remained wired for explosion.

With obvious reluctance, Sandy dragged his feet toward our walled-in front yard. As he reached the gap in the wall, he turned, raised his rifle to his shoulder, and shot the knocker off the blue door on the other side of the *strada*. We all jumped in unison and leveled our rifles over the low wall, until we realized that Sandy was acting the crackpot again. "Jerk…schmo…crackpot…jackass…nutcase. . . ." A chorus of insults pummeled Sandy, and he grinned. "Well, pardon me," he said and slunk down beside us, a somewhat relieved but indignant sharpshooter.

Sarge lowered the radio from where Mouse had placed it on the wall to a more sheltered nook beside the wall. "Let's not give 'em too juicy a target, eh, Mouse?" He pulled earphones over his head, squelched the static, adjusted dials, lifted the mike.

"Red dog calling Thin Man," he signaled. "Thin Man, this is Red Dog. Come in. Over."

Low hum, crackles, slight whistle, silence. "Red Dog calling Thin Man. Come in Thin Man. This is Red Dog. Over."

More crackling. Then a voice. "Red Dog, this is Thin Man. Read you loud and clear. Position please. Over."

Sarge studied the map he had spread on top of the wall. "Thin Man, we're at Ready H on map 214, as planned. All quiet. Has been all morning. The place is deserted. Not a soul. No one expected us. We could go on twenty miles more today. Over."

"Negative, Red Dog. Stay put as planned. Company D will be coming up in an hour or so to set up a defense perimeter. We'll make sure we can defend what we've got before we strike out for more. I'll be by in a couple of hours, as soon as we find a location for headquarters. Meantime you lay low and wait for me. Over."

"Right, Cap. Red Dog over and out." Sarge hung up the microphone and sighed. A couple of hours, probably more, the army way—hurry up and wait. By that time, the Germans would have caught on and would be on their way to make us pay for it. "Jersey," he said, "you come with me. We'll go for a brief look around. The rest of you, shake down this building, see if it's habitable, but watch out for boobies. Watch for Company D. And get some rest. We'll probably be going out tonight." He shouldered his Tommy while Jersey slung his M-1 and followed him through the gate, across the perimeter road, and into the low scrub growth that marked the challenge beyond. They walked east into the first full appearance of the white morning sun.

That left Mouse in charge, a responsibility he accepted reluctantly. His sergeant stripes came from his technical training in radio, not from leadership experience. Sergeant Tandy Schimmer had been a disk jockey back in a small backwater town in southern Virginia when he enlisted in the army the day after Pearl Harbor, as soon as he could get to Richmond. He didn't really need a nickname. Tandy seemed to fit him naturally. But Sarge pinned new nicknames on everyone, as his personal crutch for separating the Joes and Johns. Schimmer happened to be chasing a mouse around the orderly room with a push broom when Sarge came looking for the radio operator assigned to his new squad. Naturally, Sarge dubbed him "Mouse," even though his six-foot 180-pound frame belied the nickname. Schimmer accepted the new name cheerfully, knowing it could hardly be derogatory, pleased to lose the haughty Tandy that befit a radio disk jockey but not a GI Joe.

Mouse swept his hand toward the building. "Sandy, you scout out the building. Bull, check out that shed. Joe, you take up post at that east corner. Boots, the west corner. We'll then take a break 'til D Company comes by." With that exercise in command, Mouse figured he had done his duty and collapsed beside the wall.

Corporal Phelps Bricker, a former photostat operator back in Anderson, South Carolina, had earned his nickname, of course, because of his sandy hair. He carried a "fourth" after his name in important family matters, as in Phelps Bricker IV, great-grandson of a Confederate patriarch, but he disdained the title and all it stood for, and he welcomed the "greetings" when he was drafted in mid-1942, as he welcomed the nickname "Sandy."

Joe, on the other hand, had no obvious reason for Sarge to call him "Joe." Simon Coffey was a New England highschool teacher, who lost his wife and daughter in a car accident along an icy Maine coast road and had immediately abandoned his physics class for olive drab back in 1940. Even then, he was thirty years old and reasonably certain to escape the draft, but Simon Coffey was running from his past. Coffey shunned promotions and responsibility. Once back in basic training, he had been called up to the orderly room and told he'd be promoted to sergeant, mostly because of his maturity in a sea of teenagers. Thereupon Coffey swung a rounder that floored the personnel clerk, spent a week in the post stockade, and lost not only the promised sergeant stripes but his own PFC stripe. The CO got the message, and the award of corporal stripes two years later was an unannounced routine action that Coffey ignored as long as he didn't have to wear the stripes. He was assigned to C Squad, where Sarge could have just accepted "Coffey" as a nickname in itself, but Sarge reasoned: "coffee…cup of joe…GI Joe…Joe," and "Joe" stuck. Now 33, Joe was a tempering influence on us younger squad members.

My own Sarge-ordained moniker was "Boots," probably because back at base Sarge always singled me out in morning roll call for wearing somewhat less than glistening boots, and more mornings than not, he would send me back to polish my boots again while the rest of the squad went to breakfast. I was the newest member of the squad, still just 18 when assigned, and not entirely over my baby fat. Sarge took it off fast, with skipped bacon-and-eggs and extra PT. And I was lean and wiry when we boarded the Liberty ship at Newport News, happy with the nickname "Boots." I thought it also reflected my position in our scout formation where I brought up the rear, the "boot" so to speak, of our rifle squad.

We had started as the twelve-man rifle squad, C Squad, Second Platoon. Just as we boarded the Liberty ship for God knew where, one of the squad was taken off with appendicitis. Far at sea, after two weeks of zigzagging, we learned that we were not on our way to England as we had presumed, but we were to set up a beachhead in Morocco, as the backdoor to North Africa and a refueling point for B-24 bombers to follow, enroute from the US to Ploesti targets by way of South America and Dakar. Most of us had never heard of Casablanca, or even Morocco for that matter, and when we reached it, two more of the squad were too sick to get off the boat. We were then down to nine men, and we lost another one with a broken leg on the beach. The eighth man was sent as a messenger back to division headquarters where he was presumably drafted into other duties for we never saw him again either. Not a shot fired yet and we had lost five of our original dozen.

A company field officer renamed us a recon squad, gave us a map, marked off a fort to the northeast, in the general direction of Algiers, and told us to find out if the fort was Vichy French or Free French. All forts in Morocco were manned by Vichy French with an occasional German adviser, but they frequently became Free French as Allied troops approached. As sporadic fire rose from the beaches, while the Allied command searched for someone from whom they could demand a surrender, we started the six-hour hike along the deserted hard pan road. Sandy, walking left point, twenty feet off the road, signaled when the fort came into sight just around the next bend, while I, walking rear sweep in the center of the road forty feet back, signaled a jeep coming up behind us. The jeep, with a PFC driver and a First Lieutenant passenger, slowed past the squad strung out along the right side of the road and stopped at Sarge's post on the left side of the road. Sarge saluted.

"Forget the formalities in a war zone, Sergeant," the lieutenant said, but returned the salute automatically. "All it does is direct the enemy's attention to special targets. Now, who are you?"

"C Squad, Second Platoon, Company D," Sarge said.

"Recon squad?"

"Not usually, sir. Evidently we're on a recon mission at the moment, but we're just a normal rifle squad, half-strength."

"What are you after?"

"Just around that bend, sir, there's a Moroccan fort. We're to radio back whether it's friendly or might put up a fight."

"Mind if I join you?"

"As you wish, sir. But we don't know what we're in for."

"Pay no attention to me. I'll just tag along behind and take notes." The lieutenant waved the jeep over to the side of the road and told the driver to follow slowly. Then he dropped back to join me at squad tail-end, as we moved cautiously toward the seemingly deserted fort. When we reached the far side of the bend, there was clear visibility between the fort and us. Now was the time for some resistance, if any were to come. So far, French resistance had been more a soldier's reflex action than a plan. No one seemed to speak for the French forces to order either a fight or surrender, so there were two days of half-hearted but effective fire from various French forces, mostly navy. This fort, however, eighteen miles along the road to Algeria, evidently had a radio and had heard that F4F Wildcats from the carrier Santee, had made mincemeat out of a seventy-truck convoy with a thousand French troops on its way to relieve Casablanca. The French tri-color quickly dropped from the staff and two French tri-colors were raised, signifying friend, as General Eisenhower had suggested in pamphlets dropped all over the area. A soldier is reluctant to raise a white flag, but

Eisenhower had suggested he could show cooperation by raising two French flags in place of one and we'd get the message.

We marched into the fort, not certain of what we'd run into, but two score of bathrobed Moroccan fighters and rumpled French officers stood at attention before a pile of rifles and side arms. Our newly acquired lieutenant came forward to accept their surrender. Sarge unburdened Mouse of his radio and called an all-clear back to headquarters. Within an hour, truckloads of GIs, dragging howitzers, raced past us on the road to Algiers.

And that was how we met Lieutenant, soon to be Captain, Warren House, who arranged to have us reassigned to Headquarters, although still attached to Company D for rations and quarters. House, who escaped Sarge's nicknaming until he was promoted, made up the designation 714th Reconnaissance Squad, since there was no T/O for us, and dubbed us "Red Dog."

Captain House, who appeared on the Table of Organization as part of Army G2, led us through Algiers and Tunisia, completing Operation Torch, then on to Sicily in Operation Husky seven months later, and Salerno two months after that. On each invasion, Red Dog had waded ashore a day earlier to radio back to Army Intelligence what we learned of German defense layouts and to cause whatever small mischief lay within our limited capabilities. In hindsight, we were probably safer than the landing forces. By October of 1943 we were enjoying haircuts and baths in Naples, celebrating my nineteenth birthday, and wondering what Captain House had in mind for us next.

The Allies were pinned down by the brilliantly engineered Gustav line that belted the peninsula just north of Naples and halted all further northward movement. If Captain House expected us to get behind that line, night or day, he would have to find invisible ponchos for us. Instead he found a back door, and we crept into an almost abandoned town some ninety miles west by north of the Gustav line and only forty miles south of Rome. Now, if Captain House could get a bit of guts for General Lucas and the Fifth Army's VI Corps, we could have dinner tonight in Rome and we could let the Gustav line just shrivel up and fade away.

Instead, we sat on the tiles and cleaned our rifles, while General Lucas looked for a place to hang his maps. He found one, of course—a deep underground wine cellar, a flight of steps down from a walled back yard, pocked with alcoves, each intended to hold a year's grape juice and now marked as separate offices for headquarters staff, secure from bombs and shells and other inconveniences. There was no sign over the door, on the theory that those people who had any legitimate business with Corps Headquarters would know where it was. Only the MP stationed at the backyard gate gave any clue that there might be something of importance behind the stained and mossy stuccoed walls.

Antonio's equally stained and mossy stuccoed walls surrounded a basement devoid of any furnishings beyond shards of broken glass from the half-dozen shoulder-high windows and an upper floor with a zinc-covered bar and a dozen tables with chairs, along with a corner portion of the roof that had been caved in evidently by a U. S. Navy calling card. A stairway from a small landing on the patio led up nine steps to the top level, each side carrying a wrought iron railing. For safety reasons, these railings had escaped the scrap drives—unlike the fence rails that once topped the low wall around us and were now probably sinking under the shifting sands of the Sahara as parts of a Fiat tank.

To the left of the main stair, a smaller staircase led down seven steps to the basement. A lean-to shed to the right of the landing held another dozen folding tables, umbrellas, and three dozen chairs, evidently to complete the patio in better times. Sandy and Bull reported the whole layout free of booby traps, the upper level secure but somewhat exposed to the weather, the lower level good for bivouac if we wanted to sleep on a cement floor. We elected to sleep under the January sun, at least until nightfall when we'd likely find no sleep at all.

The click of an M-1 bolt brought us up on our knees as we turned to find whatever threat had alerted Joe. He stood in the center of the patio, his rifle trained on the top of a small head that appeared just above the far corner wall, framed by two clutches of dirty fingers. "Well, if it isn't Kilroy," Joe said. "Don't sneak up like that on anyone, son, especially someone with a rifle. You could'a gotten your head shot off. Who are you?"

A well-tanned boy of about ten sunny summers stood slowly and stared at Joe's rifle. "Me *Guillermo*. Willie. You Joe?"

Joe smiled and started to ask how Willie knew his name, then quickly realized that all GI's in Italy were Joes. From the pocket of his field jacket he produced a heavy bar of waxy chocolate from an earlier K ration and offered it to the boy. Willie grabbed it hesitantly at first, then avidly as he realized it was edible. "Where are your folks, Willie? Where's your home?"

Willie looked puzzled.

Joe realized Willie's English was not well rehearsed and Joe had spoken too rapidly. "Your home," Joe repeated slowly. "*Casa? Famiglia?*" Joe was surprised to find he knew even that much Italian. "*Dove?*" Joe swept his arm to take in the town.

Willie pointed across the street behind the wine shop to a row of two-story shops and apartments. "*La,*" Willie said. "You come. *Mi mama, mi zio, mi surella* Anita. You come. Anita *canta*. Eh, Joe?"

"Later," Joe said. This would be a good chance, provided it wasn't a trap, to find out how many people were left in Anzio, why the others had taken off, how they got advance word of our coming. Sarge could decide what to do. He looked at his watch. "You come back in three hours." He held up three fingers and pointed again at his watch. "*Tre oras, no? Comprende?*"

"*Si, si,* Joe. Cigarette?"

"You're too young to smoke," Joe said, but he reached into his jacket pocket and tossed a small three-pack of Chesterfields from a K-ration to Willie.

"*Por mi zio.*" Willie said. And the Kilroy figure paused for one last look at us from the top of the low wall, then ducked and scurried along the drainage ditch and around the corner.

Mouse told Joe and me to stand guard while the others caught a couple of hour's sack time. We took up posts at opposite corners of the patio, which put me in the southwest corner and first to hear the rumble of trucks. So much for sack time.

The squad stared over the wall and watched a steady line of trucks come up the boulevard, stop at the circumference road, unload platoon after platoon, and turn back down the *strada* for another load. Company D, after four hours of marshaling around the waterfront, skirmished off into the low brush and random trees to the north and east, to be followed by other remnants of the Company. One squad pitched a pyramidal tent a few yards off into the wild to serve as Company Headquarters, another squad pitched a second tent a few yards beyond that to serve as a first-aid station, and a third squad set up a field kitchen. Good. They'd get to the officer's club later. But maybe, along with the headquarters brass, we'd get a hot meal tonight.

But the boys three miles out would probably have to get by with K rations—tart lemonade powder, a small can of dog food called hash, a hardtack biscuit, and a chocolate bar that could drive nails. We visualized at least creamed chipped beef on toast with hot coffee, but Sarge scuttled that thought as soon as he returned. We'd be eating K rations, too.

Sarge and Jersey sauntered back into the patio just as the last of Company D disappeared into the scrub and Captain House drove up in a chauffeured jeep.

Mouse called: "Atten-*shun,*" but the captain waved him off.

"As you were," Captain House said. "Skip the formalities out here. Save 'em for base camp." He turned to Sarge and Jersey. "You two been out, have you? Find anything, Crafton?"

"We only put in a few miles, sir," Sergeant Roger Crafton said. It was strange to hear Captain House call him Crafton, since we knew him almost exclusively as Sarge. We sometimes played his nickname game and out of his hearing called him "Nails" when we learned he had been a roofer back in civilian life, but we seldom heard "Crafton."

Sarge shrugged. "Nothing there. No one. No defense lines, no assault troops. If our objectives are those Alban Hills over there," Sarge waved toward the northeast where the peaks of distant hills, twenty miles on the far horizon, were just emerging from the morning mist, "we can drive right up the highway and be there in an hour."

"You saw no signs of German reaction?"

"Oh, a couple of truckloads of infantry heading down from Rome, but they were shot up pretty good by our Mustangs. And there were a few patrols around Aprilia. But there can't be more than a company of Krauts in the whole area. I tell you, sir, we got an open road if we act fast."

"That your impression, too, Varlas?" Corporal Ricardo Varlas had earned his nickname Jersey obviously because his accent belied his origin, Jersey City, where he had been a gas station attendant before being drafted. He was only 20, a year older than I was, but he was as tough as a hijacked chicken roasted over a sterno fire.

"Yes, sir. You could truck dere in less'n an hour without firing a shot, march dere in a few hours. Cut da road to Rome, block any resupply to or retreat from Cassino. The British could march on into Rome in a whistle and toot." No one quite knew what Jersey meant, but we were aware that he had picked up some British expressions from his brief association with them in the *trattorias* of Naples. The intent was clear.

"General Lucas intends to stick by his orders." House said. "According to General Clark, our first objective is to prepare defense lines and divert German forces from the Gustav line. We're expecting some strong counterattacks. Only if we can contain the Germans and secure our position here can we think about cutting Highway 7."

"But there are no Germans to contain," Sarge argued. "There will be in a day or two, I bet. But right now the British on our north flank could march into *Campoleone,* the Third Division and the Rangers from *Anzio* could reach *Cisterna*, and the Five-oh-Ninth from *Nettuno* could take *Littorio*, all before tomorrow morning, probably without a casualty."

"Your strategy is interesting, Crafton, but intelligence coming into G2 suggests it's going to be tougher than your limited observation suggests. We'd better be well dug in before the Germans pour significant forces out of Rome into our sector. You take your squad out tonight and report any movements. If you happen to pick up a ranking staff officer along the way, that would be a coup. He'd be able to tell us more about what Fritz is up to than all our speculation. Incidentally, in case you haven't heard, the password is Fibber McGee, counter Allen's Alley. Set off before dark, if you can. Meantime, you need anything?"

"How about a jeep?" Sarge suggested.

"Behind enemy lines? You'd be spotted in a second. You're supposed to travel in secret as much as you can."

"We'd use it just to get a bit deeper, first. Then hide it for the return trip and go on afoot."

Captain House shook his head. "No go, Crafton. Materiel is not that plentiful yet here on the beach. You're on your own. And don't get too far out of radio range. I'll have the first sergeant monitoring the channel from twenty-one hundred hours until we hear from you." He looked around the patio and studied the building. "This place suitable as a base for you guys?"

Mouse intervened. "It's been checked out. Top floor damaged, but bottom floor secure. Could be a good base."

"Okay. I'll have your bedrolls and duffels dropped off here, along with some extra ordnance. I'll ask the MPs to station a guard near here."

"Right, sir." Sarge stood, some of the rest of us followed suit. Captain House waved a half-hearted salute and climbed back into his jeep. "Good hunting, Red Dog," he said.

The jeep was hardly out of sight before Mouse spotted a movement at the inner corner of the low wall. "Oh, ho," he cried, "Joe, your Kilroy is back."

We turned as one, and Willie presented himself. "Hello, Joe. You come see *mi mama?"*

Joe explained the appearance of Willie to Sarge and the invitation to visit his home and family. Sarge readily agreed. "Find out what you can, especially if there are any Germans hidden around here. But take someone with you." He looked around the patio. "Boots, you go with Joe. Watch for a trap, though. This town gives me the creeps. Be back in no more than an hour. Sandy, you follow 'em. See what house they go into. Wait five minutes, and if they don't come right back out and you don't hear gunfire, report back here." He turned to the rest of the squad. "The rest of you, get some sleep. We'll be going out in a couple of hours. We may be gone a couple of days, even. No guard needed with D Company practically on our doorstep. Just relax."

Joe and I, with Sandy thirty feet behind, followed Willie along the drainage ditch to a side street. Willie scurried ahead of us by at least ten feet, frequently looking back and grinning when he found us still following. He led us to a narrow alley, devoid of people, but studded with doors, no windows at ground level but a few windows above. He pushed open a weathered green door halfway along the alley and called out, *"Mama, ecco qui."*

We followed him up a flight of stairs, through a cloth-draped doorway, into a large room containing a table with four chairs, a wood-fueled range, a marble wash sink. In one corner stood a well-polished upright piano, and in an easy chair near the window sat an old man puffing on a pipe with a chubby young-teen girl trying to hide behind him. The room was dominated by *Mama* herself, short, heavy, and smiling.

"Benvenuto, " she said. She pointed to each occupant of the room, in turn, and said *"Guillermo, Anita, e mi fratello Vittorio. Me—Annetta. I make pizza."* She waved at the chairs and turned back to the stove.

"I'm Simon," Joe said, "and this is Gerry. You speak English, huh?" Joe said.

"Not really." The voice came from Vittorio, the old man in the arm chair. "I try to teach some. Annetta's husband is POW in Tennessee so good they learn some American before he come back full of strange talk."

"Where did you learn English?" Joe asked.

Vittorio grinned. "New York. Taxi driver. Twelve years. Then everything is *finito*. Taxi business no good in 1932. Come back home for visit, and Mussolini no let me go back. Too old for war, though. So I just sit. Now Mussolini gone, maybe I go back to New York after war ends. You from New York?"

"Maine," Joe said.

"Upstate New York," I offered. "You know where Corning is?"

"Oh, sure," Vittorio said. "Once drove taxi all the way to Corning when man from Berlin missed train. Two hundred dollars for one day's work, when cabs were going empty. I t'ink German had *relativos* in glass works there. If he smart, he stay there himself. But he not too smart. Two hundred dollars and twenty dollar tip big money, not smart money."

Annetta paused rolling out a circle of risen dough. Obviously Vittorio was enjoying a chance to speak English again with Americans, but he would talk all day if allowed to run free. Annetta called: "Anita, *cantare*."

Anita hesitated, turning a little red. But Annetta repeated her command, and Anita reluctantly crossed over to the piano, rolled back the keyboard cover, and timidly played a few chords that Coffey said he recognized but couldn't name until Anita began to sing. Her voice was anything but timid. It virtually boomed across the room as if amplified. She probably wasn't more than fourteen years old, still child-like, but nearing womanhood. Her body was not slight, however, and she had a voice that would fill La Scala's grand hall.

"Vissi a'arte, vissi d'amore, non feci mai male ad anima viva...
Con mai furtiva quante miserie connobi aiutai...
Sempre con fe' sin..."

The notes were clear and sustained. Coffey whispered to me, "Puccini. *Tosca*. Great opera. Listen. She's good."

When Anita finished, we didn't know whether to applaud or shout bravos, so we took our cue from Vittorio who started a mild but appreciative clapping.

"Buono," Coffey said, nodding. *"Molto buono."* Anita was embarrassed by the attention, and we were embarrassed for her. She nodded toward us, then turned back to the piano and began studying random sheet music.

"She's a no ready for *teatro* yet, but she practice good," Vittorio said.

Annetta slid her flat tomato-covered dough into the wood-fired oven, and exclaimed over her shoulder, *"Di bene in meglio, quotidiano. Megliore Maria Labia."*

Vittorio translated for us. "Anita get better every day. Better than Maria Labia." Coffey nodded. He recognized the name as a noted LaScala soprano who had a long career in Italian operas until Il Duce's ventures into Ethiopia in 1936 dampened enthusiasm for operas. To me, it was all double-talk, until Coffey explained it.

Vittorio fished the small Chesterfield box from his pocket, shook a cigarette loose, and offered one to Coffey, then to me. We both shook our heads, so he lit one for himself and muttered *"Grazie,"* for the cigarettes in the first place and for leaving all three, now two, of them for him.

Coffey cleared his throat, indicating a new subject, and said, "Vittorio, where are all the people of Anzio? When did they leave?"

Vittorio studied the rising smoke. "Two, maybe, three week ago. Nazis tell us coast to be bombed by your navy. All up and down. Not just Anzio. Most go to relatives or friends up country to escape war. Maybe a coupla' hundred *paisanos* still here. No place to go, like us."

"Then the Nazis didn't know we were going to land here," I said. It was half conclusion, half question.

"Si, si," Vittorio smiled. "Big surprise. We wake up this morning. Big guns booming, but not much. Very happy. Maybe Nazis go home." Vittorio went on for almost half an hour, describing life under Mussolini, then life under the Germans when Italy surrendered and the Nazis took over, imprisoning all Italian soldiers, and clearing the coast line. He said that some, like him, had managed to elude the occasional German patrol and had remained in Anzio, but for the most part the coast, all the way north to the cliffs beyond Rome, was cleared so patrolling German planes could bomb or strafe with freedom, not that the Germans were much worried about shooting up a few *paisanos.*

He then went on to tell of Annetta's husband, his brother Corporale Roberto Camistrata, who was a tank driver captured by the British in the Libyan desert, then turned over to the Americans in Tunis since England had no room for them. The Americans added him to a long line of other Italian POWs and herded them aboard Liberty ships returning otherwise empty to the US for more troops and materiel. He ended up in a temporary POW camp somewhere in Tennessee. He was 47 years old when captured. To get them out from underfoot, Rommel had sent the Italian troops and tanks to his southern flank, where they were quickly overrun by Australians pushing eastward across Libya.

Roberto was too old to be fighting a young man's war, but Mussolini drew no barriers, 15 to 50. Roberto's brother Vittorio, now 54, marveled that he had escaped duty in Abyssinia years ago. He maintained a low profile and guessed that the *fascisti* records were not too well maintained. Vittorio showed us two letters and a snapshot they had received from Roberto, one mailed from Cairo, one from somewhere in Tennessee. Roberto appeared somewhat disheveled, still in the uniform he was wearing when captured, sans insignia, but he seemed more content and better cared for than the rest of his family.

Annetta produced the steaming pizza from the oven. It was plain bread dough with tomatoes and olives, no additions available in food-scarce Italy, not even cheese, which was gobbled up by Germans. With a knife that could slaughter bulls, she sliced the pizza into eight parts, slid two pieces onto small plates and offered them to Coffey and me while Vittorio poured small glasses of *chianti* for us all.

We didn't realize how hungry we were, now fifteen hours past ship-board breakfast. Annetta's plain pizza was a kitchen masterpiece, a culinary triumph, superior even to the few pizzas we had tried in Naples. Pizza was a novelty food to us, unknown in bar-be-cue-happy New York State or seafood-stuffed Maine. Reluctantly we turned down Annetta's offer of a second slice. This pizza might well have been the family's total supper. We noticed that Annetta didn't insist too strongly. Anita was eyeing a second slice hungrily.

Coffey glanced at his watch—our hour was up—and beckoned to me as he rose. From his jacket pockets he produced three packs of K rations and stacked them on the kitchen table. The Camistrata family eyed the ration boxes covetously, Vittorio probably visualizing more cigarettes, Willie more chocolate, and Annetta perhaps some meat or cheese product. Anita stared at the rations as if ready to eat a whole box, waxed cardboard and all.

We explained our need to get back to the squad, praised Anita again for her commendable presentation, and thanked Annetta for her delicious pizza, trusting Vittorio to pass on our wishes and our promise to return as soon as we could. With handshakes, pats, embraces, and a kiss from *mama,* we bowed our way out and hastened back to Antonio's patio. On the way we agreed that we needn't tell the rest of the squad about the pizza. That would remain our little secret and our special source.

Sarge was pleased to hear that it was simply coincidence that the Germans had evacuated most of the coastline, that we had not been expected after all. He was also glad to hear that there were no hidden pockets of Krauts around Anzio, just a small contingent in Nettuno that every six hours sent a squad motoring through the area. We realized now what the Rangers had been firing at earlier in the morning, and that the German contingent was now captured or kaput. Sarge radioed this info in to Captain House at Headquarters, and then settled down to outline this evening's foray into the olive groves and grape vines to our east.

To tramp through D Company's terrain before sunset, we started out before supper. As we passed the newly erected field kitchen, still not operative but promising, we collectively sighed and told "cookie" to save something for our return. He replied with a tooth-short grin and a shrug. "What makes you think you're coming back?" he said.

"Your good cooking brings everyone back," Jersey said. "We'll stay out of trouble 'til breakfast."

An hour later we reached the outskirts of D Company territory and the coils of shiny concertina wire that separated GI foxholes from menacing grapes. Hundreds of foxholes in various stages of completion, with trench-tool-loads of dirt rising from them, dotted the area. Helmets popped up and down at work, while a few just nodded downward over a half-dug hole with cigarette smoke circling from beneath.

Machine guns were mounted every thirty feet or so, and mortars hid behind breastworks of knee-high dirt. M-1s punctuated the field, aimed at imagined but non-existent targets. It was a daunting array of firepower that stretched across the field, enough to give pause to any attacking Germans. But it all seemed rather futile. We all knew that if no Germans appeared before sundown, that line would move another three miles out, and all the digging would start all over again. And we were willing to lay odds that no German would appear for at least another day or two. We feigned seriousness and told them "Keep your shovels dry."

We wove our way past four-deep lines of sweating, cursing, joking GIs, stopping frequently to acknowledge an old friend or barracks mate from our Stateside training.

Sergeant Denny Blackmore challenged us. "Going out again, huh Crafton? Can't get enough, can ya'? What are you after this time?"

"Not sure we know," Sarge said. "Guess we're just going to wave in some Krauts to keep you guys busy."

"No need," Denny said. "Just wait here with us and they'll come along soon enough."

"No way, Denny," Sarge said. "There's not a German within thirty miles of here. Thought we'd run up to Rome and tell 'em we're here."

"I got a hunch they know it by now," Denny said. "Just you wait. By the way. You got the password?"

"Fibber McGee," Sarge said.

"Allen's Alley," Denny responded, and waved us through a break in the barbed wire. "Be sure to knock when you come back," he called after us, and we disappeared into rows of grape vines.

CHAPTER TWO

This wasn't a war. This was a stroll in the country.

Red Dog Patrol was bored. Under-the-breath grumbling drifted back to me and I wondered if Sarge was thinking of leading us into a firefight just to sharpen our edge.

Operation Torch had been a war. Hard to remember that the rifle squad's first battle was only fourteen months ago. Seemed as though we'd been dodging bullets, rains, mud, with a sandstorm in between, for years. But our first firefight was a surprise. A French battleship, unseaworthy, took it personally and scattered shells all over the coast. The French seemed to resent the Americans entering Casablanca more than they resented the Nazis entering Paris. As was their wont, however, the French gave up the fight after a couple of days. Vichy French suddenly realized that they had been Free French all along.

Operation Husky had been a war. Red Dog had sneaked ashore some hours before the invasion of Sicily began last July and had radioed back the positions of major German and Italian defense installations along the beaches east of Palermo, to be hit by our Navy's heavy guns. Not certain where the Allies would land, the Nazis had concentrated most of their forces on the east and west ends of the island, leaving the center beaches covered mostly by weaker Italian brigades. The naval bombardment and aircraft strafing had fairly well knocked out any serious obstacles along the central coasts, and Red

Dog had joined Patton's invading Seventh Infantry in shooting their way east to Messina.

Operation Avalanche had been a war. By last September the Nazis were beginning to wise up to defense tactics, having been mostly successful in all their own invasions over the past four years and only recently beginning to know defeats. The day before the invasion Ike announced that Italy's King Victor Emmanuel had surrendered and would join the Allies, leaving the Germans with the task of defending the whole Italian peninsula by themselves while kicking the Italian army out from under foot. It was a defense with deadly German efficiency but with insufficient manpower. The Nazis fought back long enough to enable their rear echelons to establish the Gustav line across Italy, just north of Naples, where they would hold off the Fifth Army for seven bloody months.

By now only a couple of those seven months had passed and Red Dog was fifty miles behind the Gustav line, searching futilely for Nazi opposition to the Anzio landings. The patrol spent hours and days trekking through inland farms and wastelands. We trudged through acres of vineyards, with thousands of well-tended grape vines, pruned starkly back to the trunk with two short branches crucified along wires stretched from pole to pole as far as the eye could see. We rested briefly in orange groves, all cleared of last summer's debris and holding their varnished leaves in readiness for next season's growth. We scouted olive orchards, stripped of their autumn harvest and awaiting spring blossoms. War or no war, someone was tending this land.

But for the most part, our route took us across acres of featureless, scrub-dotted flatlands that stretched unbroken to the distant hills. The winter-hardened fields were peppered with waist-high shrubs that might provide cover for a single soldier. Every quarter-mile or so we would dip across a rain-washed gully just deep enough to hide a prone soldier in a fire fight. But for the most part the frost-firmed meadowland was as hard and flat as Aunt Bessie's biscuits.

We skirted a number of isolated farm houses. Once they must have been well-off estates, and would be again when the economy returned to some normal supply-and-demand cycle. But now they were dirty, chipped, block-and-plaster hulks. After we passed a dozen darkened farm houses, Sarge was attracted to a flickering light escaping from the back of a small house. Cautiously we edged up to the back window, alert for a German billet, and found a pastoral scene of an aged farmer with wife and two daughters—no sons in sight—sitting around a kerosene lamp on a kitchen table, talking animatedly, munching apples from last fall's harvest, unconcerned with black-out precautions.

Sarge motioned to Jersey to go knock on the back door, with Sandy and Joe in back-up. The rest of us watched panic take hold of the kitchen foursome in response to the knock. Who but German soldiers would be around at this time of night? Radio Roma had told them of the invasion at Anzio but had also reported that the Allies were not advancing beyond the beaches where they were, of course, pinned down by superior German forces.

Whatever the knock might mean, the farmer hid his shotgun under a window seat—he would be shot if the Germans found it, since, thanks to King Victorio, he could now be considered an Allied collaborator. The women scurried up the back stairs to a loft. The farmer crossed to the back door, opened it slowly, and suddenly flung wide his arms in greeting. "*Americanos!*" he called, and the mama and daughters came rushing back down the stairs.

It took us half an hour to extricate ourselves from the *paisanos. Come in, come in. Stay. Mama cook supper. Antipasto. Stay. We have soft beds. Sleep. You need pasta. Come. Rest.*

Our Italian was no better than their English, but we guessed the meaning. And in return we learned that there were no significant German installations between Rome and Monte Cassino. Sarge spread out his map, and the old man, with V-spread fingers, traced a swath 40 miles wide across Italy, his index finger following what would have been the Gustav line and his middle finger tracing a line east from Rome. "*Niente,*" he said. Nothing.

The old man tapped his finger on the town of Aprilia, about seven miles up a curving road, four miles as the crow flies. "*Brigata qui,*" Brigade here. He moved his finger to Nettuno and then to Cisterno. "*Pattuglias qui e qui.*" We knew about the patrol at Nettuno that the

Third Infantry Division had tangled with for three minutes, and we were not going as far as Cisterno this trip. Even Rome held only token headquarter forces. So, except for a patrol squad here and there, most German forces were concentrated along the mountains just above Naples or held in reserve in the far north. That's all we needed, and with prolonged embraces and kisses, we finally broke away. Sarge vowed not to knock on any more doors.

We crossed over an abandoned railroad embankment and skirted the town of Padiglione. We were looking for German traffic, to get some idea of Nazi reaction to the landing, but there didn't seem to be a lot of activity. We casually strolled around for another hour or so, avoiding when we could the raised dirt roads, where every half-hour or so a German messenger would motorcycle by on some errand of imagined urgency. We didn't want to be open to any surprises, and we certainly didn't want to start a firefight if we could avoid it. Firefights make noise and attract the wrong kind of attention. We were in an environment that was not exactly a friendly picnic area, and we'd just as soon not call attention to ourselves.

The night was cold and clear, dotted with more stars than we could remember seeing since our blacked-out convoy had spent twenty days zigzagging its way across the Atlantic to Casablanca just over a year ago. Of course there was no moon. Invasion planners seemed to think that new moons provide the darkness needed to shield early morning invasions, not stopping to think that the invaders would benefit more from a full moon's illumination of strange surroundings than the defenders would benefit from a few more sniper targets. So, it would be another two weeks before Anzio saw a full moon. In the meantime, the crispness of the winter night seemed to magnify what visibility the star-filled sky provided.

From right point, Jersey raised his arm and we dropped. In silhouette against the midnight sky we could see outlines of a score of buildings that must be Aprilia and the Kraut sentry that ambled lazily around a sector of the town. Jersey drew his stiletto from its sheath on his thigh and crept forward, coming up behind the sentry. The silent approach, the quick hand across the mouth, the rapid slice of the blade, and then the quick grab for the rifle of the falling soldier in hopes of catching it before it clattered to the ground—we had all practiced this enough to appreciate Jersey's deadly ballet.

We all wore the thigh sheath Sarge had designed and had fabricated for us back in Morocco. He had found seven Spanish stilettos in a little shop in Fez. A few fifty-cent cartons of Old Golds from ships' stores along with a couple of Walther PK pistols "liberated" from German "advisors" in Casablanca persuaded the shopkeeper to offer the knives gladly. Captain House had at the same time talked the Navy out of seven Amphibious Scout assault knives to equip his newfound recon patrol. Sarge designed a special sheath that hooked on the web belt, hung below the thigh, and tied to the leg, like a western gunfighter anchors his pistol holster. We still carried the Army's all-purpose trench knife, which was good for opening K-ration boxes, but the razor sharp stiletto and the versatile Navy assault knife were more frequently used for rapid slashing and stabbing. The sheath became a badge of honor, evoking a hands-off respect from other members of Company D. So we were more than a little pleased to wear it—and grateful, for its double knives had become life savers for us in more than one behind-the-lines excursion. Best of all, they eliminated Nazis with ease.

Jersey went off to the right, and Sandy crept to the left, each looking for the next guards. We waited. They returned in a few minutes. "All clear left flank," Sandy said.

"Same right," Jersey said. "Sentries seem to be about a hundred feet apart, so we've got a four-hundred-foot gap."

"Okay, let's see what we can learn," Sarge said, and we crept into Aprilia in a closed-up trailing-seven formation. The town was a small compound of fairly new brick-and-concrete buildings, built by Mussolini in the late 1930s as a model farm commune. It provided residences for the farm families that worked the outlying fields, but also contained schools, shops, a church, a movie house, and a tall bell tower resembling a factory smoke stack. We expected the town's occupants, if any, would be asleep by this time of night, and perhaps the farm families were, but the center of town bustled with German soldiers sweeping out vacant store fronts along the main street and stacking furniture in the back. We counted almost two dozen German troops—more than we could tackle—and Sarge signaled a slow withdrawal.

Down a side alley, which seemed to skirt a sort of city hall, Sarge spotted a thin layer of light glowing from a not-too-well-shaded window. "Sandy, Mouse, keep your eyes on the cleanup crew," Sarge whispered. "Looks like they're getting ready for company. I'm gonna check out that light. Boots, you come with me. Rest of you spread out. See if you can get a line on how many more Krauts might be in town. Rendevous in 10 minutes."

The window shade did not quite reach the sill. The Germans must have known about it, since it would attract the attention of any German soldier passing the alley, but they were evidently not concerned yet about blackout precautions. Their indifference was understandable. American pilots flying Kittyhawks, Mustangs, or Mitchells out of Naples preferred their night's sleep, positing that tactical support was best rendered when they could distinguish targets by daylight. British pilots flying Spitfires and Beaufighters out of Naples welcomed night flights, on the premise that the Krauts were less likely to shoot down something they couldn't see, but they were looking for marshaling yards, trains, or convoys and wouldn't waste their ordnance on a single light in the middle of nowhere. So, until the invaders started moving out of the beachhead toward Aprilia, there was little chance that the town would be a target for tactical air support. This left a one-inch slit for us to view what was evidently a briefing by a German officer to a couple of NCOs.

The room held a desk, a few chairs, and a large map on the far wall. A German officer stood by the map with a field telephone to his ear, pushing colored pins into the map as he listened. Two soldiers sat attentively in chairs facing the map. The window was soundproof, so we couldn't hear what the Krauts were saying, but that mattered little since we couldn't have understood them anyway. The push pins indicated that the German Fourteenth Army would be receiving support divisions from northern Italy, southern France, Yugoslavia, and the Adriatic Sector on the eastern flank of the Gustav line. The officer replaced the field telephone and began lecturing the waiting sergeants. With each sweep of his open palm, as if pushing the troops into position, the officer would pause and hold up 3, 4, 5, or more fingers, indicating, Sarge suggested, how many days it would take for the divisions to reach Valletri, Cisterna, Campoleone, or even Aprilia.

"We'd better get out of here before they discover those dead guards," Sarge whispered, and we crept back to join the others in the gap we had cut in the Kraut sentry line. We moved back toward the beachhead for an hour or two, well away from the dead sentries. We passed through an olive grove that we had passed earlier. Sarge called for a short break, and sent Bull out toward the road as guard.

I tried to calculate how many miles we had covered, but I didn't even have a watch to calculate how long we'd been traveling. I knew we had left Antonio's a little after six, when it was still light, and I guessed it was now something after midnight. An average walking pace is four miles an hour, but a zigzagging rough-country pace would be somewhat less, say two miles an hour. Six hours at two miles an hour would be something like twelve miles, which seemed about right. But without a watch, it was at best a guess. Sarge wore an Army watch, all steel and plastic, presumably waterproof, and he probably had our travels figured to the yard. Joe was the only other one of us who boasted a watch, a gold Waltham that he had swathed in adhesive tape. But soldiers usually don't wear wrist watches.

A wristwatch is a nuisance, something always going out of kilter with no repair shop in sight, something to snag on sleeve or bush, something to break on the first jump into a foxhole, something to interfere with first aid if wounded. Since waiting is a major army occupation, morale would suffer if the duration of a wait was known. Time is strictly need-to-know. During the day, the only need for a watch is to check on chow times, and the sun or stomach is adequate for that. During the night, all hours are the same. And day or night, when the wrong bullet comes, the exact time of death is meaningless information.

Struggling for a passable napping position, Jersey said, "You pick the hardest ground in Italy, Sarge." He brushed pebbles and stones away from his selected bed site.

"Stay awake if you want to," Sarge said.

Jersey lay flat on his back, staring at stars. "Now, you could have taken that farmer up on his offer. Picture the soft, fluffy beds his sons must have left behind when they traipsed off to Africa. And the little one. What was her name? Clara? I think she took a shine to me. She could warm my bed anytime. But no, we had to settle for this dago cement."

"Shut up, Jersey," Sarge said. "Or you'll replace Bull and let him get some sleep." Jersey sighed and rolled over to his side. Inside two minutes Sarge had to kick him to quiet his snoring.

I was the only one still awake when Bull whistled lowly from the close-by mound. I hissed the others to awareness, just as the sound of a truck's engine began to grow to awareness. I sprinted up to join Bull, trying to hide behind a scrub bush that couldn't begin to disguise his bulk. Bull had seen the truck's silhouette on a distant rise before he even heard the soft Mercedes engine. The tarp-covered van concealed whatever it was carrying, but the flat trailer it was towing carried a mounted reel holding miles of telephone cable. The truck stopped at the edge of the olive grove, and two Germans jumped from the back of the truck. One tied a green flag to an overhanging branch of a roadside tree, which already held a blue flag, while the other pulled a few yards of wire from the reel and looped it around the branch. They returned to the truck and it moved off down the dirt road toward Anzio, unreeling the wire behind it along the side of the road.

The rest of Red Dog had joined us and lay sprawled along the crest of the hillside. "What's that all about?" Jersey asked.

"That's only act one," Sarge said. "I bet we see the second act soon. That blue flag is an early scout's recon, and the green indicates the wire connection. Now we've got to see who the flags are for. We'll wait here for them." No one returned to the gully and we all settled down to wait, which is what soldiers do best.

A distant rumble grew to a muffled roar as a line of German six-by's, with a staff car in the middle where it was shielded from land mines, crested the rise in the road and drew to a halt when the lead truck stopped opposite the signal flags. A young officer jumped down from the passenger side of the truck and began directing the trailing trucks into the olive grove. Those trucks towing artillery pieces were directed into diagonal parking places on our side of the grove. The trucks towing utility and ammunition trailers were shunted into parking slots on the far side. We counted nine howitzers, probably one-oh-fives, and a dozen support trailers. German troops poured by the dozen from the back of each truck.

"Is this going to be their permanent set-up?" Sandy asked.

"Probably." Sarge said. "It's not too far from the beach, and it's defensible. There should be a rifle platoon, though. Keep your eyes open. Anyway, it's good to harass shipping from here as well as slow down our moving out of the beachhead. We'd better back off. They'll be setting out sentries soon." Sarge turned and we followed him in a running crouch along the gully to a small rise a quarter mile away. "Moose," he asked, "are the batteries still okay?"

"Oh, we're good for another ten hours yet," Moose said.

"Set up, Moose. The rest of you, cover me." We stared at him. Was he planning on going into the enemy camp? Sarge crouched on the barren ground and fished a flashlight and some maps from his pack, and we smiled in relief. We unhooked our ponchos and draped them over Sarge's head, providing a black-out tent for his flashlight. Moose pushed the radio under the ponchos and handed the mike to Sarge, who was studying the maps and making notes. He keyed the mike and turned the volume low.

"Red Dog calling Thin Man. This is Red Dog. Come in, Thin Man. Over."

A pause. Sarge was about to repeat the call when a low crackle answered. He waited. "Red Dog, this is Thin Man. Over." Messages were minimized in fighting areas.

"Thin Man, this is Red Dog. Is Arthur out of bed? Over." Sarge was asking if artillery was active.

"Out of bed and looking for a birthday present. Got something for him? Over."

"Baltimore Orioles with all their equipment getting ready to play ball. Got a ticket for tenth row, seat five. Over."

"What hotel they staying in, Red Dog? Over."

"Oh, five or six of 'em. Got some room numbers for you." Sarge began reading a series of numbers from his notes, which transmitted the map number along with the coded latitude and longitude near us, interspersed with words like pig, basketball, seasons, or yearly. The words meant the number following would be increased by three as in three little pigs, five as in a basketball team, four as in the four seasons, or twelve as in months in a year. I had translated the other messages to myself as Sarge went along. *Baltimore Orioles*…a baseball team of whistlers, meaning nine field artillery whose shells seemed to whistle overhead. *With all equipment*…with full complement. *Ready to play*…getting set up for action. *Tenth row, seat five*…hardly disguised reference to 105mm howitzers. *What hotel*…where? *Five or six*…miles away. And then the string of coded latitudes and longitudes pinpointing their position. "Will wait for visit. Over."

"On the way, Red Dog. Keep in touch. Over and out."

Sarge turned off the radio to save its battery and settled down to wait. In the meantime, he studied the olive grove through his binoculars, which seemed to magnify the night light. The Krauts were bunking down. They had probably been on the road most of the day and evening. If this was to be their installation, they could deploy the guns and bunker the ammo in the morning, the olive trees providing natural camouflage to screen them from snooping P-51s. They had, however, unhooked the field guns from the trucks—a mistake, Sarge reckoned, but they'd never guess that they might need a fast getaway this far from the action.

Twenty minutes later a whistling artillery shell passed almost overhead and exploded in the night. We could see a short plume of flame a bit south of us and a half mile beyond. Sarge estimated the impact point on his map and folded the edge of the map along what would be the shell's trajectory from the beach to its impact. He turned on the radio again and keyed the mike. "Red Dog calling Thin Man. Come in Thin Man. Over."

"Thin Man here, Red Dog. Over."

"Pretty package, Thin Man. Half click left, two clicks down. Saturate. Over."

"Roger. Over."

"Out."

The Germans were alerted by the distant explosion, but after a bit of milling around, they seemed to settle back, attributing the noise to perhaps one of theirs, an errant bomb, or a road accident. Sarge studied them through the binoculars, then suggested we move back a bit more. Artillery is not that accurate and a dozen shells, all fired at the same settings, could lay down a pattern anywhere in a square of acres.

We'd covered another hundred yards when shells began falling steadily on the bivouac area, in rapid succession and with lethal effect. Trucks blazed. Men screamed and body parts were flung into the air. First one, then another, ammo trailer was hit, causing even more destruction among the closely parked trucks and bedded men. The German soldiers seemed at first reluctant to leave the assumed shelter of the trees, but finally a few broke free and raced away from the carnage and into rapid fire from our M-1s. Sandy and Joe circled around to catch any who might have taken to the road. Take no prisoners, Sarge indicated, unless we come across the Commanding Officer still alive. We didn't.

Sarge radioed a cease fire back to Thin Man, then stretched out in relief, but we still had no officer to march back to a waiting Captain House. We were just getting comfortable again when Sarge bolted upright. "The road," he called. "Let's go," and started racing back to the roadway where Sandy and Joe waited. "That signal truck," Sarge said. "It will have heard the noise and will be coming back to see what's up. We'll ambush it. Try to save the officer, if possible, to take back with us. No others. Sandy, Joe, Boots—you take the other side and hunker down. We'll hide here. Stop the truck before it reaches us so we won't be shooting each other across the road. Jersey, you go back along the road maybe fifty feet. Stop anyone who tries running that way. Sandy, you and I will toss grenades just as the truck reaches that rock over there."

Sarge pointed to a large rock by the side of the road, some thirty feet back. "Go for the tires and hope we don't hit the officer. The rest of you go for anything that moves, anyone with a helmet anyway. If the officer starts to run, go for his legs if you can. Okay, get set." And we scrambled into our positions.

This time the wait was short. Preceded by two walking riflemen, headlights off, traveling at no more than five miles an hour, the signal truck crept along the dirt road, more wary of attack from the skies than ambush from the sides. They had been assured that the Yanks and Brits hadn't moved from their beachheads. But they were being cautious in case the shelling of the olive grove was not an aerial attack. Alert as they were, they didn't see the grenades arcing toward the front of the truck.

The leading guards heard the grenades clatter on the road behind them and turned just in time to catch face-on the full blasts of the grenades landing five feet behind them. The blasts felled the two guards, blew the tire off the left front wheel, and spread oil all over the road under the truck. To escape more explosions, the driver jumped from the cab and three more Kraut soldiers jumped from the back of the truck and headed for the bushes. They never made it. Bull didn't even fire his BAR. Sarge's machine gun and our M-1s were more than enough firepower for the fleeing Germans. Not a Mauser was fired. Jersey came up behind the truck, certain that was the full squad but alert for anyone hiding in the back of the truck. The rest of us came out onto the road just as a white handkerchief started waving from the passenger's window. The flag holder was the only survivor, the officer we were looking for—unharmed, but scared witless. As a recently commissioned staff officer, the only gunfire he had heard so far in this four-year war was on the firing range. He had long ago determined that POW was better than KIA.

The officer stood beside the truck, trying to communicate without English and shushed by Sarge, who waved his tommy gun under the officer's nose, pantomimed a demand for a hands-on-head posture, and lifted a Luger from the German's hip holster. "Luger, yet," Sarge said. "Maybe this kid is more than he looks. Lugers are carried by upper grades. Most young officers carry Walthers. Let's see what we got here."

Sarge fished in the officer's breast pocket for his identification. He pulled out a four-by-five-inch tan booklet, the *Soldbuch,* found in the breast pocket of every German uniform. Sarge flipped open to the first page and chuckled. "Wha'd'ya know," Sarge said. "How old do you figure this boy wonder is? Seventeen? Eighteen? Doesn't look like he even shaves yet. But guess what? According to his pay book here, he's a *Hauptmann.* As I recall, that's a captain. Must be the son of someone important."

Sarge flipped through the few pages remaining in the book—pages indicating unit assignments had been removed—and turned the book sideways. "Says here he drew some pay a couple of days ago, if I read this right, in Rome. That's close. That's how he was able to get here so fast. He probably commands a desk in the signal corps. Gentlemen, meet Captain Hermann Rundestat. That name sound familiar? Anyway, Captain House will be glad to see him."

Sarge chuckled and slid the German's ID book into his own pocket. "I think we best get home," he said, and headed west on the dusty road, leaving Sandy to tie the officer's hands behind his back and prod him toward the beachhead, leading the rest of us. We left quite a mess of destroyed olive trees, trucks, and Nazis behind us, and I wondered who would clean it up, thankful it wasn't us.

We walked as a tight group, unmenacingly, openly, hoping to encounter no trigger-happy ranger or nervous repple-depple import. Everything, including us, I guess, had a distorting, trembling glow about it in the pre-sun morning light. We were almost to the barbed wire, when a voice demanded: "Halt!" but it was a shaky, almost scared, voice rather than a sharp command.

We froze, and Sarge called out, "Fibber McGee." In the edgy silence that followed, we could hear the soft clicks of safeties being released, and I sucked in my breath.

The voice chuckled, then said with more assurance, "Allen's Alley. Come ahead. That you, Crafton?"

"Yeah. Must be Denny ahead. You sound kinda' nervous, Denny."

"Still asleep, I guess. Captain House told us to keep our eyes open for you. Said you were out there causing trouble. Hope you didn't bring any of it back with you. Hey, I see you got company. Who's the visitor?"

"Kraut captain. Just down from Rome for a visit. He thought he could sit up in a farmhouse somewhere around here and watch us dig foxholes."

"Want a detail to take him over to the POW stockade for you?"

"No, thanks, Denny. Think I'll take him over to Captain House myself, soon as I change my socks. I'll bet the Captain will want to talk to this kid. You got a field phone?"

"The lieutenant over there has one." Denny pointed to a canvas lean-to that had been set up between a couple of short poles.

"Suppose he'd let me use it to tell Captain House we're back with a prisoner?"

"I'll do it for you. Gotta' go over and report to the lieutenant, anyway. Does House know where you'll be?"

"I think so. Usual place, I hope, if it's still available. That's where our packs are."

"Well, welcome back. Nothing new since you left last night. A bit more crowded as the Third dumps more ashore. Some of the Forty-fifth due in tomorrow, I hear. Then maybe we can get this thing moving. Breakfast will be up in another half hour."

The walk home is always quicker than the walk away. The distance isn't any shorter. And the steps aren't any faster. In fact, we sort of dragged along, having had less than four hours' sleep in the past thirty. But anticipation seems to compress time and space, and we were dreaming of sleep—beautiful sleep—and getting our boots off.

Denny had evidently made good on his phone call. When we reached Antonio's, Captain House was there waiting for us, with two MPs to take over the prisoner. "This is now your headquarters," the Captain said. He tacked a sheet of paper to the door of our basement quarters. It read: "OFF LIMITS. These quarters available to the 714th Reconnaissance Squad (Provisional) only. All other personnel require G2 approval for admittance." It was signed: "John P. Lucas, Major General, VI Corps, Commanding."

"Well, wha'd'ya know?" Mouse said. "We got a number. We're the Seven-Fourteenth Recon. How do you like that?"

"I made that up, Sergeant," the Captain smiled. "I had to call you something, and that'll make it easier to explain your status to Fifth Army." He led the squad into the lower quarters and waited until we'd found comfortable positions around the room. "Now, let's have the details. What did you see out there?"

Sarge handed the Captain the prisoner's pay book. "There's nothing to see," he said. "Maybe this guy can give you some more details, but as far as I can see there's nothing more than a platoon at Aprilia standing between us and Rome. We peeked in on a briefing by a German officer for a couple of NCOs which seemed to indicate that it will be at least two days before the first forces arrive in the area. More later. The first'll be from the east end of the Gustav line, then some from the North of Italy, some from Southern France, and some from Yugoslavia. But it'll be a few days before enough of them arrive to stage any kind of defense, let alone a counter attack."

"Yeah, we got a report that the Hermann Goering Division from over near Campobasso was on the move."

"Sir?" Sarge said. "If I may suggest? Now is the time to attack. We can march out this morning and be safe on the high ground in those far hills by tonight. We don't have to go into Rome, but at least we oughta go for the hills before the Krauts stake 'em out. They'll be staring down our throats if they get there first."

"General Lucas says that his first assignment is to establish a secure beachhead. The Alban Hills is a secondary objective after the beachhead is organized to defend against any German counterattack."

"What German counterattack?" Sarge protested. "There aren't any Germans to counterattack. But there will be in a couple of days if we don't take those hills."

"I take your point, Sergeant." The Captain smiled. "But you're a little out of line. You're not running this show. The General is. I'll tell him what you found out and I'll even recommend what you suggest. But he's pretty well made up his mind that we'll spend the first few days getting things in order. Now tell me about that artillery battalion you called in about and whatever else you saw in the countryside."

So Sarge began a half hour report on our scurrying about, the absence of *paisanos* as well as Germans, and the preparations for more troops at Aprilia, and before he came to the bold-but-now-defunct artillery unit, we were thankfully asleep.

CHAPTER THREE

Few pleasures in life surpass the glow of growing awareness when awakening unbidden from an undisturbed sleep. No loudspeaker, horn, bell, or chime hammers the ear drum. No strident voice jangles the nerves with breakfast announcements. No sergeant's boot prods the butt. There is just the slow realization of life renewed, creeping slowly, warmly, limb-by-limb into consciousness.

I didn't want to wake up. I probably could have slept another half-dozen hours, but the clatter of distant anti-aircraft guns reminded me that other plans were unfolding. In fact, maybe that's what really awakened me—the clack-clack-clack of British Bofors trying for the few German planes that returned hourly from bases north of Rome to strafe or bomb the steady outpouring of trucks from landing craft. Antonio's cement floor should have been enough to remind me that I wasn't home in bed. But the far-away thump-thump-thump of artillery made the point. I was in Anzio, Italy, a bit distant from Corning, New York. And thereafter waking up became a chore.

I sat up and stretched, and Varlas looked up from cleaning his rifle and called, "Lookee here. Holt's alive after all. Welcome back to our war, Boots. Now maybe we can get back to work."

For the moment I ignored Jersey and looked about the room. Sarge was missing, but the rest of Red Dog was at hand. Bull was reading a comic book. Mouse sat at a table he had brought in from the patio shed, fussing with batteries for his radio. Joe was stretched out on his bedroll, staring at the ceiling, humming to himself an indistinct tune. Sandy was prying open a K-ration box with his trench knife.

"K rations again, Sandy?" I asked.

"That's all that's on the menu, Boots. Cookie's mess is closed for lunch. Breakfast and supper only. You slept too late for breakfast and it'll be another three hours before Cookie gets up some warmed-over C-ration stew or whatever. You got a K?"

"Yeah, in my duffel."

"Well, enjoy." Sandy waved his knife back over his shoulder. "Before that, the engineers have dug a five-man slit trench just across the road, complete with shovels and paper. And the medics, I guess, have hung a couple of Lister bags from the tree out front, complete with chlorine. Just for your morning ablutions."

"Ablutions? Three syllables are more than a hillbilly from South Carolina should attempt this early in the day. Where's Sarge?"

"He went over to see House." Sandy pointed to a field telephone on the floor near the door. "Signal strung that in for us this morning. House's orders, I guess. Anyway, it hadn't been in five minutes before it rang. House called Sarge over to headquarters. Guess he's getting our day's marching orders."

"Since when do we march by day?" I pushed myself out of my bedroll, and walked off with helmet and shaving kit in hand. When I returned twenty minutes later, the scene was unchanged.

Joe hadn't altered his ceiling-contemplating position. He spoke out to anyone who would listen. "Anyone here know anything about construction? Holt? You?"

"No," I said. "I was a printer, not a builder. Ask Sarge. He was a roofer, at least. What's the question?"

"Well, what shape is this room?"

"Almost square, I guess."

"And what shape is the room above us?"

"Rectangular?" I suggested. "At least, it's longer than this."

"Exactly Now, what do you know about load-bearing walls?"

"Hey," Jersey interrupted. "This wall ain't for real." He put down his rifle and walked over closer to the wall. "There must be more space behind this. Lookee, there ain't even any mortar between these blocks. This wall ain't holding up nuthin' above it."

"Right," Joe said. "It's not a wall. It's a partition. And since there's no entrance to the room behind it, it's not a useful partition. It's hiding something."

Sensing an adventure, Jersey grinned and retrieved his trench knife from his gear. "Let's just have a look-see. Who's hiding what?" He stood on one of the folding chairs that had been dragged down from outside. He slid the point of his knife under a top block and began edging it out from the wall. "These blocks don't even reach the ceiling," he said. "There's a gap between the blocks and the ceiling."

He worked the block out to where he could get a grip on it and pulled it out. Hastily he removed three adjoining blocks, handing them down to me, until the hole was big enough to reveal rows of wine bottles stacked on their sides, shelf -by-shelf, from the floor to the ceiling and crowded up against tier after tier of wooden shelves extending to the far wall. "Well, lookee, lookee, lookee. I think we've struck gold." Jersey handed me a bottle, then grabbed two more. He handed one bottle to Joe. "Wine or vinegar?"

Joe finally removed his folded hands from behind his head and sat up. He studied the unlabeled bottle, held it up to the light, frowned. "It's white. That's rare. Anybody got a cork screw?" Mouse tossed him a pocket knife that had a corkscrew folded along its back. "Where'd you get this, Mouse?"

"Bought it in a shop in Naples," Mouse said. "It's got a can opener, bottle opener, two blades, an awl, and a screwdriver. One buck. A hundred lira in funny money. Couldn't resist it." Every month, after allotment deductions, Mouse received about thirty dollars worth of Allied Military Currency, three thousand lira, and little to spend it on. A haircut cost seven lira in a local barbershop; a shave, five lira. A hundred lira for a pocket knife hardly dented the budget. In peace time, the knife would cost twenty times that much.

"The corkscrew alone is worth it," Joe acknowledged. He twisted out the cork, tilted the bottle, and took first a sip, then a swallow. Joe smiled and passed the bottle to Sandy. "A bit too sweet for my taste, but drinkable. Probably a malmsey. Those vineyards we tramped through last night looked like they were white Malvasia grapes. That produces malmsey wine. Anyway, that's my guess."

We stared at Joe in wonder. Probably the only drinks any of us could identify by name were Coca Cola and Pabst Blue Ribbon, and god only knows what they were made from. And here was Joe, identifying by taste not only the wine but the grape that made it. He wasn't being snobbish, just reporting. Of course, Joe was a dozen years older than most of us, and he had accumulated a dozen more years of miscellany. Besides, he liked to teach. He must have been a good physics teacher back in Augusta highschool, and he carried his habits over into his present job. With slow and patient corrective reminders, Joe had even weaned Jersey from most of the *deze* and *doze* of the Jersey accent that had earned him his nickname, and Jersey's "dem two dare" became "them two there" without his awareness. Joe would work on his grammar later. But most of us, except maybe Jersey who had abandoned school in his tenth grade and vowed never to return, toyed with dreams of college after the war, so we paid attention when Joe spoke of wine, opera, continental drift, tide harnessing, potato crops, lobster pots, or whatever during our few hundred miles of trekking through Africa and Italy. Maybe we could learn something. Joe said that when you stop learning, you stop growing, and it was nature's rule that when you stop growing, you start dying. So we listened.

Sandy sampled the malmsey. "We'd better lay off this stuff until we get an all-clear from Sarge. He may pop back any minute and we don't want to march out with our bellies full of vino."

Jersey fished a musette bag out of his duffel, climbed back on the chair, and filled it with eight bottles of wine. "I've got an idea where this might be helpful," he said, "as soon as I can find Sergeant Koleski." Koleski was Company D's supply sergeant. We had no idea where Jersey might find him, but if anyone could, Jersey would. Jersey left us to wonder what scheme he had in mind this time.

I found a K ration in my duffel, pried the heavily-waxed carton open, and spread the contents across my blanket. A small can with key opener, containing a mixture of reconstituted powder eggs with bits of bacon scattered through it—we had long ago decided the bacon was *ersatz*. It tasted more like cardboard, and surely the army wasn't about to issue a line of kosher Ks for our Jewish mates. A small hard biscuit or cracker—rumored to have saved one soldier's life when he carried it in his breast pocket where he was hit by a harmless bullet. A packet of yellow powder which, when mixed with water, was supposed to make some sort of lemonade but instead produced battery acid. A small square ingot of hard dark chocolate, suitable for breaking out windows—and also good for bribing Italian street boys when trying to locate a good hotel, a tavern, or a prostitute. A small box containing three cigarettes—usually Chesterfields, Philip Morris, or Raleighs—someone once claimed to have seen a packet of Lucky Strikes, but none of us believed it. Lucky Strike green may have gone to war, but we seldom saw the country's most popular cigarette outside a PX, and not often there. And finally the little package of toilet paper—brown, not white, so it wouldn't attract attention if discarded somewhere across the landscape. The small brown box held enough to break anyone's fast, but if one was homesick enough to dream of mom's sunny-side-ups with sausage and toast, a K was enough to break anyone's heart.

As I was recorking my half-empty bottle of wine, Sarge leapfrogged down the stairs, took in the entire scene at first glance, and said, "Put it away, Boots. Time for that when we get a day off." He looked around the room. "Where's Jersey?"

No one answered. Finally, Sarge shrugged. "Okay, we'll go on without him. You guys can fill him in later. But I persuaded Captain House to brief me on the overall layout, and he took me into a room full of wall maps. Listen up."

Sarge went to the block partition and with a hunk of coal traced a line from top to bottom, diagonally to the right with a small projection curving out to the left and downward about a third of the way down. He tapped it with his piece of coal. "That's where we are right now," he said.

He scratched in a dot a few inches to the right near the top of the line. "That's Rome. About forty miles north."

He put another dot down near the bottom of the line. "That's Naples," he said, "and this—" drawing a jagged line just above Naples and extending off to the right "—is the Gustav line. Got the picture?" He waited to see if he was understood. We nodded.

Sarge blacked in a spot on the inside edge of the drooping peninsula. "That's Anzio," he said, and then, blacking in another spot almost across the bay from Anzio, "and this is Nettuno." He then drew three small semicircles—around Anzio, just below Nettuno, and a couple of miles up the coast. He pointed toward the loop around Anzio. "This is Yellow Beach, where we landed, followed by Darby's Rangers, support units, and our Company D."

He moved his finger to the loop below Nettuno. "This is X-Ray Beach, where our Third Infantry Division, some of the Five-Oh-Fourth Regiment, and some support units landed."

He then moved his finger to the loop further north. "And this is Peter Beach, where the Limey First Division came in."

Sarge then drew a line extending north from Anzio. "This is the road to Aprilia, where we were sneaking around last night, and beyond that Campoleone. That will lead to the Alban Hills, crossing highway seven to Rome."

He drew a second line leading east from Nettuno. "And this is the road to Cisterna, which is right on highway seven."

Sarge pointed to the land between the northern road to Aprilia and Campoleone and the eastern road to Cisterna. "What we need is two things—the Alban Hills, for the high ground, and, just this side of that, highway seven, to cut the Gustav line off from Rome."

He then drew a narrow arc encompassing the three beachheads . "And this is where we stand now. And will stand, I guess, until the brass think it's safe to strike. Our front's about five miles out from here and reckoning to stay five miles out, until the Krauts show up. Any questions?"

"How soon will that be?" Joe asked.

"House is arguing for tomorrow—what's that?—Sunday? Well, he doesn't sound too hopeful. Maybe Tuesday. By that time, the Krauts will be waiting for us, ten deep."

"Meantime?" Mouse asked.

"We're going out again this evening. This time we'll try the road toward Cisterna. House wants a staff officer. The captain we brought in this morning confirmed a lot of what we surmised from that Aprilia briefing, but House wants more back up on German troop movements. A truck will pick us up about six o'clock and ferry us five miles to the front. After that we're on our own."

"How long we gonna' be out this time." I asked.

"Depends on how lucky we get. Maybe a day, maybe a week. Who knows? As soon as we find us a *Gruppenfeuhrer* or better."

We stared in silence at his crude map. A spot on the coastline with one road heading north and another east. The Alban Hills lay in between the two roads, fifteen miles farther out of course. A loop cutting across the roads circled our beachhead, about halfway between us and the hills. Not much real estate to brag about.

"Okay," Sarge said. "I'm going to try for some sleep. Suggest you all do the same. It may be a long time before we sleep again."

Joe recovered a couple of bottles of wine from the hole in the wall and stuffed them into a musette bag along with some cans of C rations. "I'm going over to see Mama. You want to come along, Boots?"

"I'd like to, Joe, but I think I'd better take Sarge's advice and get a nap in before supper. I'm a growing boy. I need my sleep."

Sandy volunteered. "I'll come with you, Joe," he said. "I need some fresh air. You gonna' be out long?"

"Just an hour or so," Joe said.

I followed them up the steps and onto the patio and watched them disappear around the corner. For a moment, I regretted my decision to stay behind and I was about to call after them to wait up, but a six-by-six pulled up to the gate, distracting me from any further thought of Anita or Willie.

It was too early for the truck to take us to the Cisterna road, so I wondered if Sarge had ordered some more ammo or rations. But it was Jersey, returning without his bag of wine bottles but with a load of folding cots and mattress covers. Jersey waived me over to help carry them in, and along with the driver, we delivered the load to the basement quarters in one trip.

In ten minutes Red Dog had the cots set up, including Joe's and Sandy's. The mattress covers we spread over the cots, figuring we'd fill the covers with straw on the next home visit. With due acknowledgment of Jersey's scrounging abilities, we all settled back for an afternoon's nap. Sarge said, "Wine. Soft beds. Maybe we should call this 'Jersey's Luxury Hotel.'"

"No way," Mouse said. "I'll help you nominate him for the Congressional Medal of Honor, but I ain't sleeping in New Jersey." So we tacitly seemed to agree that Antonio's was Antonio's, and there we'd stay—at least for one Saturday afternoon—in off-the-floor luxurious sleep that even the banging Bofors couldn't penetrate.

But Sarge could. At five, he rattled our cots, shook us awake, and eventually got us back in our boots and following him across the perimeter road to where we had seen Cookie setting up his field mess.

We were still part of Company D, even though temporarily attached to Headquarters Company, and Company D had to care for us. That care included cots, probably slated for officer's quarters unless diverted by enterprising scroungers like Jersey, and food, in this case some of Cookie's notorious SOS—greasy gravyed ground beef on a shingle, a slab of toast, washed down with iced tea.

We wouldn't tell Cookie, since half of a GI's fun in life is riding the company cook, but it was actually tasty. We washed our mess kits in a series of 55-gallon drums of boiling water and returned to Antonio's in time to catch the six o'clock six-by-six ride out the Cisterna road as far as our lines had stretched. And then we were back in land no different from what we had started with twenty-four hours ago.

Again we shunned the major roads and hiked parallel to them through scrub land. Traffic on the roads was considerably more frequent than last night, and not just messengers on motorcycles. Trucks loaded with German soldiers and staff cars carrying German officers kriss-crossed the land, searching for likely bivouac areas, gun emplacements, and support stations. We stared hungrily at the passing staff cars, plotting ways of stopping one without killing the officer inside.

After a fruitless couple of hours, and a half-dozen speeding staff cars, we concluded we'd have to find a parked staff car and then search for the passenger. During one of our breaks, Sandy asked, "Sarge, what's a group fuhrer?"

"*Grupenfuhrer,*" Sarge corrected. "Or an *Oberst.* A colonel or a general would do nicely."

"How do we know when we got one?"

"Look for an oak leaf on his shoulder. Maybe with one or two little diamond-shaped pips beside it."

"That could take a week."

"Then we'll be out for a week. Hope you all brought enough ammo and rations."

Sandy just grunted. He knew Sarge wouldn't keep them out a full week. Four days max. By that time Captain House probably wouldn't need his colonel. The beachheads should be busting out by then and they'd learn the hard way what the German order of battle was going to be without a German colonel to tell them.

"So we just look for the arrival of a new Kraut unit, see which tent goes up first, and we raid the commander's tent hoping we catch a colonel. Right?"

"Wrong, you numbskull. You'll get a first lieutenant at best. When did a colonel ever show up in the front lines? Just keep marching, Sandy, and stop griping."

Ten miles in, about midnight, we got lucky. We came upon a farm house with a familiar car parked at its front door. It was a staff car that we'd seen all over Italy, a 4-wheel Steyr *Stabswagon* with an eight cylinder air-cooled engine. Noisy and not too fast, but it was a favorite of the upper ranks who didn't quite rate a Mercedes-Benz sedan.

The driver sat on a bench to the side of the driveway, puffing a pungent cigarette. Jersey drew his stiletto and started to sneak up behind the German soldier, but Sarge waved him down. No point in leaving dead bodies lying around, announcing that we were somewhere in the area, until we were sure we had our quarry secured and were on our way out.

Sarge motioned me to follow and we crept around the side of the farm house, out of sight of the driver, to a back window. We were becoming proficient at peeping through windows.

A German officer sat on a sofa with a scantily dressed Italian woman beside him and another on his lap. They were talking and laughing, sipping wine. The woman on his lap was toying with the buttons on his trousers. He wore a plain white t-shirt, no tunic.

The room was Spartan—an armoire, a small round table with a kerosene lamp, a sofa with a couple of overstuffed chairs, one of them holding a belt and holster. No coat rack and no coat in sight.

Then a third woman entered the room, carrying a new bottle of wine. She wore a German's officer's coat draped over her shoulders. A silver oak leaf and one diamond embroidered on a black field shone from the shoulder of the officer's tunic. "Gotcha," Sarge whispered.

We crept back to the squad hiding in the bushes. Sarge nodded to Jersey, and Jersey again drew his knife and crept up behind the driver. He was quiet, fast, and effective, and he dragged the body back into the shrubbery beside the drive.

"The question now is, how do we get our hands on that Kraut *Gruppenführer*?" Sarge mused. "Do we bust into the house and hope he doesn't go for a side arm and start a fire-fight? Do we wait until he's finished and catch him coming out? Or do we start a distraction and hope he comes rushing out to see what's going on out here?"

"Not a firefight," Joe said. "That may take out one or more of us and will certainly lose us our prize when we fire back."

"Wait until he comes out," Sandy said. "He'll be smug and sluggish and off his guard."

"When will that be? He may play around for hours," Jersey said.

"Probably not," Joe said. "He wouldn't leave his driver standing by if he planned to spend the night. And he probably has a job to do, anyway. Besides, with more Krauts moving in all the time, someone might think this farm house would make a good billet, and the colonel wouldn't want to be caught in his underwear by his subordinates. He'll be a half-hour, at most."

"A diversion to smoke him out, then?" Sarge asked.

"No, that would lead to a firefight, too. He'd come out with Luger in hand to find out what's going on. You don't yell, 'drop the gun' in a war. And we'd all start shooting. Pfft one colonel."

"Okay," Sarge said, "here's the play then. Boots, you go back to that window. Signal us if they move to another room. Bull, you and Mouse cover our backs from out here. The rest of you follow me. That front door is probably unlocked and we'll try sneaking up on him before he has a chance to get to his holster. Just hope that front door doesn't squeak."

Followed by Sandy, Jersey, and Joe, Sarge double-timed to the front door, pushed the door open slowly, without noise, just enough to allow the team to sidle in, and began tip-toeing, as much as Army boots would allow, across the hall toward the flickering light in the next room. On Sarge's signal, they burst into the room and the German officer found himself staring into the barrels of three rifles and a Tommy gun before even one of the women could scream.

Sarge motioned the three women over to one corner, relieving the one woman of the colonel's tunic as she passed. Sarge told Joe to watch the now cowering women to be sure they caused no trouble. Jersey grabbed the officer's shirt and lifted him to his feet, while Sandy confiscated the officer's belt and sidearm from a nearby chair.

Sarge handed the jacket to the colonel who struggled into it and quickly resumed the stance and posture of a senior officer. He stood almost at attention while Sarge lifted his *soldbuch* from his breast pocket. "Franz von Dietrich," Sarge read. "*Grupenfuhrer*. Unit assignments torn out." He returned the pay book to the colonel's pocket. "You speak English?"

"Of course."

"What outfit you with?"

The German hesitated. He was about to say something about name, rank, and serial number, but pride overcame his reticence. "Third Panzer Grenadier Division," he said. "Who are you?"

Sarge grinned. He knew he had breached the German's resolve. He had to be careful, but the officer evidently was within a sphere of manipulation. "You are being taken prisoner," Sarge said, with some pride, "by Staff Sergeant Roger Crafton, Company D, Third Division, United States Army. Where's the rest of your outfit?"

The German wet his lips. Finally, with disdain in his voice, he said, "I have already told you more than is necessary, Sergeant."

Sarge sighed. He pulled his stiletto from his right hip and held it tight against the German's chin, letting the German feel the pain of its sharp point.

"We can play this two ways, Franz. You can be a good little boy and do as we say, or you can be a sudden casualty of war. We don't care. It's up to you. POW or KIA. A pleasant camp in the United States or an unmarked grave in an Italian gully."

The German swallowed. "I am expecting reinforcements momentarily. You are the ones who will soon be dead."

"Nice bluff," Sarge said. "If you mean your driver, he's already 'killed in action,' so to speak. And if you mean the rest of your Panzer Division, you'll be dead and we'll be gone long before they get here. So, what's it to be? Do you play ball or do we drag you off into the bushes?"

The German didn't hesitate. "What do you want of me?"

"What I asked about. Where's the rest of your outfit?"

"Back in Cisterna."

"Leaving you alone?"

"They will be back in the morning. I was looking for an advance command post when I came across this farm house. The bulk of the division will be arriving about daybreak. My adjutant will lead them here. They are waiting for my report on where to take up positions."

"Then you're alone?"

The German hesitated and Sarge prodded.

"Yisss," the German muttered through clenched teeth. "Yes. I sent my adjutant back to Cisterna ."

"In what?"

"We had two vehicles. He went back with the escort."

"And you were going to make your driver stand out there in the cold all night while you played lord of the mansion?"

"He could sleep in the *Stabswagon.*"

"How kind of you," Sarge snorted. "Tie his wrists, Sandy, and bring him along. Let's get moving."

The squad reassembled outside by the staff car and Sarge asked if anyone could drive "this thing." Joe said he thought it was standard shift and he could handle it.

We pushed the German to the floor of the rear compartment, and five of us crammed ourselves into the back, showing little concern for the welfare of the officer underfoot. Sarge and Joe took the front seat, and with the slightest grinding of gears, Joe turned us onto the Cisterna road heading back toward Nettuno.

On the way we passed two sidecar motorcycles and a four-cylinder VW *Kubelwagon*, each hurrying about particular assignments and none of their occupants paying us the slightest heed. It wasn't until we approached the holding line of the Nettuno beachhead that we ran into trouble when a volley of errant rifle fire greeted our approach. Sarge hung out the side, waving a white handkerchief and shouting "Don't shoot. Don't shoot."

We slowed until we were close enough to accept the challenge. "Password," a megaphone commanded. It hadn't changed since yesterday, so Sarge shouted "Fibber McGee," and waited for the response, "Allen's Alley."

With relief, and grinning widely, we drove through the lines and across the five miles back to Antonio's without further challenge, although the well-known German staff car was the object of many unbelieving stares. We decided it would be safest if we abandoned the car at the earliest convenience, so we parked outside the perimeter road across from Antonio's and walked the short path back home just as the rising light started erasing the stars from the morning sky.

Mouse radioed Captain House who arrived within minutes along with an escort to pick up his new charge. We settled back on our luxurious cots for a two-hour nap. Later we would search out Cookie for his morning serving of powdered eggs and fried sausage with the world's best homemade bread toasted to golden richness and waxed with canned margarine. Sunday sunrise found us snoring.

CHAPTER FOUR

And of course the rains came. Not the March or April showers that steadily cleanse and refresh the land, but the biting winter rains that at higher altitudes would build glaciers but at Anzio thawed the frosted plains and turned the countryside to mud—ubiquitous, omnipresent, tenacious mud. The rains were cold but light and if left alone would freeze to ice or rise in vapor, but a thousand army boots drove the water ankle deep into the soil, uprooted any weed or plant struggling to hold the land together, and churned the countryside into mud that would coat trouser legs, spin jeep tires, and triple the weight of every army boot. Army protocols declare that whenever two or more pairs of army boots assemble, those boots would soon be standing in mud.

We had just left Cookie's mess tent and were dunking our mess kits in drums of boiling water when the first ice pellets of January's last rain began to hit us. We double-timed back to Antonio's without pausing to thank Cookie, which we wouldn't have thought of anyway. Actually, the breakfast was an appreciated change from K rations—scrambled eggs, albeit once powdered, with griddle-fried sausages, biscuits and strawberry jam, and plentiful hot coffee. That was our first satisfying breakfast since Naples, but we wouldn't tell Cookie that. Army protocols also declare that cooks and bakers are to be regarded as mis-assigned grease monkeys and fair game for sarcasm. Secretly, there are no more appreciated army specialists than cooks and bakers, and we suspect they know that, but no seasoned soldier can resist peppering the mess tent crew with insults. Jersey had given Cookie a couple of bottles of wine from our private stash, hinting that they were not in appreciation but as a bribe for better food. Cookie said we should drop by about lunch time. He was opening a can of ham and could slip us a few ham sandwiches. That elicited a snort of 'tire patches, huh?' from Jersey, which Cookie took to be Jersey-talk for "Thanks."

Back at Antonio's, most of us turned to an assortment of tasks—gun cleaning, letter writing, boot waterproofing—waiting for the jangle of the field phone to beckon Sarge back to headquarters for a briefing. I stood in the doorway watching the icy rain wash the patio. Please God, no mission in this weather, I prayed, knowing that I really meant: Please Captain, lay off for the day. One or the other must have heard me, for the awaited phone call was from House himself, telling Sarge to settle back for the day and that he would be over to talk to us soon. Sunday was to be a day of rest after all, an observance not frequently recognized in battle plans.

The rain was still holding us in when House arrived. He parked his jeep at the gate and hurried through the sleet to our basement billet. I turned from the door way to shout "Ten-HUT," but the Captain waved me down and called, "At ease," before any of us could move. He noticed the half-empty bottle of wine by Jersey's bunk as he sat on my bunk opposite. "Where'd that come from?" he asked.

Jersey hesitated, looked at Sarge, and then reluctantly pointed to the hole in top of the wall. "Antonio's cellar," he said.

"Do I get a taste?" House asked.

Jersey grinned, reached into the hole, and pulled out a couple of bottles of wine. He borrowed the opener from Mouse, uncorked a bottle, and passed it to the Captain.

After a taste, House pronounced it palatable, set the bottle on the table, and warned us against advertising its presence. "I should report this," he said, "and have the MPs confiscate it. I'll pretend I don't know about it—for a while, at least. Particularly in view of what General Lucas has in mind for you. You boys did some good work last night."

"You mean the Kraut?" Sandy asked.

"Yep. Von Dietrich," the Captain said. "At first, he was strictly old school. Name, rank, serial number. Geneva convention. Achtung. And all that crap. But we got him singing, and he seemed to have just come from a Kesselring briefing. Troop strengths, movements, dispositions. More than we had hoped for."

"How'd you get all that out of him?" Sandy asked.

"After an hour of explaining to him the difference between the pleasures of a POW camp back in Oklahoma or the grind of a POW camp down in Morocco, I couldn't get a word. I told the guards to lock him back up for a while, but I said to one of guards—low voice as if being confidential but loud enough to be sure the colonel heard—that the colonel wasn't any use to us and to call Sergeant Crafton and have you boys take him back into the countryside. That did it. He gave us answers faster than we had questions. What did you do to him, Sergeant? He was sure scared of something."

"We didn't do anything, sir," Sarge said. "I think the Kraut was just scared of our knives," he tapped the sheath on his hip, "particularly after he saw the pool of blood where he had left his driver. I guessed when I first saw him that he was a chicken colonel."

Captain House stared at Sarge for a moment and frowned. "Anyway, he gave us quite a run-down. Seems Kesselring never expected us here. Everyone thought an invasion might come, but it would be north of Rome, and it wouldn't be until March or later. Kesselring's intelligence told him that we were no where ready to launch an invasion. Even our build-up in Naples, which didn't escape his notice, was dismissed by his staff as just training or posturing."

"I bet he's gotten the message by now," Jersey said.

"He's moving everything he can get hold of to our area. By the end of the week, he'll have eight divisions in place. First in will be the Herman Goering Division and the colonel's own Third Panzer Grenadier Division, followed by the Seventy-first and Ninety-fourth Infantry Divisions. Right behind them will come the Fifty-first Mountain Corps with six light divisions, then the First Parachute Corps with five divisions, and the Eighty-sixth Panzer Corps with another five divisions. Right now we're facing maybe twenty thousand German troops, where two days ago there were a couple of hundred at most. In a week, there'll be forty thousand more of 'em. Maybe eight divisions in place, with more to come next week."

"And we sit here twiddling our thumbs while they get their act together," Sarge said.

"And with only two divisions," Sandy added.

"Sir, has the good general made any evacuation plans," Jersey asked, "or is he waiting for another Dunkirk?"

"Yeah," Sarge said, "if we'd moved out immediately, we would be in Alban Hills by now. Now we're so crowded in this pocket that every Kraut shell scores a hit."

"Now hold on, Sergeant," House said. "General Lucas had orders to set up a defensible beachhead, which he's doing. Later, he could take over the Alban Hills if feasible. You can't expect our men to set up the landing and march straight on some twenty miles deep and without a few days organizing supplies and tactics."

"Well, whether they could or not, the chance is gone now, I guess," Sarge said.

"Not quite," House said. "The Brits have wanted to break out from their forested and marshy landing zone ever since they first arrived. Besides, they want to abandon the beachhead since the water is so shallow for so far out that incoming trucks are sitting ducks for too long. German artillery and planes are having a lot of fun with them. They're going to move their supply operations down here to Anzio now that we've got the harbor cleared. Why the Germans left the dock complex intact is a mystery. They blew up the harbor facilities at a town just north of Rome, where we had feigned an invasion, but they skipped this harbor even though they had explosives in place. It would have been a real hardship if our landing craft had to sit a few hundred yards off shore to unload. Now the trucks can drive right off the LSTs onto the dock. So the Brits are abandoning their beach supply and, more than that, they are moving out of the marshes tomorrow morning."

Sarge perked up. "Tomorrow morning? Heading inland?"

"Yep. Their goal is Campoleone." House studied Sarge's crude map on the wall. "I see you've been studying the territory. This must be Campoleone." He tapped the top dot on the north road.

"Did General Lucas okay this?" Sarge asked, a somewhat incredulous tone in his voice.

"Of course," House said. Then he added in a softer, more confidential voice, "although maybe he had little choice. I think the Brits were determined to get out of their hell hole with or without the general's permission. When I told General Lucas and his staff just what Kesselring was planning, he turned visibly white, cursed the fate of a general, and fired off an urgent request that General Clark release the Forty-fifth Division for Anzio. It was then that General Penney announced that the British First Division was moving out tomorrow morning and he stormed out of the room before General Lucas could say yay or nay. Then, after some hesitation, Lucas asked Colonel Darby to take the Rangers out along the canal on the south. General Truscott will take the Third Division up the middle with the idea of spreading out to join the Brits at Campoleone and the Rangers near Cisterna."

"When does this come about?" Sarge asked.

"Starts Tuesday morning. They'll spend tomorrow moving into position. The big advance starts Tuesday. It'll take them this afternoon and Monday to get geared up."

The Captain waited for further comment, received none, and continued on another subject. "Meantime, General Lucas told his aide to write you guys up. He couldn't find a suitable medal for each of you, so he hit upon the idea of a Presidential Unit Citation for the squad. It'll be a gold-framed blue ribbon that you wear over your right breast pocket, and a ribbon to tie on your guidon, if you had one. I said you guys did a good job under dangerous conditions, and the colonel's information bears this out. General Lucas is quite keen on this, 'though it may take a couple of months to get through."

"We don't need a blue ribbon," Sarge said. "It's just a job. Medals are things you take pride in. Anyone who finds pride in this butchery and demolition is as sick as General Patton. We'd rather have a hot shower or an apple pie. Tell Lucas to hold the medals for real heroes. We certainly don't warrant it."

"Maybe you don't need it," House said, "but I suspect the Corps does. The Army needs heroes now and then—for inspiration and public relations. Let the General have his fun. He's got a lot to worry about, and a hero here or there makes him feel better."

"Or makes him look better," Jersey said.

"That's enough, Corporal. As you were," House said curtly.

"Okay. Let's drop talk of medals," Sarge said. He waved his hand toward the map. "Where do we fit into this new action?"

"What we need is someone to get into the Alban Hills. Maybe you were right. Maybe we should have taken the hills first thing. But that's past. Anyway, the Germans have set up observation posts where they can watch our every move and direct artillery fire. We need someone to get a line on German observation points in the Hills and mark them so our planes can find them. In addition, we need reports on German deployments, and if you can set up a spotter station, you could radio their movements back to us. And of course, you might be able to cause a bit of behind-the-scenes havoc as is your custom. Dangerous. And might take a few days. You up to it?"

Sarge looked around to each of us. We nodded. "Can do," he said. "When do we start?"

"Take it easy for a day. Get your gear together."

"Yeah, we need more of those wonderful Ks," Jersey said.

"See Sergeant Koleski for anything you need," the captain said. "Have him call me if there's any question."

"No problem with Koleski," Jersey said, grinning at each of us. "Koleski's on our side."

"Well then," the captain went on, "it's up to you when you start. Monday morning would seem good. You could make better time traveling by day instead of by night. Besides, the Brits will have their attention starting tomorrow morning, and you may find it easier to slip past them." House stood, turned to the steps leading up, and paused to smile back at us. "Play it safe, fellas. Please. You did good work last night. Wouldn't want to lose you this early in the game." He threw a quick salute and disappeared up the stairs.

"Palermo all over again," Sandy said. "We were out six nights while Fifth Army played yo-yo on the beachhead. Maybe if this war goes on long enough, our brass will learn how to fight a war."

"Oh, Lucas learned all right," Sarge said. "General Clark almost got his ass shot off at Palermo, extending our lines faster than we could dig in. Now it's just the opposite. And that's what's got Clark and Lucas playing scaredy-cat here."

"His orders were to secure a beachhead," Joe suggested, "not take the high ground. He's doing that just fine."

"Yeah, but then what?" Jersey asked.

"That we'll find out starting Tuesday," Sarge said. "We're in for some action starting Monday. Meantime, Jersey, you and Boots go scout out Koleski and get us some more K's. Joe, you and Bull find an Ordnance dump and get us some more ammo, black tip. I need about ten more clips. Let's hope they're already loaded, or we'll spend the evening pushing cartridges into clips. Mouse, you go over to Cookie's and see if he'll make good on those ham sandwiches for lunch. Bring 'em back if they're ready. Sandy, you stay here and mind the store. Get down a few more bottles of wine for lunch and then put those blocks back. No need advertising Antonio's stock while we're out. I'm going to see if that German staff car is still waiting where we left it. We could sure use it Monday to get started toward the hills. Meet back here within the hour. Check?"

"Check," we muttered, draped our rubber parkas over our tin hats, and moved out in various directions. The rain was letting up, but the icy mist still hung low in the air and chilled our bones. Our thoughts were mostly of tomorrow. The mud would still be there, but maybe the rain would hold off. And in fact, the sun broke out before we returned to Antonio's. It was a white winter sun with little warmth, but it drove away the clouds and promised the Brits a good day for the start of their inland march tomorrow.

During the afternoon we ate ham sandwiches, drank wine, and spread our gear out over our bunks for Sarge's okay. At the foot of the cot lay shelter half, blanket, and rubberized parka. Then a dozen Ks, twenty clips of ammo, a couple of pairs of socks, two or three packs of cigarettes, a half dozen frag grenades and a half dozen thermites, and a wire garrote which we rarely used, preferring the stilettos strapped to our legs. Most of us carried extra ammo for Bull's BAR, which could fire a clip of twenty faster than our M-1s could fire a clip of eight. And of course we each had our special loads—Mouse with an extra battery for his radio, Joe with extra maps, Sandy and Jersey with little tin boxes of battery-operated timers and blocks of the new *plastique* which they had trained with back in Naples and had promised to show us how to use as soon as we had something that needed blowing up, and me with all the first-aid materials, mostly sulfa and bandages and morphine, and my sketch book. Bull had his hands full with his BAR which weighed about twenty pounds, compared to about eleven pounds for our M-1s, and he carried a lot of extra clips. Sarge inspected all the packs, not so much to pass judgement as to remind himself of who had what.

We had just stuffed the lot into our packs and settled down for a restful Sunday afternoon when from the top of our steps came calls of *"pronto, pronto."* Mama Annetta, Uncle Vittorio, Anita, and Willie— each bearing a fresh-from-the-oven pizza wrapped in butcher's paper—stood on the edge of the patio, grinning widely, and awaiting our invitation to enter.

Sarge was closest to the door, and he had heard enough about Willie and his family to welcome them in. *"Per favore, per favore,"* Sarge said, having heard somewhere that something like that meant "please," and waved his hand in a big sweep as a greeting. Those of us who had not met Mama introduced ourselves while we gathered around Mouse's radio table and Mama spread the pizzas out for our approval. We recognized bits of Joe's Spam, some K-ration cheese, and even some corned beef hash sprinkled lightly over the tomato sauce. Jersey commandeered four of our canteen cups and filled each half-full of wine for Mama's family while the rest of us drank from the bottles. Anita was persuaded to sing, *a capella,* an aria from another opera, this one *Rigaletto,* Joe informed us. It was a fine *antipasto* for a Sunday afternoon.

Most of the Red Dog squad clustered around Mama and Anita, in almost a game of charades. Broken English, worse Italian, hand gestures, and pantomime somehow resulted in communication, sprinkled liberally with embarrassed laughter and finger-pointing as each experimented with the others' language. Anita departed from opera often enough to direct the assembly in choruses of *O Sole Mio* or *Finiculi, Finicula.*

Joe entertained Willie with a demonstration of field-stripping an M-1 rifle. Joe had dropped his rifle in the mud and had decided it was about time for a bath. He held the rifle on his hip and pulled down on the back edge of the trigger guard. The trigger assembly slid out easily, and he laid it on his raincoat stretched across the neighboring cot. He then laid the rifle across his knees, breech down, and held the rear of the receiver with his right hand. His left hand grabbed the follower rod and spring and moved them slightly toward the muzzle to lift them free and then withdraw them to his right. This assembly he laid across the top of the slicker. With a piece of scrap wood he forced out the gas chamber, and with the point of a cartridge he pushed out a pin holding the follower in place. In quick time he lined up across his slicker the upper hand guard, gas cylinder, lock and screw, follower arm and pin, the operating rod catch assembly, bullet guide, follower, and bolt. Any of us could have done it blindfolded, but Willie was a hypnotized student, following each move as a coiled cobra follows a darting mongoose.

The wonder remains that soldiers are allowed to call their rifles "M-1s."

M-1 means nothing more than Model One. The army gets an idea, studies scores of prototypes, and decides on the final production model, which is then labeled Something-or-other M-1. The Army is ever reluctant to revisit a decision and the production model usually stands, although there are a few M-2s in the chain. The helmet is an M-1, the canteen is an M-1, the trench knife is an M-1. The Thompson machine gun is a Tommy gun. The Browning Automatic Rifle is a BAR. The most frequently issued rifle, however, is never called a Garand, or even an affectionate Gary. It's an M-1.

On first being introduced to the M-1 in basic training, the recruit is verbally hammered by the training non-com to call the pieces by their right names. That little piece is not a set screw; it's a "gas cylinder locking screw." And woe be unto the novice who refers to it as just a screw, or heaven forbid, a *thing* or a *doodad.* That would call for an immediate forty pushups, reciting with each push "gas...cylinder...locking...screw...gas...cylinder...locking...screw." To drive the point home, every training sergeant at every base recites the time-worn story of the Texas cowboy visiting England and being invited on a fox hunt. After the hunt, the cowboy asks his host how he had done, and the lord of the manor replies, "Jolly good, old chap, but there is a small matter of nomenclature; it's 'tally-ho the fox,' *not* 'there goes the son-of-a-bitch.'"

Therefore it defies reason that an organization so insistent on proper nomenclature would permit the Garand rifle to be called an M-1, particularly with such affection. On the line, any reference to a "Garand" would draw blank stares as others wondered what the speaker was talking about. One soldier declared that the M-1 name was short for "Many Wonder."

Willie sat in wonder as Joe named each piece he stripped from his rifle.

Sarge had pulled Vittorio off to a corner and I joined them as Sarge was asking about the large white shell of a building that rose above the roof tops in the center of town. Its empty window spaces and roofless top reminded us of bombed out buildings all along the Italian coast, but this looked new. Vittorio said it was new—that is, it was actually six years old, but it was an unfinished structure that Mussolini had started as a casino to attract tourist lira in his plans to develop Anzio into a world-recognized resort. He drained the Pontine marshes to the east through a series of canals. This malaria-breeding swamp, became passable farm land. Then he built model farm villages like the structures at Aprilia. He planned to turn the entire area into a showpiece of agriculture and recreation for all of Europe.

Mussolini and his *amante* drove down from Rome almost every Sunday to one of the garish beach houses that dotted the mile-long sandy shore between Anzio and Nettuno. Affluent Roman vacationers visited Anzio regularly to dine on fresh sea food at one of the many seaside restaurants. The casino was to be Mussolini's show piece, like Monaco or Beirut. That was until his war in Eastern Africa began eating up his resources, Vittorio explained. Having defied the League of Nations with impunity over his aggression in Ethiopia, Mussolini could not lose face by admitting that his war was not as easy as he had hoped. Dropping bombs which burst "like budding roses" among swarms of spear-carrying natives, or dotting the mountain passes with army tanks straddling rocky ravines required a lot of steel. Hence the railroad tracks for the abandoned berm running up to Rome and the reinforcing bars for the poured-concrete casino were now rusting in other forms on the landscapes of eastern Africa. Anzio was a sleepy fishing village with only a few weekend vacationers from Rome.

"And all the people?" Sarge asked. "Where are they?"

"Germans made them go visit relatives in Roma or Milan. Most go, but many beginning to come back at night. They think nothing is going to happen here."

"It's happening right now," Sarge said. "You've heard the bombs, Vittorio. You think it's safe?

"No, but nobody gonna' listen to me. Bombs and shells land on water front, not back here where we live. *Paisanos* think life better behind American lines than behind Fascist lines. Naples more fun than Bologna."

"But you think your family is safe enough?"

"You betcha, *Sergente.*" Vittorio emptied his third cup of wine, and since none of us moved to refill it, Vittorio concluded it was time to leave. "*Annetta, Anita,*" he called, "*Tempo. E ora. Vien, Guillermo.*" After a volley of thanks for the pizza and *grazie* for the wine, Mama's family set off in the fading afternoon light.

Before leaving the patio, Vittorio paused and pointed to the German VW at the front gate. "War souvenir, *Sergento?*"

Sarge grinned. "So to speak, Vittorio."

Vittorio shook his head. "You have problem, *Sergento. Pistola, si. Ma carro, no.* No fit in kit bag, *Sergento.*" Vittorio feigned seriousness and followed his family around the corner.

We watched them pass an MP jeep patrolling the perimeter road, and moved forward to intervene if they were stopped by the police. But each waved to the others as the jeep passed by, so we assumed they had met before. We learned later that last Friday morning Vittorio had led a landing patrol from the Third Division to the hiding place of a

German squad in Nettuno. Third Division considered Vittorio an asset to our invasion, just as we considered Mama Annetta an asset to our menu.

We straightened up our billet, crossed the road to Cookie's mess "hall" for a dinner of beef stew, and were asleep by the time the evening sun had disappeared into the Tyrrhenian Sea. We dreamed of tomorrow's leisure, bull sessions with Company D comrades, maybe a haircut, and even a bath—perhaps a swim in the chilling sea if we could find a spot out of sight of frequent Nazi bomber runs and out of range of Nazi eighty-eights.

Those were things we'd do together. We each had visions of things we'd do on our own. Sandy dreamt of a crap game, probably over at the motor pool. Bull would take his last two or three comic books into Company D territory looking for swaps. Jersey would scout out some supply depots, scavenging for anything we could use to spruce up our basement home. Mouse would spend hours scanning his radio dial, looking for Armed Forces Radio, BBC, Radio Lisbon, Radio Roma, or some station unheard before. Joe would probably go over to the Camistratas to talk with Vittorio about Italy in peacetime, and I'd probably tag along.

We planned a Monday of nothing. Starting Tuesday we'd have our hands full for a week.

CHAPTER FIVE

Red Dog started its patrol in the Tuesday morning dark, hoping to be well beyond our lines before the passing *Balkenkreuz* on the sides of the staff car invited too many greetings from our sharpshooters. We would have preferred to go straight out Via Anziate, past Aprilia and Campoleone, and then cut over to the Alban Hills, but Via Anziate was slated to be clogged with trigger-happy Tommies who wouldn't look kindly on a German staff car traveling among them.

Sarge chose the dirt road to Padiglione, which we had visited Friday night, then back roads and cross country direct to Highway 7 between Genzano and Veletri. This route might not keep us out of trouble, but it lowered the odds. Our chief worry would be some snooping Spitfires or Lightnings out of Naples looking for targets of opportunity, such as *ein Kubelwagen* leaving trails across the Pontine.

Joe drove, a bit faster than normal so that we wouldn't linger too long in anyone's sights. Sarge and Bull squeezed into the front seat beside him. The rest of us crowded into the covered back seat, where we would be less visible, but we still took our helmets off and held them on our laps. Even in the dark, the distinct shape of a silhouetted helmet, American or German, readily identified its wearer as friend or foe. The American helmet had a distinct double curve along the edge. We prayed for anonymity.

On the road to Padiglione, we sped past a half-dozen motorcyclists, three major convoys of troop transports, a few random trucks dragging antitank guns or flak wagons, and even a couple of staff cars like ours. They ignored us. They were intent upon their missions, and if one or two individual soldiers did a double take, Joe's speed took us well out of sight before they could question what they had seen. The Germans were busy staking out every farmhouse, barn, and outbuilding as observation post or billet for their rapidly expanding forces. The shadow of every other building seemed to be hiding an antitank gun, a howitzer, or even a Panzer tank, in an attempt to shield the weapon from air observation.

Sarge took notes. Troop strength and disposition would be our first report back to Captain House as soon as we set up shop.

We even passed through Padiglione without raising a fuss. It was still early morning, barely daylight, and although the town bristled with trucks and troops, they were mostly preoccupied with refueling gas tanks and stomachs. From close to our left we could hear the thuds of howitzers and mortars and the muffled fusillades of massed rifle and machine gun fire. We were skirting something major—and deadly.

After Padiglione, Sarge, reading from his maps, directed us onto farm roads and wagon lanes. Now we slowed, sometimes to a walk, and we replaced our helmets and readied our rifles. From now on we would be an anomaly and could expect a challenge from any German squad we stumbled across. Furthermore, especially from here on, we could be in the scope of any observer on the hill sides where spotters could easily track any troop movements or artillery targets anywhere in the valley. It was land Sarge said we should have taken Friday or Saturday, just to keep the Germans off the high ground. Now we just prayed they wouldn't keep us off the high ground.

Highway Seven would certainly be under surveillance by both British Beauforts and German spotters, so we found a vacant farmyard and parked the staff car in an empty barn. We pulled the distributor cap and hid it on a rafter, fairly certain we wouldn't be using the staff car again, but stalling anyone else from moving it, just in case.

We took the rest of the afternoon moving to Highway 7. We dashed across in spurts as gaps appeared between slow-moving German truck convoys dodging bomb craters. We hid among the scrub bushes, grape vines, and gullies of the rising Alban Hills. Sarge's binoculars had already zeroed in on two German observation posts dug into the hill sides, and since there didn't seem to be any great activity in either set-up, we assumed neither of them had spotted us.

"Shall we take 'em out?" Sandy asked.

"Not yet," Sarge said. "They're probably in frequent contact with whatever artillery battalion they report to, and if we take 'em out, the Krauts will be up here to find out why they aren't hearing from their spotters. The hill will be crawling with nosy Krauts, and we'll be in trouble. Better wait 'til we're set to run before we think about silencing 'em."

Sarge studied each German emplacement. He counted three Germans in each dugout, fronted with low stone walls. An antenna announced the presence of an out-of-sight radio. A barrel protruded over the wall, marking a machine gun. The glint of a setting sun off a lens wreathed in darkness suggested a tripod-mounted spotting scope of significant size, bigger than the one Sarge carried in his pack.

"I would like to get hold of one of their scopes," Sarge muttered. "Bet you can see what Cookie's making for dinner with one of those."

We circled the German emplacements and climbed to higher ground, immediately above them. We found a rock ledge and, below it, a small cave that the Germans had missed. It was just big enough to hold the seven of us, and it was a better observation post than the two lower dugouts. We just hoped that the Germans weren't saving it for another artillery spotter.

Sarge pulled out his telescope and studied the valley floor, while Mouse readied the radio for Sarge's reports. The rest of us spread out to scout the surrounding area for more German posts. We located none other than the two Sarge had marked.

Anzio. I could see ships in the harbor, the smaller ones heading toward shore, three larger ships patrolling the shore. Large white puffs of smoke rose regularly from the largest ship, probably the cruiser *Brooklyn*, each puff followed by a bigger puff as a shell landed north of Aprilia, trying to prevent the Germans from sending relief forces down from Campoleone.

The battle was largely restricted to the roads and farmyards. The fields on either side were seas of mud, crisscrossed by drainage ditches that stopped any tanks not already mired, and the clouds of smoke rising west of us, from the area around Aprilia, told us that the Brits had reached the first of their objectives and were engaged in some significant gun battles. When we crept into Aprilia, last Friday night, there wasn't more than a platoon holding the town. They had one tank, but that was more for affect than effect. There was more activity now than a lone platoon could generate. Visitors had moved it.

Sarge studied the smoke puffs through his scope and gave us a running commentary. "There must be at least a full company of Krauts there now," he said. "At least a brigade or two. And I see four tanks or antitank guns, although two of them are burning. The Tommies seem to be fighting door-to-door, or even room-to-room, all over the town. There are bodies lying all over the place, but I can't tell whether they're Brits or Krauts."

Sarge swung his scope up and down the Anziate road. "There are fire fights around almost every farmhouse along the road. And a head-to-head battle at the crossroads just before Aprilia. Wow. Those guys could sure use some help."

It was like pouring fresh German troops into a funnel and getting POWs out the other end. For the next morning, anyway, the British would hold Aprilia.

I turned the binoculars back toward Nettuno. Waves of olive drab were beginning to move out from the extended beachhead. I called to Sarge and he swung his scope back toward the southern road. "I thought they were moving out this morning," I said.

"The Third is starting late, I guess. Not moving fast, either." I studied wasteland, traversable only by a few foolhardy, foot-weary soldiers who risked prolonged exposure to crossfire as they made slow progress through the ankle-deep muck.

Small forces could mount strong positions, barricading the narrow road, secure on their flanks, and pushing the front foot-by-foot ahead of them. Occasionally a lucky artillery or mortar barrage would wipe out a holding force, quickly replaced by another. It was costly—to both sides—but a battle that should have been determined in an hour or two was now stretching into nightfall.

Long strings of German POWs were being led south toward the beach, along with ambulances of British wounded, while another string of fresh German soldiers approached from the north. The Brits were facing stiffer opposition than expected.

Sarge turned his scope south and studied the advancing GIs. "Looks like the Rangers and Paratroopers are trying to sneak up the canal toward Cisterno."

"How can you tell who they are from this distance?" Jersey asked.

"Cloth-covered helmets on the Rangers. Most of us don't try for camouflage. And the troopers' boots. Laced high. Slim. Paratroopers boots. That must be Colonel Tucker's Parachute regiment and Darby's Ranger battalions."

"Why don't we get some boots like that?" I asked. "These hook-up leggings are better than the old lace-ups, but they're still a nuisance. A high boot like theirs would be better."

"You don't want boots like those," Joe said. "You're likely to wind up dead in trooper boots."

"We're all likely to wind up dead in these combat boots," I countered.

"In action, maybe," Joe said, "but walk down the street in trooper boots and you'll probably end up in some dark alley beaten, broken, and barefoot. The only way to get those boots is to go through jump school. If Rangers see someone wearing those boots and not wearing wings, they'll figure he stole them—maybe even off a dead jumper— and they won't leave him wearing them long. Maybe Sarge should change your nickname, Boots. Get your mind off boots."

"Har har," I said. I studied the distant sea, turned orange by the lowering sun.

Sarge moved away from his spotting scope and rubbed his eyes. "It's getting too dark to use that piece of junk," he said, indicating the telescope which sagged on its tripod. "We've gotta' get our hands on one of those German scopes. It's a risk, but maybe we can fake 'em out. Get some rest. It'll be midnight soon. We'll go for one of them after we're sure they're asleep. They won't be spotting much in the dark, and maybe we can catch 'em off guard. Sandy, keep first watch and wake me if anything happens. Mouse, you stay with Sandy. Call me in an hour."

"What about your idea that silence from one of their spotting crews might alert the Krauts that we're up here?" Sandy said.

"I got a plan. Make it look like something else. Maybe an aerial bomb. We'll work it out later. Right now we need the rest. You and Mouse can catch some sleep after you wake me, and we'll plan to get hold of a bigger scope about midnight."

The approaching darkness flashed with a few skirmishes throughout the valley, few of them more than patrol strength. As the land turned dark, Sandy watched one British command try to send a few tanks to protect Aprilia's flank, but the tank treads churned the fields into a sea of glue which soon held them fast. He then sent more tanks to rescue the first tanks, but the second group of tanks also bogged down in the mud, followed by another group sent to rescue the second group, and so on. It would have been a farce, if it hadn't been so deadly. Most of the tank crews, coated thoroughly with mud and each weighing some ten pounds heavier, finally waded back to the road, under heavy fire, leaving the tanks for retrieval in dryer weather. By then it must have occurred to the British commander that no German was dumb enough to attack Aprilia cross-country, so he sent no more tanks to protect the perimeter. Another newcomer to the Italian rains had learned the characteristics of the ubiquitous Italian mud.

The battle noises in the valley lessened as the darkness deepened. By midnight only a random artillery shell, aimed mostly at the docks, punctured the stillness, and the valley slept as Red Dog arose.

Sarge's plan was a bit tricky, but if we could pull it off, it stood a good chance of convincing the Germans that their observation post had been hit by a fighter-bomber. Mouse and Bull remained behind to guard the cave and the radio. Sandy, with the steady tread of a mountain man, circled the German emplacement, found the nodding sentry, and dragged him, muffled but alive, into the bushes where Jersey put him to sleep with the butt of his rifle. The two remaining Germans slept on, undisturbed until Sarge and Jersey silenced them, too, with their gun butts. No knives. Sarge wanted no unnatural cuts or holes to betray any personal intervention.

Sandy shaped a charge of *plastique,* hoping that ten pounds of the explosive, properly shaped and embedded, could simulate the damage of a 200-pound aerial bomb. Sarge shouldered his tommy gun and picked up the scope while Jersey picked up another pair of binoculars and Sandy set one of the mechanical timers for two minutes. The unconscious guard was returned to his position and nothing else was touched.

Sarge's idea was that this must look as much as possible like a lucky air strike from a Beaufort or Mitchell bomber on a search and destroy sortie out of Naples. At least he hoped that an investigating German patrol would not think of the missing scope and would conclude that the whole mess was indeed the result of an air strike. There would be no need to track possible saboteurs. This would be further confirmed by the second spotting crew being left intact and unscathed, and by the absence of any knife or bullet wounds in the bodies.

We scurried back toward our cave and were almost there when the explosion rocked the hillside and pelted us with small rocks and debris. The low rock wall had been scattered from in front of the shallow dugout, along with a machine gun, Mausers, radio, and shrapnel-riddled bodies, leaving a small crater. We nursed a few minor bumps and crawled happily back into our shallow cave to watch for the arrival of a German investigating team.

By morning's first light, we watched a German patrol trudging up the hill below the bombed-out observation post. The plan had evidently worked. In less than half an hour, the patrol had radioed for an ambulance and had slipped and skidded their way back down the hill, carrying bodies and salvaged equipment. We didn't understand why they didn't try to re-man the post, but perhaps the officer in charge had concluded that the second observation post could take over the workload. He sent a courier over to the second installation with a message.

We breathed a sigh of relief. We were in the clear, equipped with a more powerful spotting scope, and relieved of the chore of attending to yet more observers. It had been a tense twenty-four hours—and we hadn't fired a shot. Sarge said, "We'd better take out that second post soon, I guess, before they do more damage down below."

Sarge radioed Thin Man, as he would briefly every morning and night for the next five days, noting the slow progress of Allied troops, the disposition of German opposing forces, and the floods of arriving and deploying German units behind the major towns.

As sunlight spread slowly across the valley Sarge scanned the field as it came awake and gun battles resumed between farm houses and across roads. The morning began with troops beginning to change their position from last night.

To our northwest a new heavy column of German troops and tanks was moving down the road from Campoleone and beginning to challenge the British hold on Aprilia.

To our south, the Rangers continued their advance along the Mussolini Canal and the Pantano ditch toward Cisterna. It all seemed to be in slow motion.

Sarge reasoned they were marshaling forces for a major attack against the beachhead. During the day, the Germans drove the Tommies out of Aprilia and reestablished their position. That lasted most of the day before the Irish Guards took it back again. During the next three days the Aprilia sector would change hands at least five times. Back behind Campoleone to the north German activity was brisk and trucks shuttled about like ants around a disturbed anthill. The British had pushed past Aprilia to the railway junction near Campoleone, blocking any more German troops from reaching Aprilia. It had taken five days to advance fifteen miles.

In that same five days, the newly arrived 45th Division landed and immediately spread eastward, as the British First and the U.S. Third should have done last week. The 45th was now aiding the British at Aprilia and the Third at Isola Bella, but they couldn't lessen the carnage.

By Saturday, the Rangers came as close to Cisterna as the Tommies had come to Campoleone. The Tommies would be stopped at Campoleone; the Rangers would be decimated at Cisterna.

The Mussolini Canal was a broad ditch, maybe a hundred feet wide in some places, with a shallow ten-foot-wide creek trickling through the center of it. It was *Il Duce's* engineering showpiece that had drained most of the Pontine marshes, reduced malaria and other diseases, and had turned hundreds of soggy acres into arable farmland, albeit still muddy farmland, particularly in Spring. It made a good defense line and tank trap on the southern rim of the beachhead and served as a sheltered approach toward Cisterna. The Rangers considered it a sheltered alley.

Where the main canal branched off, a major drainage ditch turned left and led to within 800 yards of Cisterna. That 800 yards would be over unprotected open land, but the Rangers, advancing through the early morning shadows, counted on surprise. What they didn't count on was the Hermann Goering Division, which had set up a three-point ambush. Machine gun emplacements, mortars, antitank guns, depressed anti-aircraft guns, and tiger tanks, hiding in farmhouses, ditches, and haystacks, rimmed the ditch on all sides.

We had met the Hermann Goering Division before. In Sicily they had fought like old ladies. Their resistance was token and they fled at the first rattle of an American machine gun, leaving their Italian comrades-in-arms to surrender happily as the GIs approached. The German division sneaked back to Messina, put up a feeble fight there, too, and then escaped quickly across the strait to Italy. But by the time we met them again, a month later, at Salerno, they had become a smart, effective, fanatic fighting force, and we wondered if we were really facing the same Hermann Goering Division that had been so timid on Sicily.

A company officer captured at Salerno told us that the Division had been called to attention in front of their C.O. where they stood for five hours in the Italian sun while their commander paraded through their ranks, lecturing them on tactics, the failures on Sicily, the success of past *Blitzkriegs,* the Glory of the Fatherland, what the Fuhrer expected from every German youth, and the consequences of cowardice.

Three times during his walking harangue, the C.O. pulled his Luger from its holster and at point blank range gut shot a predetermined lieutenant and two sergeants who had been instrumental in the Sicilian fiasco. The three examples writhed in agony on the ground while the Commander enumerated their failings. Finally, he directed the entire division on a twenty-hour forced march with full field packs, followed by a full week of ten-hour close-order drills and obstacle course maneuvers.

Throughout this, officers eavesdropped on the soldiers and reported any discontent to headquarters. Every morning, the reported malcontents were called to company headquarters, stripped of any rank, given twenty minutes to pack, and were en route to the Russian front before breakfast. By the time the Americans reached Salerno, the Hermann Goering Division was a different outfit. It earned the respect of British and Americans. The Division was now a revamped force worthy of the early *Blitzkreig* armies.

Now the Hermann Goering Division had been diverted from its base in Rome and rushed into the Cisterna area as the first significant opposition to the unexpected invasion.

When Sarge spotted the pending ambush near Cisterna, Red Dog radioed Thin Man to report the location to the big guns of the *Brooklyn* and the one-fifty-fives of the Nettuno front. Their response was late in coming and a bit wide. By sunrise the First and Third Ranger regiments had walked into the traps.

Even at our distance the roar of battle was deafening, and the rising cloud of smoke hampered vision. But we could see the effects of the machine guns raking the front ranks, the mortars and medium guns mowing down the middle ranks, and the big guns and tanks firing directly into the massed troops and lobbing shells behind them to cut off retreat.

After twenty minutes of intense fire, the guns suddenly went silent, and we heard the rattle of a loudspeaker. We couldn't make out the words, but we assumed the Germans were calling for complete surrender of the beleaguered troops. We sensed, more than heard, the whine of a sharpshooter's bullet answering the call, and the tank-mounted loudspeaker went silent.

After a suspenseful pause, the clatter of the guns resumed. No white flags appeared, but the answering fire dwindled into silence. The surviving Rangers one-by-one stood up among the scrub bushes that had hidden them and held their rifles above their heads. The Germans moved among them, grabbing the rifles and pushing the prisoners toward the menacing guns. The Rangers had advanced to a few hundred yards of their goal before the Hermann Goering Division had killed or captured most of them.

Meantime, the Fourth Ranger Battalion on the left flank had met equally strong resistance from dug-in and camouflaged German battalions. There was no place to hide. By the end of the week, less than half of the Fourth Battalion remained alive, and of the nearly 800 men of the First and Third Battalions that had walked the canal, only six made it back to our lines.

Tears ran down Sarge's cheeks. In the past he had seen miles of dead and dying. We had contributed to some it. No regret, no remorse. But the grandstand view of carnage in progress left us all shocked. Sarge shouldered his tommy gun, checked his grenades, and beckoned us all to follow.

It was short work. We approached the remaining German post from above, encircled it, and on Sarge's signal lobbed seven grenades into the pit. Sarge leaped over the stone wall, tommy gun blazing, spraying bullets over already dead Germans. He emptied three clips before Bull caught him in a bear grip and hugged him into silence. Sarge's tears had been replaced with red-eyed anger. His shoulders shook in rage. He slumped, exhausted, onto a low rock, stared out over the morning valley.

Sarge turned to us, unashamed of his tears. He spoke slowly, but there was determination in his voice. "We should have taken out that second observation post. It might not have made any difference. We'll never know. But we should have taken every chance we had to cripple the Krauts."

The capture of the earlier Ranger patrols must have alerted the Germans to the approach up the ditch. But we should have made sure no one up on this hill contributed to the ambush. In battle, death is close enough to touch. It is never accepted but it is expected. If it's you, you never know. But it is often the soldier beside you or the enemy just opposite you. You wince, but you don't hesitate to go on.

From a hillside, the view of death is more exacting. It is epic. We sat as if in a stadium watching a deadly game unfold beneath us, and we could count scores of deaths at a time. It should seem more distant, impersonal than a neighboring death in close battle, but it isn't. Each falling figure pounds against the heart. A thousand hammerings left us gasping for breath. Each gun flash left our mouths dry and our eyes brimming.

We had sat on a hillside and watched a bloody ballet below us. Cleaning up. Regrouping, Trudging back to safety. The gathering of bodies. There was nothing we could do but watch. Our tears streaked our grimy cheeks unashamedly. We didn't look at one another, avoiding any accusatory or apologizing or sympathizing glance. Our M-1s lay useless at our feet, and our shoulders sagged with helplessness.

The smoke lay heavy over the flat land and spread out to hide the carnage below. Sarge pushed himself up and shouldered his tommy gun. "Let's go home," he said.

CHAPTER SIX

The bloody skirmishes went on around us as we crept through and around German troops busying themselves with preparations to repel any further assaults while occasionally trading one-for-one volleys with entrenched Brits and GIs. The Germans seemed relieved to have orders to dig in rather than trying to push farther forward. Their high voices and banter as we crept past their bivouacs told us that they were exhilarated by their success in stopping the British short of Campoleone and the Americans short of Cisterna.

Few sentries interrupted our zigzag progress. The rattle of our few brief fire fights or the blast of occasional grenades did not suggest anything unusual on the noisy front lines and did not seem to alert any tangential forces.

We waylaid two German patrols and three sentries on our return march, with less than a dozen shots being sent in our direction. Sarge seemed to invite an occasional skirmish and smiled at thoughts of fifteen-or-so Nazi bodies we left behind us.

We found a six-by that has just unloaded mortar shells and was returning, empty, to the beachhead for another load. The truck took us aboard and then began picking up walking wounded headed west along the road. By the time we reached the old lines, the truck could hold no more. It dropped us off a mile from Antonio's to make room for wounded and the swung south to the hospital area.

We dragged into Antonio's, muddy, unwashed and unshaven, sleepless, hungry, with almost empty packs, low on ammo and devoid of rations. Sarge called Captain House to report our return and ask where the closest mess tent would be now. Cookie's field tent was probably halfway up the Cisterna road, following Company D.

House said we could get something to eat at the Corps mess at headquarters and, guessing our condition, reported that the engineers had opened field showers at *Il Sole Levante,* just off the north beach. We forgot aching muscles and growling stomachs, packed changes of clothes in musette bags, and ran to the north end of the beach.

The sign at the Rising Sun bathhouse announced morning and evening hours for nurses, midmorning and mid-evening hours for officers, and afternoon for enlisted personnel. That was us. At an outside tap we forced a few pounds of mud off our boots, pant legs, and sleeves. We then stood in line for our allotted eight minutes under the multiple shower heads that pressure-washed twenty men at a time from a forty-foot length of pipe stretched along a tiled roof. Eight minutes of bliss.

We took time to shave, donned clean olive-drab cotton tee shirt and boxers, and crammed our still muddy and now wet clothing into the musette bags. After leaving a note of thanks for the Chief Engineer and protesting his failure to change the original name to something like "Setting Sun," we whistled our way to headquarters mess for double servings of hot ham and raisin sauce. Then back to Antonio's, finally, for a short canteen cup of wine and eight hours of solid sleep. This had been our first bath in twelve days and our first hot meal in seven. Joe credited Omar Kayyam for his line: *Ah, were Paradise enow.*

Tuesday morning Sarge left to brief Captain House, study the field maps at headquarters, and pick up our orders. His voice was quieter, more determined but less harsh. He offered no explanations of his decisions, sought no advice, and outlined no alternatives. His shoulders seemed to sag, his footsteps seemed slower, his smile seemed harder. I watched him plod up the steps and across the tile patio. "Maybe someone should go with him," I suggested.

"No," Bull said firmly. This caught all of our attention. Bull never offered opinions. He seldom spoke without invitation. He'd respond to direct questions and orders, but he would never volunteer comments and opinions and seldom changed expression to indicate approval or disapproval—or even indifference, although that may have been what his singular stoic stare represented.

Bull's full name was Robin Skywolf, a Navajo, a former ranch hand in Arizona, drafted even before Pearl Harbor. He had expected to serve two years and then return to ranching, but December 1941 froze that idea. Inwardly he seethed that the paleface had yet again broken his promise, but there was nothing he could do about it. He seemed resigned to being "in" for the duration.

Sarge had first met Corporal Skywolf back in Georgia where a ruckus in a little souvenir shop near Fort Stewart caught Sarge's attention. An exceptionally large man, with an MP hanging on each arm, was accusing the shopkeeper of cheating him and threatening to tear the store apart. Sarge decided to intervene.

The MPs said that the corporal claimed he had given the shopkeeper a twenty, but had received only change for a ten. A little glass deer, a five-dollar bill, two ones, and two quarters sat on the counter. The glass deer carried a two-fifty price tag, so the change was surely from a ten.

Sarge asked the corporal to show him what money he was carrying, and the corporal held out a money clip with a sharply folded ten-dollar bill and a one. Sarge then asked the shopkeeper to show him the ten-dollar bill the corporal had given him. The ten-dollar bill lifted from the top of the cash-drawer slot was curved, as if having been carried in a thick folded wallet. But it wasn't creased. Sarge asked to see the top twenty-dollar bill in the cash drawer and pointed out to the MPs that the twenty had a sharp fold, like the corporal's other money-clipped bills. It was obvious that the cash register's twenty had come from a money clip and the ten had come from a wallet.

Sarge mentioned something about having certain stores declared off-limits, and the shopkeeper hastened to apologize for his error and quickly added the ten-dollar bill to the change on the counter. The corporal folded the bills, added them to his money clip, pocketed the quarters, and rescued his glass deer. "For Alva Deerrun," the corporal said. "A going-away present."

"She's going away?" Sarge asked.

"No. Me. We sail soon, don't we?"

No announcements had been made, but scuttlebutt was rife and the corporal seemed to ferret out the right scuttlebutt with confident accuracy.

The MPs agreed to forget the incident, as the shopkeeper's apologies became more and more profuse. The corporal followed Sarge from the shop. In fact, the corporal followed Sarge for the rest of the day until, just to get him off his back, Sarge finally agreed to see if he could get the corporal transferred from F Company to D Company. Sarge admitted his rifle squad could use a BAR-qualified sharpshooter to fill out the roster.

Thinking of the havoc the oversized corporal could have caused in the souvenir shop, Sarge nicknamed him Bull and welcomed him into the squad. It was plain that Sarge had earned Bull's loyalty forever.

Now we all waited for Bull to say something more than "No." Nothing was forthcoming.

"Why not?" I asked. "Sarge might need some company."

"No," Bull repeated. "He needs to be alone now. He walks with a heavy step. Much to think. Leave him to work it out his way." Bull turned back to his comic book, signifying he was finished with conversation. At that, this had been more words than we had ever heard Bull speak at one time. I shrugged and decided not to push it, particularly since no one else seemed inclined to take up the cause. I stared out the door at the darkening rain clouds.

It rained lightly but steadily for three days and then opened into a drenching downpour, as if emptying the heavens once and for all. Fortunately, Captain House had left us alone most of the week, and we were free to come and go as much as rain drops would allow.

Joe went to visit the hospital area, now dubbed Hell's Half Mile, to look for an old friend who had lost an arm to artillery on the road to Cisterna. Jersey and Sandy went in search of an ordnance depot that could replenish our supply of plastic explosive. Mouse looked up the

Third Signal Company to see what was new in radio transmission. And I found a perch on a low hill where I could sketch views of the landings below. Bull stuck to Sarge.

The rains hampered the German *Luftwaffe* runs over the beachhead. They had been aiming mostly at the shipping, forty or fifty sorties a day, with fighter-bombers dropping guided rockets all over the navy on their southward run and strafing the beaches on their northward return. They had a couple of sinkings chalked up, but their most serious effect was to drive the Navy further out to sea.

The rains did nothing however to stop the round-the-clock artillery shells that peppered the beachhead. The German shelling was not as intense as Allied artillery return. Hitler seemed to be conserving artillery ammo for the expected invasion of France while the Americans were offloading tons and tons of 105mm and 155mm shells in Italy. But the main difference was that our artillery had a wide valley to cover while the Germans could concentrate their fire in a tighter landing zone. And they had the better observation posts up in the Alban Hills. Although well back from the front lines, the streets of Anzio and Nettuno were often as deadly as the Via Anziati.

In late afternoon we were sitting on our bunks, reading *Stars and Stripes,* writing letters, waterproofing combat boots—just putting in time before supper. A low rumble started from the east and grew rapidly to a deafening roar as if a heavy freight train was about to plow right through Antonio's. We ducked, instinctively, just as a tremendous boom erupted from the beach below us, and the ground shook.

"What the hell was that?" Jersey demanded.

"*Kee-rist*, that was close," Sandy said.

We hurried up the steps to see if we could figure out what it was, where it had come from, what was the explosion that followed. A large column of black smoke arose from a supply dump near the shore. We searched the clouded skies for a bomber, but the rain made that unlikely. It had to have been an artillery shell—but unlike any we had heard or felt before.

We retreated from the rain, not inclined to return to reading or letter-writing, when the freight train barreled through a second time. Again we ducked. And again the roar that seemed to come in through one window and out another was followed by a deep booming explosion farther westward.

We rushed back up the stairs, and a second billowing cloud of black smoke rose up from the beach below. It remained unspoken but each of us wondered what kind of a new weapon the Nazis had come up with this time.

We waited for a third freight train, but it didn't come. Almost every evening thereafter, two major ear-rumbling explosions punctuated the normal daylong shellings from the large caliber guns somewhere well behind the lines. What kind of gun fired the screaming, roaring shell that arrived most evenings about dusk was beyond our comprehension, but we began referring to the evening shells as "the Anzio Express" and the gun "Anzio Annie." Captain House told us they were railroad guns, bigger than the big guns of a navy destroyer, but hidden on railway cars somewhere in the hills.

Friday's break in the weather allowed the fly-boys out of Naples to pinpoint and bomb some of the artillery installations, but most were too well camouflaged to be spotted from the air. Aerial photos indicated probable areas for hidden guns, but the air squadrons wanted more positive identification.

Saturday Captain House came by to tell us that was our next mission. Get back to work. Locate the batteries. Wait for a clear day. On hearing the approach of any fighter-bomber, we were to release a smoke grenade—green for a battery east of the smoke plume, yellow for west—one smoke grenade for one kilometer away, two smoke grenades for two kilometers. The fly boys would take it from there.

So we requisitioned a dozen smoke grenades and set out Monday morning for an excursion into the Pontine again, just as the Germans began a renewed assault on Aprilia. The Brits had pulled out of the Campoleone suburbs four days ago and had moved back to their base for a bit of recuperation from the heavy losses they had suffered, leaving Aprilia to be defended by the Forty-Fifth. We knew better than to look in that direction for artillery installations. The Germans had some around there, but we couldn't get near them.

Where the mud was not too deep, we tried cross-country. Near one dirt road we found scores of bodies evidently cut down by artillery. They were bloody, dismembered, and three ambulance crews were rounding them up, always hoping to find one still alive.

We kept our eyes fixed straight ahead or down as we walked by. We were not squeamish; we had seen enough carnage. But these were men we had trained with back in Georgia, marched with across Algiers and lower Italy. We didn't want to see any we would recognize. Instead we spoke of the guts it must take for a medic to enter into artillery range. An artillery shell does not discern the difference between a tank and an ambulance, does not recognize the red-and-white cross. We could duck; an ambulance couldn't.

By nightfall Monday we had found a farm path that skirted the little settlement at Carano, and we bedded down for the night in a half-filled drainage ditch a good mile behind the German lines. An artillery barrage every hour or so told us we were not far from at least one of our goals. There was no point in stumbling around in the dark looking for it. We would most likely trip over sleeping Germans and end up in a fire-fight. We split into two patrols, one to guard while the other slept, alternating every three hours. Sarge went off into the darkness to do his own snooping. By dawn Sarge was back with fixes on two heavy-gun installations and an idea of where a third might be. We were in business—if the sun would cooperate.

It didn't. Tuesday morning drizzled for endless hours and by the time it started to clear, it was too late for patrolling Marauders or Mitchells to respond to our smoke. We settled back to wait for another day when a low rumble started in the distance and grew into a deafening roar, approaching us from the southeast. We moved to vantage points clear of overhanging brush and watched an armada of large sleek bombers fly over, accompanied by squadrons of fighters, headed north of Rome. They were still climbing from their bases on the eastern shore, gaining altitude to escape German anti-aircraft guns. We guessed there must be as many as two hundred planes above us—Joe said they were mostly B-24 Liberators, some B-17 Flying Fortresses—headed, we learned later, for the airfields at Orvietta and other small towns in northern Italy and southern France which spawned the *Luftwaffe* bomb runs over Anzio.

"That's the life," I said. "No mud. Wish I was with 'em."

"Be careful what you wish for, " Joe said. "You might just get it. It's mighty cold up there. You wear forty pounds of leather, fleece, and flak jackets and you still freeze. You breathe through an oxygen mask. And when German shells start bursting all around the plane, you have no place to hide. Once hit, especially in a Liberator which has a gliding angle of about zero, you plummet like a rock."

"How do you know so much about it?" I asked.

"Got a nephew up there," Joe said. "He flies in a B-twenty-four. Cramped up in a little ball turret hanging beneath the plane for six hours a day. I visited him in Charleston just before we sailed. Went up with him on a training flight. Believe me, a muddy foxhole is comfort compared to a ball turret at sixteen thousand feet."

I watched the formations disappear to the north, losing my feeling of envy and increasing my feeling of admiration. "No place to hide, huh?" I said softly, not thinking I'd be overheard.

"And you can't run, neither," Jersey said.

"Well, we've got a couple of hours of daylight left," Sarge said. "Let me show you your posts for tomorrow. I have a hunch this clearing might stay with us." We picked up our packs and our rifles and followed Sarge to where he had spotted the first artillery installation. There were fourteen large guns, maybe one-seventies, and each one seemed to fire no more than one shell an hour, conserving ammo. Each gun nestled under yards of camouflage netting. They waited for any more advancing troops, but were content harassing the supply lines periodically, as they stockpiled shells for their anticipated German counter-thrust.

Sarge found a hiding place a kilometer west of the battery and stationed me, along with Joe and Jersey, for overnight watch. If the skies were still clear tomorrow morning, we should listen for the approach of a light bomber or two from Naples, alerted by Captain House. We were to release a green smoke grenade some distance away from us and then hurry back and take shelter. Sarge then led Sandy,

Mouse, and Bull to the second gun installation, where they would go through the same procedure. We started digging a bomb shelter, since in every four or five bomb runs, one is likely to spread shrapnel wide of the mark.

The next morning dawned brightly. We nibbled on K-ration biscuits and listened for approaching aircraft. It was a five-hour wait.

Jersey scooted out, tossed a green smoke grenade, and jumped back into our shelter. Two Mitchell B-25s came in low, growling overhead, loosening bomb clusters just above us. We watched the bombs glide across to the targeted olive grove where they burst through the gun emplacements. Some must have hit ammunition carriers since the big blasts were followed occasionally by even more blasts. In all there were a couple of dozen explosions in the targeted area.

We saw more green smoke rising a mile farther south, and then a third green cloud beyond that. More Mitchells zeroed in to the east of those plumes, but we didn't stay to watch. We could hear guttural commands from an approaching German patrol searching for the source of green smoke. We ran.

That night Red Dog slept deeply. During the night the occasional booming of a German gun suggested that the Mitchells had not been one hundred percent effective, but the less frequent firings meant that some of the guns had been silenced.

One of the installations we came across had only three big-caliber guns, and Sarge reasoned we could take that one out ourselves, using some of Sandy's *plastique*. That night we crept up behind the four sentries, one on each corner, and cut them down, silently. Then, while the rest of the German crews slept, we plastered explosive to the hinges of the three breech locks, Sandy set the mechanical timers, and we hurried away. We were well out of range but still within earshot when the three charges warped the block hinges of the one-seventies.

The next day we smoked two more gun emplacements for the circling bombers. These hurt. Sandy caught a piece of shrapnel in his left shoulder at the first bomb run, Mouse lost the radio to a sniper's bullet, and Sarge took a Mauser shot through the arm from the same sniper before we located the German. He had been hiding on the roof of a chicken coop. Bull's BAR put a volley right through the peak of the shed roof, and the German slid lifeless to the ground behind the coop.

The noise attracted a small platoon of Germans who approached warily, strung out across the neighboring field. We ducked into a drainage ditch, bent low, and ran as far as the ditch would take us. Grateful, we were well away from the chicken coop by the time the German patrol discovered its dead sniper.

I dressed the wounds with a liberal cloud of sulfa powder. Sarge's bullet hole was clean and neat. The bullet had passed on through. Sandy's shoulder had a rugged gash and a small piece of shrapnel, a splinter really, was still embedded. I couldn't get it out. The sulfa would have to do until we found a battalion aid station or a real medic.

We still had a ten-mile trek ahead of us, most of it through actionless territory still held by the Third division. We went first to the hospital where wounds were treated. Properly cleaned and bandaged, Sarge and Sandy were released with instructions to return tomorrow for re-dressings. They had earned Purple Hearts, but at Anzio, Purple Hearts were a dime-a-dozen. The battle lines were often manned by more bandaged than unscarred GIs.

Midnight neared as we returned to Antonio's, and we had little sleep before the following morning light met us with polite knocking on our posted door. Sarge called, "Come in," from his cot and turned to watch the door open and two MPs come into our nest.

"Sergeant Crafton?" one of the MPs asked.

"That's me. What's up?"

"We'd like to talk to you and your squad for a few minutes."

"Now?" Sarge said "We just got to bed, for Pete's sake." Sarge would not abide swearing. More than once in basic, one or more of us pulled extra obstacle course tours for using traditional army language. "For Pete's sake" measured the depth of Sarge's exasperation with inconvenience, and he probably wouldn't even have used that if he had been told that it might show disrespect for Saint Peter.

One of the MPs pulled a chair over to Sarge's bedside while the other stood imperially at the door. "This won't take long, Sergeant. Just a couple of questions."

"Yeah," Sarge said. "Get on with it."

"Well, we understand you and your crew know the Camistratas."

"Who?"

"Camistrata. A mother, Annetta. An uncle, Vittorio. A girl, Anita, and a boy, Guillermo. Know them? "

The name Vittorio registered. "Oh, yes. Corporal Coffey met them first." He nodded toward Joe. "Three or four of us have been to their house. And one day, they all came here. Why?"

"When did you see any of them last?"

Sarge thought back. Time loses distinctions in war. "I guess it was more than a week ago. Sunday, I think it was. They came here with some pizza for us."

The MP rose from his chair and walked around our cots. "And you?" he said, pointing to each of us in turn. We all agreed it was about ten days ago. And we all asked why he was asking.

"The girl—Anita—she's dead." The MP looked around at each of us, watching our expressions. "She was murdered. We found her body day before yesterday. In a deserted bunker down on the beach. Attempted rape, we think. Her neck snapped. We understand you guys are pretty good at hand-to-hand."

"We use knives, usually," Sarge sneered. "Easier and surer. But murdered? That's monstrous. Why come here?"

"We want to talk to anyone who might have known her. The scene suggests it was someone she knew who took her there."

Stunned silence flooded the room. "So, none of you have seen her since a week ago Sunday? Right?"

"Right," we nodded in unison.

"We've been up at the front for days," Sarge offered.

The MP's headed for the door. "We don't know yet how long she'd been dead. The autopsy should be available by this weekend. Let us know if anything occurs to any of you. I'll see you all later." And they were gone.

Sarge sat up in bed and looked around at each of us. "I hardly even noticed the girl," he said. "But she did sing like an angel, didn't she? Joe, you knew them best. Should we do something to...to . . .?."

"Condolences?" Joe said. "Yes, I want to do that. Should we all go?"

We all murmured regrets, somewhat embarrassed. Death we knew. Intimately. Often. We were steeled against it. But war and murder are two different things. Crimes, maybe, but one ordained by higher powers and condoned by world assemblies, the other condemned by all moral beings. Perhaps they should both be condemned, we thought. But war comes naturally to men, murder takes more effort. Death by war begs regrets, death by murder demands atonement. Especially the murder of a young girl.

CHAPTER SEVEN

The next few days seemed suspended. Artillery shells kept cascading back and forth. Patrols kept herding POWs back to the beach. Ambulances kept ferrying the maimed and bleeding to first aid stations. Aprilia was recaptured by the Forty-fifth and then captured back the next day by the Nazis. But we sensed an intermission between the acts. Things changed, but nothing changed.

We hung around Antonio's most of the time, mending our wounds, with occasional trips to the hospital for new dressings, to Captain House's office to study the now static maps, to Mama Annetta's to console her and to bring her some mess hall plunder, and to the showers to wash away not just the mud but the slime that cloaked everyone in war. We even stayed clean-shaven for a whole week.

I took up my sketch pad and drew blood-and-guts battle scenes that carried tones of resignation and despair. In all the gore, where was the glory? Joe looked over my shoulder a couple of times and shook his head. "That's not healthy," he said. "Your pictures don't need to be so dark."

"It's the rain," I said. "No sunshine to brighten things up."

"That's not what I meant," he said, "and you know it. You're young yet. When this is over, you have a good life ahead. Think of this war as a necessary step to the good life. Make the best of what must be, not the worst."

I folded my sketch pad, pushed it aside, and lit a cigarette. "That carnage we saw was a step toward a better life?" I asked. "If that's so, maybe I don't want a better life. Let's just go back to what we had."

"Ah, the callousness of youth," Joe said.

I felt resentment rising in me as I watched the smoke rising in the air. Perhaps it showed on my face, for Mouse came over to interrupt my thoughts. "Boots," he said, "you got a cigarette I can bum?"

I handed him the little pack of Pall Mall that came with my K-ration breakfast. "You smoke too much, Mouse," I said. I seldom saw Mouse without a cigarette dangling from his lips. "They're gonna kill you yet."

"Suppose so," Mouse said. "Guess that's why they call 'em 'coffin nails.' But I gotta die of something. I guess the army's out to get me one way or the other." Mouse lit the Pall Mall and blew a stream of smoke into the air.

"Y'know," he said, "I didn't smoke before I joined the army. But the army pushes 'em on you. In basic, every hour the drill sergeant barks out: 'Take ten; smoke if you got 'em.' Makes it sound almost like an order."

Mouse studied his smoke rings. "Look," he said, "a pack of cigarettes outside costs a civilian twenty cents; the PX gives 'em to you for a dime—five cents aboard ship. Every pack of C rations or box of Ks comes with free cigarettes. And what are the first PX supplies to reach you overseas? Razor blades and cigarettes. You can't get toothpaste but you can get coffin nails. It's intentional.

"The army means waiting. Chow lines, short-arm lines, pay lines, shower lines. And if there's not a line, you wait anyway. By the side of the road, in a foxhole, standing at ease. The army figures they have to keep us busy doing something or we'll get into mischief. So they offer cigarettes to fill waiting time. Believe me, it's an army plot."

"Joe doesn't smoke," I said. "The army isn't making him do it."

"But he's the only one of us who doesn't smoke. There's always an exception. But more than that, I've asked around, and only two of us smoked before getting in the army. The rest of us picked up the habit in uniform. It's a scheme, I tell you. If a Mauser doesn't get you, cigarettes will. It'll cut down on veteran claims and costs."

"But those cigarettes will tear your lungs out," I said. I knew they would tear mine out. They felt like it with every puff. I tried to keep smoking to a minimum.

"So will a Kraut machine gun," Mouse said. "I tell you the army's out to get us. One way or another. If I get out of this in one piece, I'm gonna sue the army. I didn't smoke before. The movies didn't convince me. Remember Paul Henreid lighting two cigarettes at a time and passing one to—who was it—Bette Davis? Sexy, but no sale. No movie star ever persuaded me to smoke. No magazine ad convinced me to walk a mile for a Camel. Few guys I knew smoked before. No, it was Uncle Sam did it. When I can't breathe any more, blame him."

I laughed. My funk had left me. Mouse was a good tonic. I told him to keep the little box that still held one Pall Mall, and Joe, who had been listening to the monologue, tossed Mouse another trio box of Pall Malls from his morning pack. Sarge came down the stairs, returning from headquarters, just as the packet of Pall Malls sailed toward Mouse. Sarge intercepted it in mid-air, pulled out a cigarette for himself, and passed the packet on to Mouse.

"Get ready to move," Sarge said. "The Captain hasn't any mission for us right now, but air observers report lots of Kraut activity on their side. They maybe getting ready to attack in force as soon as the weather clears. We're being detailed back to D Company to help hold the center. We've got foxhole duty."

It started to clear just as Sarge spoke. A week of relentless rain had turned the fields into even deeper mud plains, but if German tanks were to be constricted, so were our defenses. The growing frequency of artillery shells streaming over our heads announced the beginning of the German offensive Wednesday afternoon. And we heard that the Forty-fifth, which had just taken Aprilia back for the third time, had lost the town again.

The British Commander of the battered First Division prowled the front lines on our left flank, spewing out encouragement, orders, and cuss words to egg on the Tommies trying to hold back the German First Parachute Corps on the northwest side of the Via Anziate.

On the east side of the road to Aprilia, Sherman tanks of the First Armored Division fired point blank volleys of 75mm shells directly into the advancing German battle group. Our Forty-fifth, now clustered along the railroad embankment that paralleled the Via Anziate, couldn't move forward and wouldn't move back.

Farther to the east, the battered Third Division, including Red Dog, held off the half-hearted and mostly diversionary attacks of the German Seventy-Sixth Panzers. They were trying to keep us pinned down so we couldn't help the Forty-fifth Division on the Aprilia road. The odds were three-to-one against them, but the Germans gave no ground.

The main German thrust, however, was along the Anziate road. The advancing tanks were temporarily stopped a few miles north of the fly-over bridge from which the British brass had reviewed the parading First Division on their initial advance up the Via Anziate a week earlier,

Here, the Germans introduced another of Hitler's secret weapons—remote-controlled "baby tanks." These were two-foot long models of actual tanks, with tiny treads, a radio-receiving turret, and a full load of explosives. They didn't work well. The one or two baby tanks that didn't flounder in the mud were easy targets for a sharpshooter. Most of the tanks just stopped in their tracks—mud, of course.

The British commander conscripted every available man—clerk, dockhand, cook, or truck driver—to shoulder a rifle and reinforce the British First Loyals. They held. And General Lucas then reluctantly sent the reserve forces of the Third Division across the unused railroad bed and the just-arrived One-sixty-ninth Infantry Brigade up the Via Anziate. The Germans were stopped, but the same forces, sent earlier, could have kept the Germans from even getting started.

The chief instruments of the battle were the artillery battalions. The Germans laid down intensive barrages on both the British Fifty-sixth and the American Forty-fifth. Most Allied losses, especially the Forty-fifth's, were due to German artillery. But German losses to our artillery were greater. For every shell the Germans fired at our lines, our artillery returned ten.

During the four-day battle, the Allies counted more than four hundred killed, almost two thousand wounded, a thousand captured, and sixteen hundred other casualties, mostly trenchfoot from days in rain-filled foxholes and mud-filled ditches. The aggressive British First Division alone had lost more than two thousand Tommies, now mostly POWs. And we heard reports of more than four hundred Rangers being paraded through Rome by grinning Nazis. If the Germans were really stopped now, they must have made mistakes equally as serious as those made by General Lucas.

Given the high water table and the constant rains, we knew the Germans were in for a trenchfoot treat, too. We called for some artillery, but they were mostly occupied with more threatening advances, and by the time a few shells fell on the far side of our concertina wire, the Germans were too well dug in to be much annoyed. Our biggest challenge was to keep our feet dry.

By Monday morning only sporadic shell fire punctuated the day. We were relieved by a platoon from Company D, and we were summoned back to VI Corps headquarters for another assignment. No rest. Just straight to the Captain's Office. We gathered around the array of maps in Captain House's underground cell and stared in amazement. Was that the way it looked today? After two weeks of attack and counter attack, two weeks of sweat and blood, we were just about where we had started.

Captain House mentioned the casualty figures with all the feeling that might accompany a recital of boxcar loadings or wheat production. We put faces on the statistics. We had marched with some of the Third Division dead. We had bantered across mess hall tables with some of the Forty-fifth dead. We had swapped insults with some of the now-dead Scots Guards. We tried to put the captain's statistics out of our minds. A thousand dead was a number. One dismembered body, recognized as that guy George who swapped mismatched boots with you during basic, was a reality. Grown men do cry, even if it's not obvious.

"The Germans seemed to have let up," Captain House was saying. "The artillery barrages seem to have returned to normal. Most of their tanks have been destroyed by our artillery or planes. We think their casualties are running twice that of ours, but we have no way of making sure. Anyway, they seem to be digging in. Air recon suggests some behind-the-front maneuvering, but we can't determine what it's about. That's where you guys come in. Can you get us another senior officer who would appreciate a vacation in Tennessee or Louisiana?"

"If there are any left," Sarge said, "maybe we could find one. How soon do you need him?"

"By the weekend maybe. The sooner the better. You did such a good job with that last German colonel, we kind of hoped you could get us another one, more up to date. We've screened all the POWs—almost three thousand of them last count, I think—but there's not one among them high enough up the scale to know what's really going on. They're a ragtag lot, suggesting that German battle groups are badly chewed up and they're scraping the bottom of the barrel. The Brits, though, caught a fresh German sergeant who has suggested that something's in the wind, but he's not saying more than that, assuming that he knows more than that. What we need is someone who's in on the planning."

"What did the German sergeant say?"

"He said something about after the fifteenth we'd be the prisoners. So we suspect something's up, and soon, but we don't know what exactly. What we need is someone higher up, someone who's in on the planning."

"We'll start out tonight," Sarge said, but he said it slowly, looking at each of us in turn to make sure there were no objections.

"How's your arm, Sergeant?" House asked.

"Just about back to normal," Sarge said.

"And your shoulder, Bricker?"

"Functioning," Sandy said. "Smarts a bit, but I guess that means it's healing."

"Good," House said. "We can scrub this if there are any complications."

"No sweat," Sarge said.

"General Lucas wanted to meet you guys, but he's off on some recon. Guess he wanted to pin a purple heart on you two."

Sarge shook his head. "Tell him to hold off. We don't need any sudsing. If we're in a hospital bed sometime, come visit us. But our scratches just hurt. They don't cripple. Tell Lucas to take the medals down to the hospital where there are a lot of pillows needing some decorating. If war's a career, the medals would be part of the trimmings. But we aren't in it for the long run, just for the ugly moment. The medals are for special needs. I understand Company E saw fifty percent of their buddies crippled by German artillery attacks. Those are the guys that need some special attention, a pat on the back. Not just bandages. Medals might suggest the brass knows that. Medals are for their wounded, not us."

"The purple hearts are already on their way there, sergeant. That was quite a speech, and I don't believe you mean all of it. A medal might be of some help to you later. You never can tell, and it costs you nothing. No reason to pass it up."

House sat on the corner of his desk and read our faces—grungy, tired, unshaven. "If it helps any," the captain said, "I'll tell you about one German brigade—maybe twenty-five hundred men. They were spotted marching down from Campoleone, en masse. The observers called in artillery, and some three hundred guns zeroed in on the Germans. They seemed to have fired simultaneously at that one designated spot. *Bah-room!* One big volcanic upheaval and the whole brigade just disappeared. Does knowing that help any."

"Not really. Even if every Kraut in Italy was killed, we'd still remember. Always."

The captain stared at us. Whatever he read in our faces left him frowning. "I think I understand, Sergeant. Can't say I disagree."

He turned back to the maps on the wall. "Pick your target, Sergeant. I'll send a truck to pick you up at sundown. You can tell him where to take you. He'll take you as far as he can, and then from there on it's up to you. Good luck."

We shuffled back to Antonio's to ready our gear for the evening's march. I noticed Sandy wincing each time he stuffed a new ammo clip into his back pack. Sarge noticed, too. "Your shoulder hurting more than you let on, Sandy? You can stay home this trip if it'll help. We can manage."

"Not a chance," Sandy said. "You ain't leaving me in this hell hole. I gotta get out of here and into a good fight."

"You walk out of here with that chip on your shoulder and it might just be your last fight," Sarge said.

"Sorry," Sandy said. "I'm just mad at everything. This war is just a butcher shop on wheels. The sooner we get back out there, the sooner it's over. You're not leaving me behind."

"Gung-ho, huh?" Sarge said. "You keep thinking like that and by the time we reach Berlin you'll be a basket case."

Sandy grinned and flopped back on his cot. "Just kidding, Sarge. Pay no attention to me."

"I wish I could," Sarge said. "I wish I could."

CHAPTER EIGHT

The first trick was to find a gap in the German lines so we could squeeze through. We spent two hours scouting along our front, questioning sentries, ducking cross-fire. There were many blank spots in the German lines, but they were thickly mined. Sarge decided on a gamble. We'd walk out along the bottom of the Mussolini canal. Considering the manslaughter that greeted the last group to try the canal three weeks ago, the Germans might figure that no one would be so foolhardy as to try it again. Sarge guessed right. We were almost to Cisterna before we ran out of ditch. We hadn't seen a single German and, and since we walked most of the canal in the dark of night, we guessed they hadn't seen us either.

The second trick was to cross eight hundred yards of open country, unprotected, without tripping an alarm or a land mine. Darkness and speed helped, and we were soon on the outskirts of Cisterna.

We found a deserted stone barn on the edge of town just as first light began to break in the east. With sighs of relief, really prayers of thanks, we climbed to the loft, unslung our packs, and settled back for a day of quiet observation until the onset of nightfall provided a mantle of dusk for the next trick of our mission. We had hoped for a day of quiet, but it was interrupted midmorning by the now familiar roar of heavy bombers returning for another saturation of Highway Six.

The first wave of Liberator bombers dropped sticks of anti-personnel bombs. They flew low enough for us to see the clusters of bombs leaving the bomb bays, five clusters to a stick, four sticks from each bomber. Each cluster split into nine small contact bombs that spread out on their descent. Each of sixty planes salted the land with some two hundred oversized grenades that exploded on contact and strewed shrapnel like popcorn, cutting down anyone not thoroughly shielded or dug in. They caught few Germans fool enough to be out in the open with Liberators overhead.

We implored each bomb to overshoot our barn, and I guess we were too far south of the main targets to gain attention. But now no traffic moved over Highway Six north from Cisterna toward Rome, chiefly because there was no more Highway Six. Just craters. And Cisterna itself was half rubble, so there were probably few occupying troops hiding there. Still, cringing in some basement as the bombers flew overhead, there must be a few headquarters companies, where we might find a *Grupenfuhrer*.

As the bombers disappeared toward the east coast, we settled back again only to be startled by another roar, this one smaller but closer. From the loft gate we watched a Tiger tank wheel out from the shadow of a small roofless, half-walled building and head directly toward us. There was no place to hide. One shell from the eighty-eight would sweep the loft clean. We held our breath, hoping it hadn't seen us, waiting for it to stop and fire. It kept advancing. At the barn door it turned about, facing the approach road, and backed through the barn door. It was looking for a better hiding place.

Three black-clad crewmen climbed from the tank turret, stretched, and spread blankets on the straw in one of the side stalls. One stood in the doorway looking out over the open fields while the other two stretched out on their blankets. This tank had evidently been assigned to guard the southern approach to the city but had been interrupted by the bomb runs. They had been hiding from the bombers and arrived late at their assigned post. Sarge signaled Joe, Mouse, and me to keep each crewman in our sights while Sandy, Jersey and Bull slid noiselessly down the stone steps. On signal Jersey and Bull fell on the napping tankers with their Navy knives while Sandy grabbed the sentry from behind, left hand clasped over the German's mouth and right hand drawing the stiletto across his throat. The bloody incident took less than a couple of seconds.

But we now had the barn to ourselves, and we had a tank, to boot. The machine gun would discourage any further inquirers, and Sarge thought he'd be able to handle that. But could anyone drive a tank? We all shook our heads. None of us had even seen the inside of a tank, let alone a German one. Movies had told us that it was run by moving levers back and forth, but how and why never was explained. Sarge registered obvious disappointment. Evidently he was thinking of reconnoitering the city by driving a German tank right in among the Nazis. I was inwardly pleased that not a one of us knew how to drive a tank. At the moment, a Liberator looked like safer transportation.

Toward dusk we set out to scout the damaged town. We just had to hope that no one discovered the dead tank crew before we returned, but it was necessary to track down a possible target while it was still light, possibly while everyone was concentrating on the dinner hour. We darted from rubble to rubble, wall to wall, door to door.

On turning one corner we found ourselves in the middle of an ambulance crew dragging bodies from a bombed building and loading them in the ambulance. We were out in the open before we realized what we had stumbled upon.

Sarge signaled "forward" and we marched by as if on a parade. We paid no attention to the ambulance crew, but they stopped in their tracks and watched us, open-jawed, as if they were unsure of what they were seeing or uncertain what to do about it. We turned another corner quickly, and Sarge sneaked back to watch the crew go on about their business as if we had never existed. Sarge frowned in disbelief, shook his head, and hurried back to our squad. "How much luck can we get in one day?" he said. "Forget the colonel. Let's go for a general. Maybe even Kesselring himself." We knew Sarge was kidding. Well, maybe we didn't know for sure, but we hoped so.

From a narrow alley, the squad neared the town square and ducked into a half-building half-brick pile adjoining the square. The bottom floor had been a market, the top floor—now a pile of roofless bricks on the first floor—apartments.

We climbed to the top of the rubble and looked out on a cobblestoned plaza surrounded by alternating stone buildings and rubble piles. The pattern suggested the heavy bombers had not been exactly aiming for the center of town—most bomb craters were to the north—but since they drop the 500-pounders en masse on signal and not by individual sightings, fringe bombs could drift anywhere.

The church and city hall still stood, pocked by shrapnel and without glass, but otherwise intact. A third of the surrounding buildings were roofless and windowless, most with at least one wall crumbling. A clean, brightly painted ambulance sat in the center of town square. It was unattended, and probably not concerned with transporting dead or wounded. It was positioned to dissuade bombardiers or artillery spotters from targeting the town center. Unless it was a recent arrival, it was not effective.

Two staff cars and two troop-loaded open trucks with a dozen soldiers in each waited on the cobblestones in front of the city hall. On the steps of the *municipio,* a group of German officers stood quietly, almost at attention, watching two other officers on the steps above them. One seemed to be doing most of the talking, gesturing wildly, pointing westward, slicing menacingly, pounding emphatically, while the second stood calmly listening, hands behind his back. Sarge studied their collar tabs through his field glasses. The gesturing officer wore an oak leaf with one pip; the listener, no oak leaf but four pips.

"I think one's a lieutenant colonel," Sarge said. "The quiet one is a major. The ones on the steps below are wearing three diamond-shaped pips, one with a silver bar added. The bar is first lieutenant, I think; the others, second lieutenants. Next question: how do we separate the oak leaf from the pips?" He turned away from his post and handed his glasses to Sandy.

As Sarge spoke, the major saluted, turned and walked down the steps. He stepped into the lead staff car while the lieutenants dispersed, two to the first staff car, three to the second, and one to each of the trucks. The convoy turned off the square and onto a side road leading west, away from the cratered highway. The colonel stood on the steps, watching their exhaust.

"By God, he's alone," Sandy said. "How do we get to him?" Sandy paused. "Oops. Spoke too soon." Two soldiers with slung rifles came out of the building, walked down the few steps to the colonel, and stood beside him, while two others stood in the doorway. Obviously their colonel was not to be left alone. As if on signal, the three turned back and marched into the city hall. "Guess that's his headquarters," Sandy said. "And he's probably gone down to the basement for some supper and beddy-bye. Must have at least a platoon in there. He'll never be alone."

"How about when he's sleeping?" Mouse asked.

"Or when he goes to the crapper," Jersey added.

"When he's sleeping," Sarge said, "he probably has his duty officer and radio operator right outside his door. As for the crapper, the latrine is probably in the next room off his. It'd be different if he had to get to a slit trench or an outhouse."

"How about during an air raid? Where would he go?" Sandy asked. "He'd probably bunker down right where he is. If anything, he'd go deeper and tighter. Any other ideas?" His question was met by silence.

After a few moments with no further activity in the plaza, Sarge started to get to his feet. He was about to suggest that we return to the barn for the night and resume surveillance in the morning. But Joe raised his hand to interrupt him. "Can we smoke him out? " Joe asked. "What would he do if his building caught on fire? He probably doesn't have enough men to put it out. I bet he'd come out and look for new quarters, maybe even in the church. He'd have his headquarters squad with him, but I'll bet there aren't any other units staying in the city. Not with these daily bombing patterns. Bet we could ambush the squad and isolate the colonel."

Sarge thought a minute. "Front door or back?" he asked.

"Front," Joe said. "Easiest escape route and easiest access to other quarters."

"Worth a try," Sarge said. "Boots, you, Bull, and Joe go back to the barn. See if you can wrestle that machine gun loose. With the stand if that'll come. And bring any jerry cans the tank might have been carrying. Full I hope. Sandy, Jersey, and Mouse, we passed some bombed out vehicles back a few blocks. Go see if any of them were carrying jerry cans. If they haven't burned, siphon out all the gasoline you can get. I'll keep a watch on our retiring bird."

By midnight, we had accumulated a machine gun, half its mount, and six jerry cans of gasoline.

Jersey crept around the back of the buildings and eliminated the sole guard watching over the deserted square from the city hall doorway. Bull and Mouse mounted the machine gun in a pile of heavy stones, the swivel pinion braced with stout blocks herring-boned around it. Sarge, Sandy, and Joe crept into the unguarded hall, moved quietly to the back, and poured gasoline liberally over the back and side walls, keeping the inside staircase and front exit clear. Sandy set a one-minute mechanical fuse to a thermite grenade. And we all took up positions in the rubble on the south side of the plaza.

"Remember," Sarge whispered, "go for anyone carrying a rifle. If any are unarmed, leave 'em alone—one of 'em will be our target. Don't be too liberal with that machine gun, Bull. Wait for my signal. Joe, you and Boots cover the door in case there are any stragglers and to cut off retreat—although I don't think any will be rushin' back in. Start picking 'em off from the back forward. Sandy and Jersey, pick off the front. Our colonel will probably be in the middle somewhere." Sarge pushed back his sleeve and studied the faint glow of his watch face. "Get set. That gas is going up about now."

The words had just escaped his mouth when a giant WHOOSH of air swept across the square and a large fireball blossomed inside the city hall, spouting beacons of flames through every window. It wasn't an explosion like an artillery round or *plastique,* but it took our breath away. We had underestimated what thirty gallons of gasoline in an enclosed space can do. We stood gaping, even as the spurts of flame subsided, until the rush of German soldiers called our attention back to the job at hand. There must have been thirty Germans in the rush out the front door. Most carried Mausers, one carried a bulky radio, and three in the middle were running while pulling tunics over their white undershirts.

"Now!" Sarge hollered. A fusillade of M-1 fire began dropping men, front and back. Sarge trimmed stragglers from the sides with short bursts from his tommy gun. The machine gun from the tank gave a quick burst that dropped a large part of the German platoon. With the machine gun chatter, the still-standing Germans hesitated, looked around to see where the fire was coming from, and raised their hands in surrender. This was just as well, for the machine gun had "walked" out of its makeshift mount and was useless for further firing. Mouse and Bull dropped the machine gun, picked up their rifles, and dropped a few more who had not raised their hands. Only five men were left standing, calling *"Kaputt! Genug! Halten Sie!"* We had our prize.

Sarge led us out into the square, rifles ready. We herded the five prisoners to one side while Bull walked among the dead and wounded, kicking aside weapons, prodding bodies for possum-players.

One of the five wore the insignia and arm band of a medic, and Sarge motioned him forward to attend the wounded. All but three were dead. With signs, Sarge motioned a *schutse-grenadier* from the standing group to help the medic load the wounded into the ambulance. He directed the medic and the private into the front seat. *"Krackenhaus"* he asked, and the medic pointed down the road. Sarge waved them off, and half in fear, half in doubt, the medic drove the ambulance quickly into the night.

"We'd better get out of here," Sarge says. "They'll be sending a whole battalion back here to get their officers. Let's go." And we herded a hands-on-heads group of three German officers back toward our stone barn

"Krackenhaus?" Jersey asked, as we marched.

"Hospital," Sarge said. "Old sign on the hospital in Naples. Used to be a German hospital before our medics took it over, I guess. Could have meant latrine for all I know. But it worked.

"Just like that gasoline," Jersey said. "Wow! When you start a fire, you do it up big."

Sarge smiled sheepishly. Joe intervened. "Gasoline usually just burns," Joe said. "But when the vapors mix just five percent in air, they become explosive. That's what runs an automobile."

I grinned at Joe. "Is there anything you don't know something about, Joe?"

Joe was not apologetic. "You forget, Boots," he said, "I was a physics teacher."

"It's not just physics," I said. "Everything."

"Well, don't forget, Boots. I've had thirteen or fourteen years more than you in which to learn."

"Don't you ever forget anything?"

"More than I can remember," Joe said.

Sarge let us ramble on. Bull and Mouse argued over whether a machine gun could be fired hand-held. Bull claimed he'd seen it done in field practice. Mouse argued that the recoil of the rapid-fire German gun would pull it right out of your arms.

It was obvious to Sarge that we were working off tension, burning off adrenaline, looking for escape. Small talk and banter kept us from thinking of the risks we had taken and the messes we had made. Or the problems we had ahead. Sandy voiced them. "How we going to get these three guys back through the German lines?" he asked. Sandy tended to worry details more than most.

"Same way we got here," Sarge said. "The canal. We'll stop at the barn long enough to gag and shackle these three. Then try to make it back to our front before daybreak."

That would be fast moving, Sandy thought. It was only a few hours to daybreak. We'd had luck on our side at every move today. Pray God it lasts five more hours.

We gagged the three officers to keep them from alerting any German patrols we might encounter, and Sarge ran a rope from the lashed wrists, joining them together with less then two feet between them. If one fell, they'd all fall. And if one found some way to set off an alarm, they'd all die. Individually, any one of them would be easy to intimidate, but collectively they presented a show-off front, each trying to impress his fellow officers with his bravado. More than once Sarge yanked on the rope sharply enough to send them sprawling in the mud. With prodding from his Navy knife, the three would regain their feet and lose a bit of their hard shell. If it weren't for the gags, they'd be screaming Geneva conventions, officer courtesy, and POW handling.

Three hours later we were half way down the canal, well within our lines, and ready to climb out and look for some transportation. We climbed up the bank and started across a field toward an artillery battalion where we would probably find a truck unloading 155 shells. Halfway across the field, the Germans stopped short, bracing themselves against the pull of the rope and almost tipping Sarge off his feet.

"Now what are you three up to?" Sarge said. "Piss call? What?"

The senior officer, the colonel, nodded toward a little wood sign planted in the field just before us. Sarge read: "*Minen!* We almost walked into a mine field. Dandy. Now what?" We realized that the edges of the canal were probably mined most of the way from Nettuno to Cisterna.

The colonel led us to two hardly noticeable markers, about three feet apart. There was another pair ten zig-zag feet beyond, and another set ten feet beyond that. "Single file," Sarge said, "and stay between these markers."

Three hours later we were through the mine field, and on our way to turn the German officers over to House and his staff.. By mid-morning we were back at Antonio's, hoping to find a late breakfast or early lunch at Corps mess and get in a couple of hours sack time. It had been a lucky night and started out to be a lucky day.

That afternoon Captain House assigned us back to Third Division to help protect the eastern flank once again. We were back in the foxholes again, fending off cursory attacks from German platoons, while the land to our north trembled and the night skies blossomed in blood red-orange clouds of artillery barrages, and we knew we were lucky again. The unlucky Forty-fifth Division, as usual, was absorbing the bulk of the battle.

CHAPTER NINE

Scuttlebutt had it that we had a new CG. We had spent six days in foxholes near Cisterna before Lieutenant Pelski's platoon had relieved us, and all along the march back to Antonio's we'd heard from a dozen sources that General Lucas had been axed and that General Truscott was now commanding Six Corps.

We met General Truscott the next morning. We were among the last on the beachhead to meet the new CG. Truscott had been spending most of his daylight and half his nighttime hours patrolling the front lines, the rear echelons, the incoming ships, and hospital wards, shaking hands with awe-struck GIs and Tommies, asking each of them where he was from, what did he need, or how was he being treated. Each quick-to-gripe and quicker-to-sound-off soldier offered little more than "everything's fine, sir," at first. But Truscott probed.

His predecessor, General Lucas, had spent most of his waking hours studying orders of battle, bills of lading and harbor reports, or tables of organization and equipment. General Truscott studied the tired, unshaven, and often bandaged faces of riflemen, armorers, sappers, signalmen, and artillerymen—and learned as much.

When we first heard of Lucas' getting the axe, Joe muttered under his breath, "Thus exits Flavius."

We stared at him, awaiting further explanation. "Who?" Jersey asked.

"Flavius?" Joe said. "He was a Roman dictator. He was in charge when Hannibal brought his elephants from Carthage to attack Rome. Flavius wouldn't attack him. While Hannibal sacked towns all over Italy, Flavius would snipe at his heels, raid his supply lines. But he always postponed any confrontation with Hannibal. The Romans named Flavius the 'Cuncator.' That's Latin for 'delayer.' The Romans finally booted him out and brought in a new commander who would fight."

"You're saying Lucas is this Flavius?" Jersey asked.

"To a point. I don't want to stretch the analogy too far. The successor took Hannibal head on and was slaughtered. The Romans had to ask Flavius to return. But Hannibal gave up the campaign and sailed back to Africa before Flavius could do anything about it."

"Everyone's heard of Hannibal. How come we never heard about Flavius?"

"Losers are quickly forgotten," Joe aid. "Same with Lucas."

Jersey started to press for more information, but Sandy interrupted him. Sandy had been standing in the doorway, looking out over the tiled patio. Two jeeps stopped at the gate, and Sandy turned away to call back, "We got company. Brass. Big brass."

Captain House was the first down the steps. He grinned and stifled a call to attention, for we were already standing by our bunks in quasi-attention. Behind him came the General who called out "as you were" as he surveyed the crowded basement. Behind him came a handful of staff officers, dressed in sharp-creased wools and clean, crisp field jackets while Truscott sported mud-flecked pants and a well-creased leather tank commander's jacket.

Truscott motioned his staff to stay back. The small basement room was beginning to resemble a circus telephone booth. He turned to us and smiled. "So this is the Red Dog patrol I've heard so much about."

"This is Sergeant Crafton," House said.

Sarge started to salute, but Truscott thrust out his hand and Sarge swung from salute to handshake in a smooth and natural motion. He also turned a little red around the collar.

"I understand you and your squad are proficient with those knives." Truscott indicated the double sheath that lay at the foot of Sarge's cot, and in a deep, hoarse voice asked, "Where did they teach you that?"

"Mostly just practice, sir," Sarge said. "Some hand-to-hand back at Fort Stewart. But not like this."

"So you learned the hard way."

"By doing. Yes, sir."

Truscott studied the sheathed knives, shuddered, and turned to the next cot—mine, just across the room.

"And you?"

"Private Holt, sir," I said.

"How old are you, Holt?"

"Nineteen, sir."

"Kinda' young to be learnin' this trade, aren't you?" Truscott smiled.

"My mother thinks so, sir."

"In your next letter, tell her I said you've got good watchdogs." Truscott's arm swept wide to take in all in the room. "The sergeant, of course, but especially me," he added.

Then alternating cots back and forth, Truscott first greeted Sandy. *"Corporal Bricker, sir... From the south, no doubt...South Carolina, sir...Thought so. Nice accent."*

Then Jersey. *"Corporal Varlas, sir... They call you Jersey?... Yes, sir. How did you know?...You've got an accent, too."*

Then Mouse. *"Sergeant Schimmer, sir... Football player?... No, Sir. Disc jockey. Radio. Virginia, Sir...* Well, you'd make a great tackle. Try the University of Virginia after the war."

Then Bull. He didn't smile. *"Corporal Skywolf, Sir...Skywolf? Indian?...Yes, Sir. Navajo...From Arizona, then?...Yes, Sir...God's country...Used to be ours, Sir."* We all gasped. Bull had exceeded his daily allotment of words. Truscott just smiled. "Indian country, huh? Who's was it before you got there?"

And finally Joe. *"Corporal Coffey, Sir."* Truscott held onto his hand, looking into Joe's eyes, wondering why the "corporal" came out kind of swallowed. "You used to be a sergeant?....*No, Sir...*Proud of being a corporal?...*No, sir...*Rather be a private, then?...*Yes, sir...*How about a field commission?...*An officer? Heaven forbid, sir..."*

Truscott shook Joe's hand, slowly, almost thoughtfully. "I've been in this army twenty-six years, Corporal, and I never met anyone like you. I'm going to look forward to talking with you again when we have more time. Right now I have an appointment down at the docks. We'll meet again." Truscott turned back to Sarge. Then stopped and briefly surveyed the seven of us still standing almost at attention.

"You fellows have done a remarkable job. Especially that last trio you came back with. How you do it, I'm not sure I want to know. But we're all grateful for your efforts—and some of us are probably alive today because of them."

He turned back to Sarge. "Your squad provided us with one of the keys to a successful defense against Kesselring's last attack. And I'm almost sure it was his last. The next move is all ours. Anyway, Major House here will tell you all about it. I just want to say keep up the good work. With guys like you, we're gonna' win this one."

Truscott turned toward the door, then stopped and turned back to face us. He threw us a hasty salute, spun on his heel, and vanished up the steps, to his waiting entourage of assorted colonels. Captain House remained with us, to explain Truscott's parting remarks.

The captain sprawled in a chair, lifted his tin hat and dropped it on the table, and motioned us to sit on the bunks nearest him. "You never met the General when he commanded Third Division?"

"We saw him from a distance," Sarge said. "He took over Third Division just as you pulled us out of Company D, back in Morocco. We still trained with the Third, however, and he was a driver. But a good one. And fair. He got results."

"He does that, all right. He has the British thinking they're finally on the same team with us. They never liked Six Corps. Thought Lucas was a bit aloof. But Truscott's been in so many front line skirmishes every time he visits the men of the British First that they think he's one of them. Once he lost his helmet, rolling down a hill to escape some German machine gunner, and he came back wearing a British tin hat. They made him an honorary Grenadier."

"He needs a rest," Jersey said. "He's lost his voice almost. Barking out too many orders, probably."

"Or he smokes too much," Sarge added.

"He doesn't smoke," the captain said. "And his orders are soft, but certain. No, he hurt his vocal chords when he was a kid. He's sounded like he's whispering from a foxhole ever since."

House waited until he was sure we had no further comments on our new commanding officer. He sensed we liked him.

"So, to give you an example of his orders," House said, "the General spelled out, quite calmly, what each battalion or regiment was to do when we learned where the Germans would attack. He was absolutely right. It was a bloody day, but we stopped the Germans. For once and for all, we think. Too many of them are now dead or captured for them to mount any more attacks in strength. It all started when you brought in that German colonel."

House turned to the charcoal map Sarge had drawn on the block partition. "Is this what I think it is? It's as good as many of the maps we have at headquarters. I'd add two lines though."

House picked up the lump of coal that Sarge had dropped to the floor, and scratched a curving line from left to right across the bottom of the map. "That's the Mussolini Canal and the ditches. That's where the Rangers were shot up a couple of weeks ago."

He then drew a second straight line, running northwest to southeast, parallel to the seashore, about five miles inland from the beachheads. "And that's the raised railroad bed that you've climbed over more than once. Most of the action took place within that box formed by the Canal on the south, the railroad bed on the west, and the Via Anziate heading north. Not much on the eastern edge, where you guys were stationed with your old Company D for a few days.

"And here, where the railroad bed passes over the Via Anziate," House tapped the intersection, "is where the Germans were stopped. It's along this railroad bed that the British First held them from going south into Anzio. They were a short jump from overrunning our entire rear echelon." House dropped the charcoal to the table and resumed his seat.

"All this began," House continued, "when the Scots Guard brought in that *Gefreiter,* a German sergeant. He was an arrogant son of a bitch.

He wore a clean, sharply pressed uniform, so we knew he was new to the front, but all he did was sneer at his captors. He told them to enjoy themselves because he would soon be freed and they would be the prisoners. At one point he said that his captors had until the fifteenth of February to enjoy their freedom, and then he realized he had probably said too much and shut up."

"Where's he now," Jersey asked.

"Probably in a POW camp in Morocco by now. Anyway that's why we sent you guys out for some scouting. Air observers had reported a lot of German maneuvering, so we sort of suspected they were ready to attack again. But we couldn't figure where. They might come down the coast from the north and get behind the British, but we figure they had little access to the coast north of us and a lot of the terrain was marshy. Then we thought they might come through the ditches and canals to the south, but they had already mined the area thoroughly, which would slow down troop movement, and they might just get ambushed as they had done to the Rangers

"So that left the south-west route into Nettuno from Cisterna. So we concentrated your division in that area.

"There was still, of course, the much-used direct route to Anzio along the Via Anziate, where they'd been seesawing around Aprilia with the Forty-fifth for more than a couple of weeks now. We never thought that they would try that again after two attempts thwarted earlier.

"Then you guys came back with that German Colonel. He was a character, an old-school baron. He was one of that group of German officers who think Hitler is a madman. He almost cried when he described the effects of the bombing raids over Germany from England. And now that we're establishing heavy bomber groups over near Foggia, the bombers from Italy will provide the one-two punch with the bombers from England. They can reach targets the bombers from Britain can't quite get to. Romanian oil fields, especially. But the German said that if the war doesn't end soon, all of Germany will be nothing but one vast pile of bricks and stones."

Sandy filled the pause with a question. "Then why do they fight so hard? They're only prolonging the war."

"Corporal Bricker," the captain said, "you have to understand the Prussian devotion to duty. Before you joined this army, you were free to question authority, even encouraged to sometimes, and probably did more often than you should have. But in basic, you were taught to follow orders, whether or not you agreed with them and even if you didn't understand them. And I'll bet you don't always do that. But the traditional officer corps in Germany is made up of career officers who have had drummed into them from the cradle that the Fatherland is the supreme cause. The tradition goes back for generations. Duty surmounts all considerations. It's a matter of honor. Can you sense their motivation?"

Sandy hesitated. "That's deep, sir. I'll have to think on it."

"Fair enough. I can't understand it all the time, myself. But anyway, back to the colonel, he said that the German offensive would come down the battered and bloody Via Anziate for the third time. Actually, it's the best route for tanks and battalion-strength troops, even though it's pretty well shot up. The goal would be to break through to Anzio itself and split the beachhead in half with the British Divisions on the northern side, and the American Third and Forty-fifth on the south. The fifteenth was the marshaling date, when all attack units had to be in position. The actual attack began just before daybreak on the sixteenth."

"And by then," Sarge added, "we were with D Company."

"Every man who could handle a rifle was on the line or in immediate reserve. You got one of the easier posts. Any trouble?"

"Not really," Sarge said. "The six-by you sent took us to a battalion aid station on the road to Cisterna and we hiked a mile to D Company. They were stationed straddling the road, and there was a built-up driveway extending to the left, with the ruins of a farmhouse on a little hill at the end of a peninsula. We were assigned to Lieutenant Pelski's platoon, and he assigned us to hold that farmhouse—or what was left of it. The wide fields between the farm house and the Forty-fifth

Division on our left flank were muddy swamps. But the fields to the east were passable. That's where the Germans would come from."

"But not in great force," the captain said.

"No, sir. It seemed like they only wanted to tie us down so we couldn't interfere with their main thrust down the Via Anziate. On our left flank we could hear the *carrumph* of artillery shells and see the sky brighten with flashes. Sometimes we could even sense the earth move. The artillery barrages must have been overwhelming."

"But mostly ours," House said. "We probably got off a dozen shells for every one they fired. According to the colonel, Hitler had ordered a 'walking barrage' to precede the troops down the Via Aziante, but he wouldn't release enough ammo to do it. He's hoarding his shells to meet an invasion from England. Did you get any artillery where you were?"

"No, sir. A few mortar rounds, but they were mostly aimed at the brick pile that used to be a farmhouse. We dug in on the perimeter, so the mortar shells flew over us. Most of the action, what little there was, came at night."

Sarge paused to judge House's interest. Evidently the captain really wanted to know what action we might have met.

"We heard noises ahead of us, shot off a Very flare, and the night turned into brighter-than-day black-and-white. A platoon of German soldiers was coming across the field toward us, but in less than twenty minutes they were dead or scampering.

"At first light, we'd watch a German stretcher squad come out and retrieve bodies. We left them alone. But the next night, the Germans would start the same thing over again. That went on every night for six nights before we finally got through to those thick-headed Krauts that such tactics were stupid. And then Lieutenant Pelski sent some other squad to relieve us—we were about out of ammo and flares anyway."

"Right. The battle was about over. The Germans had hoped to strike down the Via Anziate right into Anzio and split our forces in half. They got as far as that railroad bed where it passes over the Via Anziate. The Forty-fifth had fought them all along the way, and that had given the British time to set up an almost impregnable defense line just at the overhead bridge.

"The British call it the 'fly-over' for reasons known only to them. But the Germans had been hoping to break through to Anzio. The British thought otherwise. They had planted bombs all around the bridge and were prepared to blow up the whole works and everything around it if they had to. All this they had surrounded with dug-in antitank guns and artillery aimed point-blank at anything that passed under the 'fly-over.' Not even a turtle was going to get through."

"And that broke it?" Sarge asked.

"Not quite. Here the Germans introduced another of their secret weapons. Remember the little two-foot radio-controlled tanks they tried earlier? Those had been easy prey for snipers. But now they had a tank-tread open truck, about half the size of a regular tank. It was like an open box on tracks with a smaller closed box hooked on the front.

"The idea was that the driver would take it as close to the target as he dared, hop out, and direct it the rest of the way by radio. At the target, he would release the smaller front box which was loaded with explosives. He'd back off the mother truck to be used again with another front-end load. Then he'd detonate the placed load.

"When it first appeared, it was scary. But it soon became funny. First of all, the response to the radio signals was erratic, sometimes turning the 'tank' in circles or driving it into a mud puddle. Second, it was easily crippled with a well-placed bazooka round. It had no defense. Above all, it couldn't find any targets worth its payload. You don't use a weapon like that against foxholes. Two of the remote tanks were stalled right under the bridge, blocking the Germans themselves."

"That was yesterday?" Sarge asked.

"Day before. Yesterday was the start of the German retreat. Blocked by the British, the German forces turned east and started streaming down the unused railway bed. They had the idea that if they could sweep through to the canal area, they could cut off the Forty-fifth and the Third Divisions completely and reel them in like fish in a net. Tanks and troops rolled down the railroad bed with command of the high ground and with little opposition. Most of our troops were spread out along the Via Anziate or in the pocket over where you were. Then the Germans came to a blown-out bridge.

"They milled about for a while wondering how to cross the gap. They didn't want to send their tanks into the fields on either side since the fields were all mud and the tanks would never get up the other side. They waited for some engineers to bring up some bridging.

"Meantime, one of our platoons dragged an anti-aircraft gun up onto the railroad bed opposite the German tanks, lowered the barrel, and began shooting point-blank into the clustered troops and tanks. The first round utterly destroyed the lead tank and left a clear field of fire to the second tank. As the first shell hit home, someone in the platoon shouted '*STRIKE!*' And repeated the cry with each succeeding round. They killed most of the attacking force and drove off the remaining Germans, now without their tanks. That raised railroad bed, flat and straight, is now known as the 'bowling alley.'

"And that was the high-water mark of the German offensive that your colonel had called Operation Fischfang, whatever that means. The Germans beat a hasty retreat back along the road to Campoleone. They still held the costly Aprilia ruins, but that was mostly because we were too spent to pursue them. We're guessing they lost more than five thousand men in five days of fighting and we lost maybe half that. That's grim."

"We should have chased them," Sarge said. "When we had them on the ropes, we should have finished them off."

"We're badly shot up," House said. "We need time to recover."

"We evidently weren't as badly shot up as they were," Sarge said.

Joe said. "Excuse me, sir. I don't mean to interrupt. But I understand army officers from all over the world come to our battlefields to study the Civil War. Isn't this something like Gettysburg? The Confederate Army wore itself out in three days of assault on Union lines. They failed. Decimated, they straggled back to Virginia to regroup. If Meade had pursued them, instead of just sitting there and licking his wounds, he could have destroyed all that was left of the Southern forces. End of war."

"That's not quite comparable," House said. "Lee had most of his army concentrated at Gettysburg. The Germans have a lot of reserves spread all over Italy."

"They'll keep trying," Sarge said. "Kesselring knows he has to knock us out. The longer we stay, the stronger we get. Maybe we couldn't get to Kesselring, but we sure could have buttoned up the Alban hills and captured a lot of that Kraut artillery."

"As usual,"House said, "I somewhat agree with you. But the colonel you brought in seemed quite convinced that this was Kesselring's last try to wipe out our beachheads. The powers that be seem to agree with him. Any other questions?" He looked to each of us in turn, and we shook our heads.

The captain reached into his pocket and drew out a small square of cardboard. "Then there's one more thing," he said. "I think I have you to thank for this." He held up the card. It held a shiny brass maple leaf.

"This morning General Truscott gave me this. He said he had long agreed with me in staff meetings that we should have acted sooner, and I got those ideas mostly from you. Events proved us right. If we had moved on to the Alban hills as soon as we came ashore, we might have prevented a lot of German action.

"Anyway, he gave me a field promotion. He wanted to pin this leaf on me before we came out here. But I begged off." House stood up. "Sergeant, I'd be in your debt if you would pin this on my collar while Red Dog looks on."

Sarge took the card from House and unpinned the brass leaf. "My honor, sir." He removed the captain's bars from House's shirt collar and pinned the leaf in their place. "Congratulations, sir." He stepped back and saluted, as we all did.

Major House returned the salute, looked from one to the other of us, and grinned sheepishly. "Thanks. Get some rest. I'll have another assignment for you in a couple of days. But for now, take it easy." He turned sharply and hurried up the stairs to his waiting jeep.

We gathered in the doorway and watched him drive off. Joe was the first to speak. "He's hooked now," Joe said. "No turning back. He's an officer through and through, and there's no salvation in sight. Probably join the reserves after the war, poor guy. From now on, each mistake he makes will get costlier and costlier."

"Someone's got to do it," Jersey said. "Better him than some ninety-day wonders I could name. We gotta' have officers, and I'll take House any day."

"Wasn't thinking about us," Joe said. "I was thinking about what a commission does to otherwise nice guys. A lot of good men have been ruined by scraps of metal pinned to their collars. They confuse responsibility and authority."

"Let's not get into that, fellas," Sarge said. "House'll be okay. Let's hit the showers. We're beginning to smell like last month's dirty underwear."

We gathered our gear and headed for the water line at the engineer's bath house. We were lucky. Our second shower in the five weeks since we left Naples. We knew some Company D guys hadn't seen more than a helmet-full of water at any one time since they last saw the Mediterranean.

CHAPTER TEN

The call from Major House carried urgency and we double-timed to his cavern where the Major paced nervously in front of a large wall map. He didn't bother with any greetings, but waved us over to the map and remarked: "You guys are supposed to be good at sneaking through German lines, right?"

"We've been lucky so far," Sarge said.

"Okay. Here's your biggest challenge. See this area here?" He circled a section of land to the west of Via Anziate and half way between the unused railroad overpass and the ruins of Aprilia. "When the Germans gave up and retreated back to Campoleone, they evidently didn't give up entirely. Some of our forces had been holding this area. Mostly the Second Battalion of our One Fifty-seventh Regiment and some British. The Germans have them surrounded. They're trapped."

"It'll take force to get them out, won't it?"

"If we could get them out. We sent the Fifty-sixth Division in, but they were fairly well cut up by German machine guns. Then we tried the Queen's Royals, and they fought their way into the area, but now they're trapped, too. We've lost god knows how many tank and infantry companies trying to break them all out. The British Fifty-sixth sent an armored force to open up an alley, but they lost three tanks and an anti-tank gun and they never even got close. The Germans have the area so surrounded, so infiltrated, and so blanketed that nothing can get in and nothing can get out."

"And what do we accomplish if we sneak past the Germans?"

"You carry ammunition. As much as you can load on your back. Drop your gear. Nothing but rifle ammo. They'll have to fight their way out—you with them—but they're running out of ammo. We tried airdropping them some, but the Germans got more of it than the Second Battalion did. We're trying every way we can think of to get ammo to them. You're one of our bets. It's slave labor, I know, but it has to be done."

"Is it open land like that we've been working in."

"Oh, no. This is special. Highly eroded. Deep ravines, gullies, ridges, caves. Not like anything you've seen yet. And you can't trust the caves. The Germans have infiltrated some of them, cleaned out our troops, and set up crossfire between alternate caves. It's a mess, from what I hear."

"Let's give it a try," Sarge said, and we nodded.

"Okay, here's an order for the ordnance depot where they have backpacks already loaded. Take your weapons, but little else. There's a truck outside to take you as close as we can get up Via Anziate, but the biggest part is up to you. Can do?"

"Doesn't sound as easy as most of your assignments," Sarge said. "But if we can help, we'll do what we can. Any passwords?"

"None. It's all too confused. Every other machine gun emplacement could be one of ours or one of theirs. Any password is compromised in a minute."

"Okay, then. We're off."

After the truck dropped us off just past the unused railroad overpass, we went out into the brush. Progress was slow since we were each carrying a hundred-pound backpack of M2 ball cartridges, as well as pockets full of our own reloads. We found a shallow gully heading north and dropped to our knees. We could hear sporadic rifle and machine gun fire on our right flank. The Germans were too engrossed in engaging the Queen's Royals to pay much attention to their backs, but we wanted a low profile in case one of the Germans looked around. We weren't there to get into a fire fight with the Germans; we were there to deliver ammunition .

We probably could have caused a lot of damage since we were coming in behind the encircling Germans, but eventually they would have realized where the back fire was coming from and we wouldn't get a step farther. On hands and knees, with frequent rests, we crawled the half mile of narrow gully in two hours, avoiding the dirt road on our left and the encircled British on our right.

The gully passed under a single-lane dirt road. We huddled under the low bridge while Sarge and Mouse studied the maps. To reach our objective, we would have to take the farm road, or something parallel to it. And the road was spiked with frequent German platoons moving to new positions surrounding the beleaguered Royals.

"There's a farm house up ahead," Sarge said. "Can't tell whether we hold it or they do. Let's assume the Germans have it. But we've got to get to that farmhouse before we can get to the ridge where the second battalion is trapped. And the only way to that farm house is this road." Sarge pointed a thumb toward the bridge above our heads. "If we run into a German platoon, it'll have to be them or us. Sandy, take forward point. Let's go."

Sandy crept out from under the bridge first and then signaled an all clear. We followed about forty feet behind him, but we hadn't trudged more than a hundred yards before Sandy signaled for cover and ducked into the scrub alongside the road. We scattered, finding hiding places in shallow rain gullies or behind leafless shrubs.

We heard the tromp of boots first, and then a squad of maybe a dozen Germans rounded the curve, not marching in unison but bunched too closely for their own safety, their guns slung and their attention elsewhere. Sarge waited until they had passed Sandy before giving the signal to fire. The bunch crumpled under a hail of bullets from Sarge's Tommy gun and our M-1s. Our only concern was to avoid hitting our own squad members across the road, so we fired at angles.

The German in the center of the bunch was the last one standing and he seemed confused. None of them had even unslung their Mausers, and he seemed to realize too late that rifles should be held at the ready when approaching enemy lines. A single shot from Sandy crumpled the last of the German squad, and we began the task of dragging their bodies into a nearby ravine, while Sandy and I took opposite points on the road to see if the brief skirmish had attracted any attention from either direction. No activity. Our brief fusillade seemed to have been swallowed up in all the other gunfire to our right and ahead.

In a few hundred yards, the dirt road ended at a farm house, substantially and surprisingly intact, rare in a landscape frequently raked with artillery barrages. We circled the farm house, keeping cover in narrow gullies, behind minor outbuildings, and under still-leafy olive trees. Sarge studied all sides of the farm house, wishing he had brought binoculars, to see if it housed any German ambush.

He was almost convinced that the farm was deserted when he spotted a movement behind a small half-moon attic window in a gabled roof. "Someone's there," Sarge whispered. He pointed to the upper story, and we followed his line.

"Yank," Bull said.

"How do you know?"

"I caught the shape of a helmet," Bull said. "American."

"If you're wrong," Sarge said, "I'm in big trouble. You guys stay here and watch for my signal."

Sarge shed his backpack and strode openly toward the house, He was half expecting a volley of machine gun fire at every step. His Tommy gun was held at the ready but would be useless if a German gunner or sniper were in the house.

The front door was open, unattended, and Sarge found himself in a littered first floor where evidently both Germans and Allies in turn had at one time or another found refuge in the farm. The interior walls, like most of the outside walls, were unmarked so Sarge concluded that no skirmishes or fire-fights had taken place in or around the house. Evidently opposing patrols had come and gone, unmolested, at different times, since the litter included ration wrappers and boxes imprinted in both German and English. Maybe each side had tacitly agreed to leave one piece of civilization unscathed as a reminder of what peace once looked like.

Sarge found the staircase to the second floor and then the trap door to the attic above. With his gun barrel, Sarge pushed the trap door aside and called up into the blackness, "Hello up there. Red Dog recon squad here. Are you hiding or working? Need help?" Silence greeted his question, and for a moment Sarge wondered if he and Bull had been deceived by reflections in the small glass pane.

Then following some shuffling and grunting in the low-ceiling attic above, a face appeared in the small square.

'How did you know I was up here, Soldier?"

"We were studying the house. Saw a movement behind the attic window. That you?"

"Yeah. Dammit." A pair of boots swung through the trap door, followed by a dusty olive drab uniform. The back of the helmet bore a small silver bar. "Lieutenant Duschak. Sixty-ninth Armored. You?"

"Sergeant Crafton. Company D, Third Division."

"How many of you are there?"

"Seven. We're on an ammo relief mission if we can find the Second Battalion."

"Well, I'm disappointed you spotted me. I'm trying to stay hidden. I've been holed up here for five days now, directing artillery fire. Half a dozen patrols, both ours and theirs, have passed through here without detecting me, and I'd like to keep it that way."

"Yes, sir. If that's the way you want it, we'll move on. Can you point out the way to the caves where the Second reports they're penned in?"

"Come over to the north window, Sergeant. Stand back in the shadows and look slightly to your right. See that ridge? There's a six-foot-deep canyon running along this side of it. The caves are on either side of the canyon."

"Man-made caves?"

"Augmented, of course, but natural. Probably that ravine held running water at one time that ate out soft spots in the banks. The whole valley is pocked like a wheel of Swiss cheese."

The lieutenant pointed to some burned out tanks at the far end of one of the gullies. "See those three burned-out tanks to your right? Mark Fours. I'm proud to say I did that. Our artillery is cracker-jack. Those tanks could have driven right up the ravine and fired directly into the caves where we're holed up.

"Second Battalion is down to one Company, I think. Two others have been just about wiped out. But they've been joined by some British, and now they're all trapped. I don't dare throw any artillery in there, because the Huns are pretty well mixed in with our lines. But I can keep the Germans from moving more forces into the area. Meantime, I'm waiting for a relief force to come up or for the trapped troops to start to back out, and maybe I'll be able to soften up the path ahead of them."

"There's no relief force in sight," Sarge said. "Two attempts to break into the circle have failed. I think headquarters is telling the Second to shoot its way out. That's why my squad is here. Bringing in some M-1 rounds."

"Well then, your best way into the ravine is to your left there, where those olive trees end. Most of the Germans are east of that. Good luck. By the way, you carrying any extra rations?"

Sarge wondered how long the lieutenant had gone without food and he handed the lieutenant his two lone K-rations. He turned and started back to the lower floor. "Good luck to you, too, sir," he said. Sarge felt the Lieutenant would need it. If the Second and the British could fight their way out, there seemed little chance that the Lieutenant could join them.

From the edge of the olive orchard, Red Dog watched stretcher crews criss-crossing the valley floor under white flags. The valley was heavily salted with dead and wounded, both Allied and German, but mostly German. Under a two-hour truce, multiple teams from both sides, wearing red-cross arm bands and carrying stretchers, passed by each other, unacknowledged, as they gathered first the moaning wounded and then the stiff dead. We hadn't heard any recent large gun battles, just sporadic volleys, so the bodies must have been there since yesterday.

Were these the remnants of Second Battalion's C and D Companies? Most of them had surrendered when attacked in their holes by flame throwers but a few had charged the surrounding Germans.

Jersey suggested we blend in among the American stretcher bearers and sneak by the Germans while the truce was still in effect. Joe quickly talked Sarge down.

"No way," Joe said. "Those rescue teams are under close scrutiny while they're in the open. We'd be spotted in a minute, and we'd all be wiped out, stretcher bearers included, in a flash. Our best hope is to study the layout for the rest of the afternoon and wait until dark."

"There's a small cave on the other side that looks empty," Sarge said. "Think a couple of us could make it? We need another angle so we can get a reading into this side of the ravine."

"As I said, most attention is on those stretcher bearers. The rest of the line is using the white-flag time to catch up on sleep or get something to eat. I doubt if they're looking toward this end. I'll try it. Who's going with me? Boots? How about you?"

"Two of us enough?"

"Yeah, two," Sarge said. "What we need is some kind of reading on where the Germans are throughout the ravine. I'm assuming the far rim of the ridge is fully manned, and I've seen enough Kraut helmets on this rim to know that this side of the ravine is pinned down. The only way out will be either back in this direction which leads away from our main forces or the other end which will be like running a gauntlet. In the dark, the Second can avoid the attackers on the rims, but those down in the ravine will be dangerous. We need to know where the Krauts are holed up so we can sneak by them, both in and out."

"That cave seems to have a good view down the ravine," Joe said.

"Okay, you and Boots make a run for it. We can't give you any support, since we can't see where the fire will probably come from. The rim forces on our right will probably be the ones most likely to spot you. Let's hope they're sleeping. Leave your packs here. We'll lug 'em over after dark. Good luck."

Almost flying, lightened by the release from our ammo backpacks, Joe and I slid down the hill, raced across the flat valley floor, jumped the small creek that wavered through the ravine, and clambered up the ridge to the small cave. Along the way we jumped over two unrecognizable blackened bodies that had swelled to bust the buttons of their jackets, meaning they had been there at least a couple of days, shot down and ignored in the confusion that must have accompanied the torched surrender of hundreds of Second Battalion troops. But we were west of most of the problem. Not a shot followed us. "Cheated death again," Joe said as we rolled into the shallow cave in safety. "And they say cats have nine lives. Hah! We've got that record beat." Red Dog's luck was still with us.

The cave was not more than four feet deep and not high enough for us to stand. But it was wide, as if someone had run a giant ice cream scoop along the side of the ridge. It would help to hide the rest of Red Dog when they joined us after dark.

We sprawled on our bellies at the edge of the cave and studied the south side of the ravine. From the other rim, we had seen perhaps twenty or thirty caves along the ridge, and now from this side we spotted nine more caves along the sloping hillside opposite the ridge.

After an hour's study we had pegged GI helmets in six of the caves, German helmets in the other three. From each of the German caves, a machine gun barrel stuck out over a pile of rocks at the cave's opening. Occasionally, but seldom, a sniper shot echoed from one of the German caves toward the opposite embankment. It looked like stalemate, but the massed German troops along each rim announced with frequent gunfire that stalemate would not last long.

After sunset, a voice whispered, "Joe, we're coming in." It was as good a password as any. Sarge and the rest of Red Dog crawled into the slot. Each of our back packs were slung between two of the squad. We were not pleased to see them again, but we still said "thanks" to the four who had carried our packs in addition to their own. Red Dog was united again, and we looked forward to some rest. But Sarge had other ideas. We would have to locate the Second Battalion in the next hour or two. We couldn't wait until dawn. Nothing moved in the valley after the sun came up. We had to move at night, and we had little left of it.

"From what we could see," Sarge said, "the biggest cave on this side of the ridge seems to be about two hundred feet down the way. I figure that's probably headquarters. Dirt outside the cave means it's been enlarged to hold more. That's what we gotta' get to. There are two caves between us and them. They look quiet, but I suspect a few GIs may be holed up in them. We've gotta' skirt them or get them to identify us. Sandy will lead.

"Sandy, your job is to get to the big cave and get recognition, so skirt the closer caves.

"Jersey, you're next. See if the small caves are empty. Remember, if they're occupied, the troops probably need some of the ammo we're carrying. Let 'extra ammo' be your password if you need one. That oughta get their attention.

"I'll come next. Then after me, Mouse, Bull, Boots, and Joe, in that order. I've moved Joe to the rear since he and Boots already tempted fate. The fate we tempt tonight will probably be from our own side. The Krauts can't see us, but the GIs will hear us and think we're Krauts. We'll need some Red Dog luck. Any questions?"

None. Darkness deepened. Sarge signaled 'move out' and we tried for a noiseless march along the slope of the ridge.

When Sandy neared the large cave, he called out in an a stressed whisper "ammo coming in," hoping his whisper would be heard inside the cave but not carry across the ravine or to the rim above. No response. Sandy crept closer, and repeated his stressed whisper "ammo coming in."

"From where?" came a response.

Sandy sighed. These guys were tense. "All the way from Brooklyn, you jerk. Where do you expect?"

"Come ahead."

And Sandy crept into the cave. "There's six more behind me," he said. He slid his pack from his back and rotated his shoulders in repeated exercises. "We got almost half a ton of some M-1 balls, and I ain't gonna carry these a step further."

A captain came forward and offered his hand. "Glad to see you. . . uh?"

"Corporal," Sandy said.

"Yes. Corporal. Very glad to see you."

The captain nodded to a couple of guards who moved to the front of the cave to welcome the rest of the squad. "Now that you got in—don't tell me how—do you know a way to get out, Corporal?"

"Not that I've seen, sir," Sandy said. "May I sit?"

"Be my guest," the Captain sighed.

Sandy studied the cave. It was deeper and taller than the cave he had known. Perhaps eighty men, a third of them Italians caught up in the German sweep, fit comfortably within its confines. Along one wall, a medic changed bandages on a score of wounded. At the rear a soldier fiddled with a crackling radio set, unaware that his depth at the back of the cave would hamper reception. Mouse would correct that when he came in.

Sandy smiled in satisfaction. He had accomplished his mission. He'd worry later about what he'd do next. For the moment, getting rid of the heavy backpack was worth a smile.

The rest of Red Dog joined Sandy, and we, too, smiled in relief as GIs quickly relieved us of our extra ammo. Sarge introduced himself to the captain, who seemed to be in command. A company usually numbered somewhere between a hundred and two hundred men. This was evidently the company headquarters for what was left of the one company remaining in the Second Battalion. The rest of the men—those that hadn't been captured or killed—probably filled the adjoining caves, looking for salvation.

Sarge told the captain that Six Corps expected them to fight their way out, and the captain said, "Thanks a lot. The radio already told us that. You have any idea how to do it?" And Sarge admitted he didn't even know how Red Dog would get back, let alone a company.

"As I see it," the captain said, "we have three choices. We might try breaking out along the route you say you took coming in." The captain pointed to the west. "That, however, takes us in the opposite direction from where we want to go, and although a squad might be able to worm their way through the German build-up, I doubt if a company could sneak by. Second, we could strike out straight across the valley and try to hook up with the main body of the British just south of us."

The captain pointed to the south, indicating the bank opposite the cave. "But that side is bristling with a battalion of Nazis, and we'd get chewed to pieces. Or third, we could head for the end of the ridge and strike the Via Anziate."

The captain pointed to the east, straight down the valley. "If we can reach the road, we can maybe tie up with some relief column and head south from there. We may run past a line-up of machine guns, but if we traveled in small groups in the dark, we might stand a chance. That strikes me as the best bet."

"Whatever you order, sir. But I'd like to lead my squad back along the way we came, if I may. We may even be able to set up some diversions that would draw the Krauts away from the hillside."

"You're on, Sergeant. Stay the day and take your squad out at first dark tomorrow, if you need some rest. Or you can head back now before the sun comes up. I'll leave it to you. We'll wait until tomorrow night and then we'll start for the highway. You'll be well away by then. Good luck…and thanks for the ammunition."

We would have welcomed some rest, but Sarge led us out, crawling and scuttling along halfway up the ridge to our starting cave, then across the valley floor and up the other side, and finally into the olive orchard where we waited for daybreak.

Getting past the German machine gun emplacements aimed in our direction was best done in the dark. By-passing the larger German forces facing in the other direction would be best worked out in daylight when we could keep German movements in sight. We nibbled K-ration biscuits and settled down for a brief nap. Sarge stayed on watch.

As the first light of morning painted the sky, we fell into our usual roadway formation, Sandy at left point, Sarge and Jersey in the lead, and me following Bull at the rear.

Morning light also permitted renewed firing from our rear and from the Queen's Royals now on our left flank. The clatter of German machines had a rapid-fire clicking noise. Unlike the distinctly metallic clacks of the Browning machine gun, the German gun had a hollow rattle like a stick being dragged along a picket fence. It was easy to pinpoint German machine gun emplacements surrounding the gully on our left, and we reasoned that as long as we had enough ammunition, we might just sneak up behind a German nest, wipe it out, and retreat back to the west before neighboring German troops could pinpoint our presence.

The task was made easier by the German deployment, which stationed riflemen in front of the machine guns, with their backs to us.

With six quick shots, we eliminated the three men manning the gun, crippled the gun with a grenade, and faded back into the brush before the forward troops had time to look up from the foxholes.

We then moved sixty yards down the line and came up behind another machine gun placement. We took out four machine guns that way before Sarge began to worry about having enough ammo to shoot our way through any road block we might encounter.

As we headed south, we skirted two German patrols without their detecting us, and even without our heavy backpacks, our progress was still slow since we had to duck into the scrub at every curve and corner. We were tempted to take on the patrols, but they outnumbered us three to one and Sarge wanted to save our fire power for more certain targets.

We stopped at noon near what had once been a prosperous farm but was now a leveled brickyard. Mouse and Joe took points along the road while the rest of us rested against a low stone wall, not napping, for we were in the heart of German traffic. I thought I heard a scratching behind me and I stood up alongside just as a single figure rose with me on the opposite side of the wall, not three feet away. I stared in disbelief. I was looking in a mirror. The same wide brown eyes. The soft cheeks that could avoid a razor for two or three days. The down-turned mouth. It was me, except for the boxy helmet. For a second we stared at each other, our rifles at half port.

The roar of a BAR over my shoulder startled me into awareness and set my head ringing. I watched my mirror image crumple backwards and I heard the clatter of his fallen Mauser. My head throbbed, my ear hurt, and I fell to my knees. I would have fallen over on my face except for Bull's massive hand grabbing the back of my jacket and lifting me back to my feet.

"I. . . I froze." I murmured.

"So did he," Bull said.

"But I. . . I just stood there." Tears rolled down my cheeks.

"Yeah. I noticed."

"But he was me."

"Not anymore," Bull said. "Snap out of it."

Sarge had watched the play, alerted by the discharge of Bull's BAR right over my shoulder. He motioned the others to be alert since the German soldier probably had companions nearby. Our line of rifles capped the stone wall.

Sarge pushed himself erect, put his arm around my shoulders, and motioned Bull to lie low. He offered me his canteen. "Here, Boots. Have a drink. And sit down." He spotted a row of German helmets in the rubble of the farm house. "Krauts at nine o'clock," he called to the others. And immediately we were in a fire fight.

The distance was too great for much accuracy, but the volleys kept both us and Germans pinned in place. Sarge nudged me. "Boots, follow this wall over to that small shed on the side there and see if you can get behind those Krauts. I can't tell just how many there are, but I judge about eight. See if you can flank 'em." I hesitated, started to protest, but Sarge pushed me to the side with more than usual force. It was his way of bringing me back to the war.

I crept around the rubble pile and noticed Joe to my right and Mouse to my left also trying to infiltrate the side fields. The fire exchange continued over the stone wall and kept the Germans' attention, and we were well behind them before they looked around. Too late. Volleys from our three rifles in unison cut through the Germans caught off-guard. They didn't get off a single shot in our direction. Red Dog luck continued to hold. And my freeze-up was never mentioned again.

We circled around to where we had left the Via Anziate the morning before and started south with a plodding, dragging step. We were picked up by a returning six-by and dropped off near Antonio's, too tired to even call House and tell him of our return.

Two days later, rested and fed, we learned from Major House that few had made it out. The Second Battalion had lost two of its three companies and a good part of the third. The Seventh Queen's Royals had lost almost four hundred of its officers and men. All told, counting wounded, dead, and captured, the two major forces caught in the gullies and caves had lost eighty-five percent of their strength. And we were right back where we had started.

CHAPTER ELEVEN

That year February carried an extra day. It didn't fool the weather gods; they had stored up enough rain to soak Italy for thirty or thirty-one days a month, so February's twenty-ninth used up all the rain they had left.

It didn't slow Kesselring either. He knew he had to act before we grew stronger. Having failed three times along the Via Anziate against the British First and the Forty-fifth, the Germans picked the last day of February to throw their battered Fourteenth Army against the Third Division farther east.

By the first of March, Kesselring knew that the situation was hopeless. The unexpected heavy rains of February had made Panzer operations impossible. Most of the fighting was small arms fire as crawling Grenadiers clipped barbed wire or slid bangalore torpedoes under concertina coils. The Allies fired more than eighty thousand artillery shells at the rain-soaked German infantry and the next day, when the rains lifted, nearly four hundred heavy bombers saturated the Cisterna-Velletri road with fragmentation bombs. Kesselring's third major attack against the beachhead had strewn hundreds of olive drab and gray-clad bodies across the Italian land, and like the earlier two assaults, accomplished nothing. So much for February's extra day before Mars took over the calendar.

Red Dog didn't even have time to respond to the attack. We were packing our kits for a return to D Company fox holes when Major

House reported that the battle was just about over.

"Stand down" was the order. "I'll have another assignment for you later. Meantime get some sleep." And most of us went back to bed. With the sun breaking up the constant February rain clouds, March seemed to be coming in like a lamb, but artillery barrages made it more like a lion. Constant and dense artillery saturated front lines and beach operations. It was a good day to spend in bed.

Jersey woke us up for lunch. He bounded down the steps, his arms cradling packages and envelopes. "Ho! Ho! Ho!," he called. "Guess what I found at company HQ? It's Christmas." We woke grudgingly, but frowns turned to grins when we saw his armful. This was our first mail since we left Naples six weeks ago.

Jersey paced the aisle between our cots, tossing first the bulky boxes, then the envelopes, on the foot of each bed. "This big one's for Corporal Simon Coffey. Don't salivate, fellows. It's not edible. It's from the Down East Reader's Book Shoppe. No chocolate chip cookies there."

Jersey moved over to my bunk. "But this one here, fellas, for one PFC Gerald Holt, from Corning, and the handwriting suggests it's from dear old Mom. Rattles like cookies. Be advised, Boots, that there is a minor delivery fee, payable in cookies."

He crossed to where Mouse was strapping on his leggings. "And here's a box for Tandy Schimmer. And another for Tandy Shimmer. And another for Tandy Schimmer." He dealt three dissimilar boxes onto Mouse's cot. "See what you can reap, fellas, when you have a radio fan club? Get an audience, plead hardships to come, and ship off to Italy. All the girls will spend their lonely Saturday nights making up cookie packages just for the golden voice that introduced the latest swing records—all for you."

The envelopes followed like a blizzard.

"Bricker. From South Carolina. Looks like a bill....Crafton. Hmm. Perfume. Ooh la la...Me. A tax statement...Crafton, again. This is better. Purple-lined envelope...Mouse. Mouse. Mouse. Mouse. All addressed in feminine hand. You're a rat, Mouse...Corporal Robin Skywolf...You know someone who knows, how to write, Bull?...Gerald Holt. From Mom I'll guess. Oh, here's another for Holt.

131

From Florence yet. Not the town. The girl. What'd'ya know. Boots has a girl back in Corning..... Joe, again. From the book store. A bill. And here's another from Augusta School District. Looks official....And Sandy...Sarge...Sarge...Joe...Me...Sarge...and Boots once more."

We settled down to read. Mail call is the soldier's link to sanity in an otherwise mad world. The mud, wet feet, biting smoke, ear-piercing noise, splashing blood, pain, body parts, and death of recurring battle may seem real at the time, but the soldier preserves his sanity by relegating these to a world of fanatic fantasy and relying on a letter from mom, wife, a girl friend, or buddy to provide the needed life-line to the true reality.

A younger brother's baseball sailing through the livingroom window is more a disaster than a mortar round landing on company headquarters. Little sister's list of A's on her Junior High report card is more to be applauded than a company list of bronze star winners. Dad's strained back from shoveling snow from the sidewalks is more painful than the soldier's stiff legs from six nights' sleep in a damp foxhole. Mom's winning twenty dollars at Thursday night Bingo was a more appreciated windfall than a GI's take of two hundred dollars from a floating crap game. One was reality; the other make-believe. Without the ability to label the murder and mayhem of war as fantasy, the dogface would sink into unimaginable neuroses. Mail call preserves his sanity.

"Hey, listen to this," Mouse said. "Peggy writes me that the number one song these days is 'As Time Goes By.' Remember that movie we saw at Special Services in Naples last December? *Casablanca?* Humphrey Bogart and Ingrid Bergman? Well, that song that Bergman asks the piano player—Sam, was it?—to play has now become a number one hit. *You must remember this, a kiss is still a kiss, a sigh is just a sigh...* That's a relief. I was getting mighty tired of songs from *Oklahoma!*"

"I'd have guessed that the number one song is 'Don't Fence Me In'," Jersey said. "At least it's the only American song the Ite-eyes seem to know. In every *trattoria* in Naples all the bands play 'Don't Fence Me In.' Every hour on the hour. Maddening. Maybe they'll learn a new one now."

Mouse turned to Joe. "What's the book you got?"

Joe looked up from his reading. "A Philip Wylie book. *Generation of Vipers.*" He flipped the book to hold up the cover.

"About what?" Mouse asked.

"Us," Joe said. "Everything that's wrong with society today, Wylie ascribes to the little red schoolhouse, moms, social clubs, and I haven't read enough of it to know what-all else."

"Serious?"

"Wylie thinks so. I think it's fun. Clever writing. Thought-provoking, too. Here..." He reopened the book. "He writes: War 'represents an unreasoned and inarticulate attempt of a species to solve its frustrations by exploding.'"

"Never heard of Wylie."

"Ever read the *Saturday Evening Post*?"

"Read it? I used to deliver it. Back when I was in the eighth grade. Every Thursday after school. Got a penny a copy for every one I sold. Had a route of about thirty regulars, so I had ice cream money for the week. And of course I read the ones that didn't sell."

"Well then, you probably read one of the stories about Crunch and Des, a couple of deep-sea fishermen off Florida who solved murder mysteries in *Saturday Evening Post* stories. Written by none other than Philip Wylie."

"Let me see it sometime when you're not reading it, okay?" Mouse hesitated, wondering how to approach his next subject. Finally he just pointed a finger at Joe and said, "And what was in the tin box that came with the book?"

"Not for us," Joe said. "It's for Mama Camistrata—Annetta. I thought I'd try to cheer her up. These are maple sugar candies from Vermont. Mama said she's never tried one. Came through fast. I just ordered them by V-mail about three weeks ago. But Mama needs something to take her mind off her daughter. Maybe sugar candy will help. Why don't you try Boots, over there. I smell chocolate chip cookies."

Attention immediately shifted from Joe to me. I grinned and pushed the box to the foot of my cot. I knew it wouldn't last long anyway, but darned if I was going to serve them. If anyone wanted a cookie, he could damn well get off his bum and come get one. They lined up to help themselves—but they each took only one—although they then looked back at me, hoping for an invitation to a second. It was an unwritten rule of "goodies sharing" that one was expected as one's due; a second required an invitation.

To divert attention as I closed the box for later recall, I mentioned an item from my mother's letter. "Incidentally," I said, "I hear from back home that a town in New York called Asheville, has instituted an all-women fire department. Seems all the eligible young men in Asheville are out looking for Tojo or Hitler. If you were worried about Rosie the Riveter taking over your job, looks like nothing's off limits for what we used to call the weaker sex. If they can fight fires, they can do anything."

"As long as they still function in the kitchen and produce cookies like these," Mouse said, holding up one of my chocolate chips, "they're welcome to the heavy lifting."

"And in the bedroom," Jersey added.

"That goes without saying." Mouse pushed a couple of his opened boxes toward the foot of his cot. "Try one of these," he said. "There's peanut butter cookies from Jennifer, and Marybelle's version of the chocolate chip. Not as good as those from Boots' mother, but passable."

In turn, we helped ourselves from the boxes, muttered thanks, and began exchanging letters for others to read. Jersey's letter told of the benefits to renters from the new rent control bill. People were earning more money than ever but had less to spend it on. But they certainly weren't going to spend it on rent, according to the government. With little available, they bowed to Uncle Sam's drumming of war bonds. Even school children bought ten-cent savings stamps instead of Milky Ways. Everything else was either rationed or absent. Among other restrictions on spending, Campbell's soup was scarce since Campbell couldn't get tin cans, there was no more sliced bread since the steel slicing blades had gone to war, and new sneakers were non-existent since Jeeps need tires. Most of the letters were full of trivial reports, spiced with phrases of longing or sympathy, but this trivia was the measure of reality.

Sarge moved to the center of the room and began reading aloud a report that his family had received a Christmas card. This was rare. Paper shortages had curtailed the production of Christmas cards. Few cards showed up on merchants' counters, and those were somewhat sleazy. Christmas postcards, popular twenty years ago, were making a comeback but even they were few and far between. Sarge's card was addressed to Roger Crafton and family, and was sent from Wilhelm Brucker's Meat Market, their local butcher who seldom had enough meat to satisfy even the 28-ounces-a-week meat ration but evidently thought it vital to maintain good customer relations as an apology for his German heritage.

Sarge was about to comment on Wilhelm's anti-Bundist activities when his eye fell on Bull, sitting impassively on his bunk, and his pause directed us all to the object of his attention.

Bull sat on his cot, his forearms resting on his knees, his stare fixed on an unseen spot on the floor. His hands dangled limply, his left hand holding a folded note. He hadn't moved since we began our mail exchanges. He hadn't participated in any cookie raids. He seemed unaware of all our banter and he didn't move when Sarge came over and sat beside him.

"Bad news, Bull?" Sarge asked.

Bull's posture didn't change. His eyes didn't waver from whatever spot mesmerized him. He turned his wrist and held the letter as an offering. Sarge lifted it slowly from his mild grip, unfolded the page, and read slowly to himself.

"Read it aloud," Bull said. "Does it really say what I think it says?"

Sarge hesitated. "Okay," he said slowly. "I guess we all should know." Sarge cleared his throat and read with lowered voice. "Dear Robin. I hope you don't get mad at me, but I can think of no better way to say this than directly. I'm getting married next week. He's Charles Friendly, from the Otter Clan. He is a reporter for the Navajo Journal and a stringer for the Daily Star. We met at a Tribal Ceremonial in Tuba City a couple of months ago. He is a tall, handsome, kind, and considerate man with a slight limp from a childhood accident. Maybe you know him. Anyway, we fell in love immediately. And I'm so sorry, Bull. I couldn't help myself. I know you were planning many things, so forgive me if this comes as a surprise. I'm glad I've known you. You will always be an important part of my memories. But right now I hope we can carry your blessing into the ceremony in Tuba next week. With affection, Alva."

Sarge folded the letter and placed it carefully on the cot beside Bull. He looked around at us. Silence hung heavy in the room.

A "Dear John" letter is a demolition bomb. The girl-back-home dream world often exists more in a soldier's wishes than in reality. In a world where buildings crumble, bodies fly, and pain abounds, the slightest deference shown by a back-home girl provides an antidote to a way of life too gruesome to contemplate. Escape from a world too mad to accept is possible only by building mental palaces and pleasures around the image of the girl-of-one's-dreams. Over time the promised Xanadu becomes all embracing, enlarged beyond rational proportions. But it sustains sanity. That is, until a "Dear John" letter arrives at the front, revealing that the dream was all in the mind of the soldier alone. One block-busting demolition bomb completely levels the grandest of castle walls, leaving the dreamer no place to hide from the real demolition around him.

Sarge cleared his throat. "I guess it wasn't meant to be, Bull. The sooner it's over, the better. If you did love her, you'll want her to be happy. I know a 'Dear John' letter is hard to take, but it's for the best in the long run. Better to find out now than a year or two from now." Sarge paused. Had he said too much? Bull didn't move. "Do Indians cry, Bull?"

"Not so you'd see," Bull said.

"A good cry is like a relief valve. Vents all the pressure."

Sandy interrupted. "Let's get some lunch. That'll take your mind off anything. Sometimes what they serve for lunch around here could make you cry more than a letter could."

Sarge pulled Bull from the cot and we headed out toward the headquarters mess. Canned ham loaf, watery beans, thick slabs of fresh-baked bread, and syrupy pears. The pears were mushy. A large can of apple butter on the table lubricated the coarse bread. The beans tried to imitate Boston baked beans but required liberal doses of catsup to give them any flavor. Nothing could help the processed ham, which tasted like tin.

Cookie probably had the same menu over at the D Company mess, but he would do tricks with the ingredients, such as a raisin sauce for the fake ham or molasses and brown sugar for the beans, that would make the headquarters cooks cringe in shame. Some cooks deserved medals; others, a firing squad.

After lunch, we scattered around Anzio in our own pursuits. Jersey headed for the supply room, not that we needed anything, but Jersey thought it important to maintain good relations with the supply sergeant. Sandy went searching for—and found—a sizeable crap game, run by a motor pool mechanic who had worked on a pleasure boat before the war. Sarge headed for the hospital to reminisce with old friends from D Company awaiting evacuation to Naples or even stateside. Mouse scouted out Special Services to see what the latest big-platter recordings from Armed Forces Radio had to offer.

We didn't know where Bull disappeared to. We knew he had a Navajo friend over in the Forty-fifth, but he never accompanied us on any of our excursions and he never suggested any of us accompany him on his. Skywolf was really Lone Wolf.

Joe and I picked up his tin of maple sugar candies and headed for Mama's. It had been more than a week since we last saw Willie when he delivered our last set of clean laundry. We hoped everything was all right.

Mama's apartment was festooned with olive drab clothing like stalactites hanging from the roof of a cave. Mama had set up a lucrative laundry business. Willie would collect the dirty clothes, label them with the soldier's name and a shorthand that told Willie where they belonged, and deliver them to Mama. With a forced devotion that took her mind off other things, Annetta washed clothes all morning and ironed all afternoon.

Vittorio would hang the clothes to dry, over the back roof when the weather permitted, which was seldom, or on lines strung from wall to wall across the livingroom. A score of parallel lines of olive drab boxer shorts, olive drab tee shirts, olive drab wool shirts, and olive drab wool trousers, even olive drab handkerchiefs, each line carrying a folded paper label with the owner's name, filled the livingroom.

The sunless clothes would never quite dry, so Mama had to press them a bit longer with her charcoal-heated brass flatiron. Willie would tie them up, add the name label, and deliver them to behind-the-lines support troops. At forty lire a bundle, military currency was accumulating copiously in a large carton in the corner. But again, there was little to spend it on.

"*Ah, Signores Simon e Gerry,*" Mama cried in greeting, "*Benvenuto. Entrare. Entrare, amicos mios..*" Mama was smiling again, something she had not been able to do on our last two visits. She still wore black, as did Vittorio and Willie, but the loss of Anita was becoming more acceptable as time passed.

More conspicuous than the ranks of army clothing was the vacant corner where the piano once stood. Was this an attempt at out-of-sight-out-of-mind therapy? Joe didn't think this was the best way to adjust to Anita's death. He would try to get Vittorio aside later on and raise the question.

For now, he smiled, embraced Mama, and proffered his tin box of candies. "Maple sugar, Mama," he said, certain she would understand. "From Vermont."

Annetta set the box on the table, motioned us to chairs beside Vittorio, and hastened back to the kitchen to put aside her hot flat iron. Vittorio offered us his hand, in turn, and beamed a welcome. "Good to know you are safe, my friends. Tell me, do you see any end to all this bombing and shelling?"

"Afraid not," Joe said.

Vittorio looked at me. I nodded agreement. Vittorio looked into our eyes for an extended minute, then sighed in resignation. "I hope *turistas* return some day to Anzio and I can drive taxi again. Now I only good for hang laundry."

Mama returned from the kitchen and set a tray of home-made bread and a wedge of cheese on the table, along with a bottle of Antonio's wine that she had evidently saved from our last visit. She joined us at the table, and with Vittorio's translations, we persuaded her to try the maple sugar candies. She seemed to admire the maple-leaf shapes, as if gathering courage to bite into one. Finally she gingerly selected a piece, nibbled at an edge of the leaf, and stared at the piece in her hand while her mouth worked at the grains of sugar. She admitted it was good—well, interesting anyway—and it was clear than she was more puzzled than enthused.

She asked what Vermont was and when she remembered that Joe was from Maine, she remarked that Joe had no obligation to encourage consumption of Vermont products. Vittorio took a piece of candy to see what the discussion was all about and pronounced it more than good. He had in fact tried maple sugar when he was in New York and considered it a treat. Joe thereupon pulled the tin box back from Annetta and handed it to Vittorio.

"For you, then," Joe smiled. "Not for Annetta."

Annetta grabbed the box from Vittorio. She insisted it was her present, and she would determine who could have a piece. Truth be known, she confessed, she found the aftertaste intriguing and maybe her initial judgment had been too hasty. It was no substitute for *cioccolatto* of course, but she was at fault for expecting it to be.

The banter had been light, the bread and cheese filling, and the wine warming. I felt Joe tightening, as if ready to change the subject. Finally he pointed to the empty corner and asked what had happened to Anita's piano. Mama lowered her head and stared at her lap. Vittorio explained that Annetta had thought it best to remove as many daily reminders of Anita as possible.

Joe held Mama's hand and made her look up. No, he insisted, it wasn't fair to Anita. Mama played the piano, too, and Anita would not want Mama to abandon the piano just because something had happened to her. It would be better—healthier, Joe said—to honor Anita's memory by playing some of her favorite songs now and again. Vittorio nodded in agreement. After some pause, Annetta conceded. She would have Vittorio and Guillermo move the piano back that evening.

"Not this evening," Joe said. "Now. Boots and I are more able than Vittorio and Willie. We'll move it now. Where is it?"

Vittorio indicated a back room, and Joe beckoned me to follow as he headed for what had been Anita's bedroom. I don't remember anyone asking me my opinion, and I was ready to suggest that damp laundry hanging all over the room might not be the best environment for a piano, but I swallowed instead and helped Joe wrestle the piano back into position.

Vittorio helped, and while we were pushing, he asked if the MPs had made any progress in investigating Anita's death. We said we had heard nothing but were certain they were still working on it. We changed the subject as Mama approached the piano and idly punched a finger at a few keys, as if checking it's tune.

We stayed until Willie came home. Willie said he had stopped by three or four times, but we were never there. He would walk back with us and collect what washing any of us had ready.

As the three of us reached the bottom of the stairs and stepped out into the alley, the sound of the piano echoed down the staircase behind us. We paused for a moment and listened. "*La donne e mobile*," Joe said, "Woman is fickle." Willie looked back up the stairs and a wide grin brightened his face. His sister was home again.

CHAPTER TWELVE

The sun from the east drove through the upper windows of Antonio's bunker and startled us into grudging awareness. We hadn't wakened to sunshine many mornings in the past two months. The light seemed surrealistic and we experienced a strange feeling of unease. Something was not right. And then Sarge called our attention to the source of our unease.

"Where's Bull?" Sarge demanded. We turned to stare at Bull's empty cot. It was neat and tidy, his sheathed knives lying across the foot and his BAR along the side. The bunk had not been disturbed since yesterday morning.

Normally Bull commanded little attention. He was largely silent, unobtrusive. His size was commanding, but it was accepted as a normal part of the team's composition. He was most noticeable in his absence. Probably any missing team member would focus our attention, but maybe just because of his size Bull's absence was especially disturbing.

"Anyone seen him?" Sarge asked. No response. "When was he last seen? Sandy? How about you? When did you see him last?"

Sandy hesitated. "Yesterday," I guess. "Lunch time. He had lunch with us. Then we all went off in different directions, I think."

"Yeah," Jersey seconded. "He didn't say anything about where he was going, but that's not unusual. I thought maybe he was heading for a shower. He had a musette bag and went off in that direction."

We all agreed that lunch was the last any of us had seen of Bull. That was yesterday. We usually kept each other posted if we were going to be away any length of time, but two- or three-hour breaks were not accountable. Bull had been away more than a dozen hours.

"Okay," Sarge said, "after breakfast, we're going on a search. Maybe he's hurt or even sleeping off a drunk in some alley. Indians can't hold their liquor, I'm told. Any wine missing, Jersey?"

"Last I looked it was all intact. Doesn't seem to have been disturbed."

"Okay. I'll check battalion aid and the hospital in case he's been hurt. Jersey, you check D Company. See if anyone at headquarters has seen him. Check Cookie, too. Sandy, you scout out the waterfront. Bull has always been fascinated by boats."

Sandy interrupted. "I know Bull had a friend, another Navajo I think, over in H Company. Maybe I should check over there, see if I can locate his friend."

"Good idea," Sarge said, "you do that, Sandy. Boots, you take the waterfront and the beaches. Mouse, wander around Corps headquarters. Check Special Services. Look up the Chaplain. Check especially with the MPs. Mouse, look around Nettuno. Check out any restaurants that may be open and not off limits. No, check even off-limit places. Bull won't be hard to miss. Describe him to anyone who'll listen. If anyone has seen him, they'll remember him. Six-foot-two Indians are not everyday sights. We'll meet back here at noon. If any of you get a lead on him before then, come back and leave a note before going on and we'll follow you. Any questions…? None…? Okay, let's grab a quick breakfast first."

I spent three hours scouring the waterfront. Sailors seldom left their ships to come ashore, so a few questions to waiting crews determined that he had not been on or near any ship currently near shore.

SPs and MPs directed traffic at nearly every street corner, separating in-bound trucks loaded with ammo, POL, or rations from outgoing empty trucks on their way back to Naples for more supplies. I walked the line of empty trucks that waited impatiently for a chance to get away from the beachhead shelling and bombing. It seemed futile since they had arrived during the night and Bull had been missing since yesterday afternoon. But a driver might have seen something, and it was a necessary inquiry. A sailor wearing an SP armband stood to one side of the line, watching for a signal from the LST at the quay. He studied me with suspicion as I patrolled the line and finally stopped me.

"Looking for something?" the SP asked.

"Yeah," I said, "I'm missing my buddy and I wondered if any of these drivers had seen him."

"Any luck?"

"Nope. But how about you? Were you on duty here yesterday?"

"I been here three days now. Going out with this load, I hope. What's your buddy like?"

"He's pure-blood Indian. A giant. Six-foot two. With a face like a hatchet."

The SP grinned. "Y'know, you're the second guy that I've caught patrolling these lines of trucks."

"Oh? Who was the other?"

"Your buddy, I reckon."

"When was this?"

"Last evening. About sundown. He'd been going up the line, talking to three or four of the drivers. I was about to go over and ask him what he was up to, but I turned my back for a second and he disappeared."

"You sure it was him?"

"Fits your description. Big guy. Dark. I particularly noticed his hands as they hung on the truck's window edge. He could squeeze the milk out of coconuts with those paws. Why you lookin' for him?"

"He didn't come home for supper last night," I said. I felt like saying it was none of his business. "We thought he might be hurt somewhere."

"No one hurt around here I know of. Hope you find him, though. But you best step back. The flagman tells me these trucks are ready to roll." He pointed to another SP at the head of the line, waving a yellow flag.

"Did you notice what direction he was moving to?"

"Nope. As I said, he just disappeared." The trucks started moving slowly toward the ship, and the SP swung up onto the running board of the last truck in the line. "Hope you find him," he called back.

I stood there watching the tail end of the truck cross the dock. I turned slowly, looking for an inviting route that Bull might have taken. Nothing. I started back toward Antonio's bunker. Maybe I had a lead, but nothing definite.

I was the last to return. The others sat on the cots, silent, with long faces, which told me that they had no better leads then mine. They looked up expectantly. I told them of the SP directing traffic at the dock, and his guess that a soldier he saw fit Bull's description.

Sarge stood while I recounted the shoreline meeting and then sank slowly back on his bunk. A quiet followed my story which Sarge finally broke with an under-breath exclamation: "That dumb Indian!"

When nothing further explained Sarge's epithet, Sandy said, "What?"

Sarge looked up. "That dumb Indian! He's gone AWOL. He's gone back to Naples."

"Some chick back home dumps him, and he dumps us, huh?" Jersey said. "He's in heap big trouble."

"You bet he is. If the MPs pick him up—and they probably will—he'll be charged with desertion."

"What are we gonna' do?" Jersey asked.

Sarge rose from his bunk. "We're going to Naples. Boots, come with me. The rest of you stay here. I'll get back as soon as I see Major House." I followed Sarge up the steps and toward Corps Headquarters.

Sarge cautioned me not to mention Bull. Just follow his lead, as he asked Major House for a three-day pass to Naples for each of us. "The guys are beat," Sarge said. "They can't sleep—or they have nightmares. They get the shakes every once in a while. Just three days' change of view ought to snap 'em back into shape."

The Major stared at Sarge, and then me, searching for a way to say "no." He leaned forward on his desk. "Look, I can't let you just take leave. There are some foxhole guys who have had it just as bad as any of you—maybe worse. You can't just walk in here and say you're tired of the war and want to go back to Naples for a little R and R."

"I thought that would be your answer, sir," Sarge said. "I don't know how to argue this, sir, but I was hoping I could find some way

144

to talk you into it. Please don't ask me for details, but it's of vital importance to the squad that we get a couple of days in Naples. We could fall apart as a team if we can't get this break. I don't know what more to say. It's not for me, or for just a few of us. It's important to our functioning as a unit. Without it, it could be the end of Red Dog as a team."

"What's the real reason?" The Major asked.

"I was hoping you wouldn't ask. Trust me, sir. I'll spell it out when we get back, but you really don't want to know before hand. I'm not pulling a fast one, sir. I've never steered you wrong before. Please accept my declaration that this is vital."

Major House leaned back in his chair and tossed his pencil onto the desk top. "No, you've never steered me wrong, Sergeant. But I can't give you passes. No way. We just can't issue exceptions from the war." The Major leaned forward again. "But I'll tell you what I can do. Maybe I'm sticking my neck out, but I'm going to put you on orders. We've been wondering why PX supplies, such as Gillette blue blades, Zippo lighters, Pepsodent toothpaste, or Pabst Blue Ribbon, seem to reach us just in trickles. We'll authorize you to make inquiry into Fifth Army G3 to see if they can't expedite PX supplies for the front. It would help morale here at Anzio if a few creature comforts, as well as a few necessities, could squeeze in among the ordnance they keep sending us. How does that sound? Can do?"

"Sounds wonderful, sir," Sarge said.

"Okay, I'll make up the orders. You guys leave your weapons here with me and report back to me as soon as you get back. I don't expect you to do a hell of a lot of good, but you might just put a bee in their bonnet. Rattle their supply lines, so to speak. I'll have another assignment for you that'll get you out of earshot if there's any noise following you back. All seven of you going?"

"Yes, sir."

"Okay, come back after lunch. I'll have your orders ready. And Sergeant—don't hang me out to dry on this one. My neck's way out. So play it square. Okay?"

"Yes, sir. You won't regret it, sir."

As we left headquarters, I asked Sarge why he insisted I come along. "Moral support," Sarge said. "And to give Major House the impression that this was a team action, not just me. Fortunately, the Major didn't press me—or you—for details. If we'd told him about Bull, he would have had to step in officially, and Bull would be up on charges. I don't know how much the Major suspects, but he's given us a free hand. Let's hope we succeed."

We lunched on beef stew and canned corn, with thick slabs of freshly baked bread. We left our weapons with Major House and picked up a dozen mimeographed copies of VI Corps orders sending the seven of us, listed by name, rank and serial number, to Naples to explore supply lines and report back to VI Corps G4 in three days. Why it took seven of us to ask a simple question like where's-our-cigarettes would be hard to explain, but we hoped no one would ask.

We checked in with the harbor master who studied a clip board of papers and assigned us to an LCT then unloading at the quay. Papers in hand, we presented ourselves to some naval CPO who seemed to be directing things from the boat. He studied our orders, nodded agreement, and told us to get comfortable anywhere out of traffic. "We'll have this stuff unloaded in half an hour more, and then give us another half hour to take on the empties. We want to get out of here before the evening bombardment starts or a Heinkel comes looking for us."

By dusk we were out on the Adriatic, circling south to Naples. It was a short ride, but rocky. The high sides gave us no view of the horizon, and to thwart seasickness, we couldn't fix our eyes on the horizon. We stood and tried to keep our bodies erect by springing our knees like a skier. We kept our eyes steadily on a selected rust spot. LCTs are not for sightseeing and hardly for heavy seas. Jersey said, "Rub-a-dub-dub, seven men in a tub," and that started a light banter on bath tubs, butter tubs, sailing tubs, that diverted our attention until we heard the prow scrape against the dock.

Sarge seemed to know where he was going. We left the harbor and headed east into town, toward the Palazzo Reale. Sarge avoided main-street traffic where possible, sticking to narrow alleys and side streets.

It didn't help. We turned one corner onto Via Toledo and were stopped short by a couple of MPs, who demanded to see our passes. Sarge handed them a copy of our orders.

"Staff Sergeant Crafton," the MP read. "That you?"

"Yeah."

"Where's your stripes, Sergeant?"

"We're just in from Anzio, Corporal. We don't flash stripes up there. Too good a target."

The Corporal grunted. "But you're in Naples now, not Anzio, and you're out of uniform. Says here you're on a supply detail. That's down by the docks. What are you doing this far inland?"

"Headed for supper. I know of a nice trattoria up the way. Used to be stationed here in Naples a couple of months ago. Looking for some veal parmigiana that as I remember was the best in the world."

"You're a sad bunch for Naples," the MP said. "Your boots could use a bit of polishing. That mud's okay for the front, but not for town. And now you'll need neckties. You got neckties with you?"

"Neckties?" Sarge echoed. "At Anzio? Don't be silly. I haven't seen a necktie since last Christmas."

"You'll need them now. Fifth Army's trying to spruce up Naples a bit. It was getting too slovenly. All restaurants not off limits must require that GIs wear neckties for service. No necktie, no service. Fifth Army order."

"You're kidding," Sarge said. "We're still at war, aren't we?"

"Not in Naples, Sergeant. Better not challenge this. We're authorized to run you in if you try to eat in a restaurant and you're not wearing a tie. Better get a tie, pronto. Some restaurants keep a stock of 'em just for guys like you," He started to hand the orders back, but hesitated and studied them again. "Wait a second. It says here there are seven of you on this detail. You're only six. You lose one? Where's number seven?"

"He's back at the dock," Sarge said. "He's setting up a meeting with the Supply Depot for tomorrow morning." The lie rolled glibly off Sarge's tongue, and the MP seemed to think better of challenging it.

"Okay. Carry on. But find some ties." He handed the orders back to Sarge and waved us by. We were a few paces beyond earshot before we took a deep breath.

A few blocks up the Via Toledo, Sarge turned left into a side street and then another, to Via Montecalvario. After turning the corner, Sarge paused and we studied the building across the street, where an unobtrusive sign denoted the *Albergo Toledo.* The street was lined by small shops, mostly shuttered, again with unobtrusive signs: *farmacia...macelleria...panificio...florista.* Between each of the shops was a colored door leading to a stairway to second-floor apartments. The doors were green, blue, brown, rose—the paint now chipped, worn, dirtied by years of war-time neglect. In the 1930's Mussolini had decreed a face-lift for Italian cities. He distributed paint by the gallons and in some cases erected brick, marble, or plaster veneers over older structures. The tourist traveling Rome, Milan, or Naples was impressed by the crispness of Fascist efforts, unmindful of the creaky-floor, leaky-roof apartments behind the new facades. Similarly, the Duce's boast that he made the trains run on time applied only to the tourist trains; the daily commuter and goods trains were still catch-as-catch-can.

The shop to the right of the *albergo* was one of the few store fronts still open this late evening. A window sign read, *"Ristorante Toledo,"* and the door between the restaurant and the adjoining hotel was a clean unmarred purple, probably painted many years ago but still crisp since it was unused. A stairway descending from the two floors above ended in a landing from which one could turn right into the hotel lobby or left into the diningroom. The door was fastened shut since it was not used as access to the rooms above the two fronts and therefore retained its freshness along a street that was rapidly getting more and more seedy each year. It lent the hotel and restaurant an air of class and cleanliness that contrasted with their more neglected neighbors along the Via Montecalvario.

"This is the place," Sarge said. "Stick with me. Let's see if our luck is still holding." We followed Sarge across the street and into the hotel where a sleepy clerk looked up from his newspaper and broke into a wide grin. *"Sergente Crafetono, amico mio.* How say longa time we no see. *Benvenuto. Benvenuto."*

"Bono sera, Alberto," Sarge said.

"You need room tonight?"

"Probably. If we can find our *paesano*. You remember Skywolf, Alberto?"

"*El Indiano. Naturalmente.*" The porter pointed to the ceiling. "He here now. With Constanzia. Room *venti due.*"

Sarge held out his hand. "Key?"

"No key. Locks all broken now. *Beones.*" Alberto spit to the side.

Sarge turned and headed for the stairway. We followed. On the second floor he stopped in front of Room 22, raised his hand to knock, then thought better of it and lowered his fist. He turned the doorknob and strode into the room. We didn't want to miss a word of this so we crowded in behind him.

Bull lay in the bed, staring at the door, his right hand holding a half-empty bottle of *chianti.* Another wine bottle, empty, lay on the floor beside the bed, and a full bottle stood ready on the night stand. Next to Bull lay a well-painted, black-haired woman of indeterminate years. She sat up suddenly, letting the blankets fall as they would, making no attempt to shield her naked breasts. We stared in wonder.

"*Sergento,*" she frowned.

"Constanzia," Sarge acknowledged. "How've you been."

"So-so. You looking for Robin, no?"

"That's right," Sarge said.

Constanzia shrugged. "*Certamento.*" She threw back the coverlet and stood so she could reach her clothes on the nearby chair. She seemed unaware, or at least unconcerned, that she was completely naked. She was shapely, long-necked and long-legged, with free-standing breasts and taut hips. We stared in appreciative amazement. For me, Constanzia was the first nude woman I had ever seen, and I suspected that was so of most of us. We were mostly virgins, despite our braggadocio, and we were torn between a hasty retreat in embarrassment or a *voyeur's* stance in appreciation. We chose the latter, as Constanzia stepped into a skimpy set of briefs and bra and pulled a flimsy, flowered dress over her head.

I knew Sarge had a wife back home and Joe had been married. And of course Sarge must have rescued Bull from this position at least once before. But of the other four of us, I suspected we were all naive. Mouse talked a good line about all the fans a radio personality attracts, but I suspected his conquests were nothing more than wishful thinking. And Jersey was too much talk to have that much action. Sandy was quiet, reticent to enter into banter on sex. Recalling past barracks talk, I'd lay odds I was not alone in not knowing what to do with a naked woman.

During basic, barrack's talk invited exaggeration, a certain amount of bragging, an unabashed accounting of past encounters, more imagined than real. Women were playthings, and boys liked to play. The chatter after lights-out consisted of stories that would make Lady Chatterly blush.

In the foxholes, however, attitudes changed. A certain reverence enveloped any mention of the opposite sex. Women were our mothers, our sisters, our fiances, or our wives. No slurs. No dirty jokes. No back-alley talk. We wanted our stateside links modest and pure.

Bull interrupted our thoughts. "You comin' back, Connie?"

"You gonna' be here?"

"Yep. Sarge is just visiting."

"I'll spend a few hours at the club, Robin. I need the money. But I'll check back with you after the club closes."

Sarge stepped aside and let Constanzia pass on her way to work. He then turned back to Bull who so far hadn't even acknowledged our presence. He pulled out a chair, turned its back to Bull, and straddled it, resting his arms on the back of the chair, his chin on his arms, waiting for Bull to speak.

"You make a good tracker, Sarge," Bull finally said.

"I've dragged you out of here before, you stupid Indian. What do you think you're doing? You looking for a firing squad?"

"No firing squad."

"You bet firing squad. This is desertion. In time of war yet."

"Not an Indian war. Pale-face war. Not my business."

"Oh, it's Indian business all right. If Hitler wins this war, what do you suppose he has in mind for the Indians and the Negroes, after he wipes out the Jews. You've seen enough of the "Why We Fight" movies. Remember what he did to the gypsies in Romania? You're in line. Hitler thinks Indians are misplaced Asians, from the Mongol hordes. The Super Race has no room for Indians."

"You'll stop him, Sarge. You don't need me. I am Chief Joseph: 'I will fight no more forever.'"

"Not the same thing, Bull. Chief Joseph was beaten. You're a winner."

"Tell Alva that."

"Oh, don't drag her into this. You were playing around with Constanzia long before Alva ever threw you over. You've got no complaint."

Bull closed his eyes and lowered the Chianti bottle to the floor. "Guess I screwed up, huh, Sarge?"

"Royally."

"What do I do now?"

"We're going to try to get you out of this. You just do what I tell you. First, no more wine." Sarge moved over to the bed, picked up the half bottle from the floor and the full bottle from the bedside table and passed them back to Jersey. "Now, you get dressed and we'll go downstairs and get some supper. It's too late to head back now, so we'll stay here the night and get down to the docks first thing in the morning. Meantime, you stay close at hand."

"What about Connie?"

Sarge sighed. "Well, I hate to see you earn a reward for what you've done, but I guess Constanzia will help you forget Alva. I'll think of something special for you when we get back to Anzio. Maybe a week's straight KP duty. I'll have to level with Major House who stuck his neck out so we could get you out of here. He doesn't know about you yet. But he will. And AWOL charges are a piece of cake next to desertion in time of war. I suspect your corporal stripes are the price you'll pay for Constanzia. Enjoy it while you can."

It was better than a firing squad.

CHAPTER THIRTEEN

Sarge called Major House to set up a meeting with Bull, and the Major told Sarge to bring all of us. He'd deal with Bull first and then brief us all on a recon mission he had in mind. We sat on the floor in the Major's "cave" while he and Sarge and Bull went off to a private "cell"for a separate meeting. Sarge later told us what had happened.

Sarge reported Bull's escapade, carefully avoiding the word "desertion," and Bull sheepishly nodded his *mea culpa*. House called the D company commander and received the colonel's order to conduct a company courts martial at the major's discretion. During Sarge's reporting of Bull's escapades, House had listed a score of possible charges. Now, with perhaps a moan of resignation or perhaps a sigh of relief, the Major crossed them off one by one and said he was reducing the charge to four hours AWOL.

The Major told Bull that there was a way out. If Bull was proficient in his native language, Bull had a chance to volunteer for a transfer. Headquarters was recruiting for an all-Navajo platoon to be set up in Hawaii for deployment somewhere in the Pacific theater. No one would say for sure what the platoon would do, but if Bull accepted and if he was fluent in Navajo, he'd be transferred to the Navajo-speaking outfit in the Pacific. He'd be free of Anzio, and the courts martial would be dismissed. Bull shook his head. He would stay with Red Dog—with Sarge really. He'd pay for his mistake—and he did—with his stripes, a reduction in pay, and a courts martial on his record. We were pleased it had worked out so simply and proud that Bull had opted to stay with us. Bull's standing with the army went down two grades but his standing with us went up even more.

Major House then clustered us around a wall map bristling with push pins and colored strings. "Somewhere in this area," the Major said, pointing to a relatively blank area on the map, "is a very mobile German artillery brigade. Must be at least a dozen big guns—at least one-fifties. They fire about three salvos every day, and they've caused all sorts of havoc. They must have a good spotter somewhere that directs their fire right to our command posts and supply points, because they're more accurate than pure luck would allow."

"And you want us to find the spotter?" Sarge suggested.

"Nope. I want you to find the artillery. Eliminating the spotter would help, but it wouldn't cut into their fire power. The problem is that every time we get a fix on the battalion, they somehow hop out of the way. As I say, they're mobile. Very mobile. They fire a salvo, and by the time we zero in on them, they're a couple of miles away.

"We've been chasing these guys with return fire for a week now and we've blown up a lot of empty fields. They stay within four or five miles of the front, because that's their effective range. Could you locate them so our one-five-fives could clean them out?"

"What area are they operating from?" Sarge asked.

Major House drew a circle just north of Carano. "Somewhere in here. The fixes we get on them when they fire are mostly centered in this area. Maybe they scoot back across the railroad lines, but there are no real facilities for rapid movement. There are some farm lanes, but they hardly seem adequate to move an artillery brigade with the speed that gets them out of the way of our return fire. Maybe enough of the fields have dried out so they could go cross country, but that wouldn't work for a big convoy of what must be three or four dozen vehicles. And there's no place to hide."

"So we should find 'em and spike 'em?" Sarge asked.

"Two or three you might get to, but not a dozen. No, I see two possibilities. First, you can get us the real coordinates of wherever they are at any given time if they're not dispersed. Or maybe you can somehow scuttle their transport so they can't move for a while. We've got the fire power to take them out, if they'll only sit still long enough for us to zero in. If you spot them in the clear, we could maybe call in some A-twenties from Naples to chew them up, but we haven't spotted them from the air yet. Either they have lucky cloud cover or damn effective camouflage. The Fifteenth Air Force tried to saturate the area with hundred pounders from the heavies, but the later air photos showed nothing but big holes and dead sheep."

"We're lookin' for a ghost battalion, huh?" Jersey said.

"I'd think so," Major House said. "Their first barrage usually hits late afternoon, followed by another an hour later from a slightly different angle, and a third just about dusk. There just may be three ghost batteries out there, but the patterns are all the same. We think it's the same one, changing its base after each firing without our being able to spot a large convoy. I'd like to know how they do it. Air recon should spot any movement that large. A concentrated movement would leave a major dust cloud. But every time our Grasshoppers go after a suspected location, the guns have disappeared and the dust has settled."

House shrugged in resignation and moved away from the map.

"Before you set out tonight, get up on a rise somewhere near the marshaling area and watch for a barrage. You might get an idea of just how accurate they are in hitting vital spots."

So we were off on a ghost chase. First we climbed a small hill that rose from the mud flats nearer the shore than our front lines. The hill was less than forty feet high and covered with dense sedge, but we had a full view of the troop dispersal. Below us, small clusters of men and vehicles marked a command post. Occasionally trucks paused near a netted sand-bagged lot, unloaded rapidly, and scurried back to the beach. About four o'clock, a single enemy round landed in an open field not far from the unloading trucks, followed five minutes later by a dozen shells bracketing the storage area. The first had evidently been for range, the others for effect. Someone was directing the fire.

We didn't see any point in waiting an hour for the second barrage, so we started back down the hill. Bull raised his arm to signal a halt and closed his fist, signaling silence. Bull pointed to faint wisps of smoke that rose erratically from the sedges just to our right. We probably wouldn't have noticed them, but Bull was instinctively alert to anything out of order.

We readied our rifles while Bull stepped silently through the brush toward a small hole, hardly bigger than a rabbit hole, in the side of the hill. He snapped a grenade from his suspenders, pulled the pin, counted four and tossed it into the hole.

A three-foot square of boards, dirt, and brush rose from the side of the hill and folded downward, exposing a shallow cave with a chopped-up German soldier, still with a cigarette between his lips. Beside him lay a shattered radio, a twisted spotting scope, and a flurry of empty ration wrappers.

For at least a week the spotter must have been holed up right there in our own back yard. He probably knew that his chances of getting out alive were slim, but he couldn't have expected our stumbling across him just by chance.

"Next time, for sure, he won't smoke," Bull said.

Sarge radioed Thin Man to report our find and the elimination of the German spotter. A half-hour later the hill was crawling with shoulder-to-shoulder riflemen looking for more rabbit holes.

We waited for the second salvo. Was there another spotter hidden nearby? Could a spotter in the Alban Hills see this far with any accuracy? Or was the German artillery without eyes?

A half-hour later a solitary shell landed on the flat land below us. With no spotter to radio corrections, the German guns waited silently for five minutes and then fired off a hit-or-miss salvo that did little damage to anything that wasn't already damaged. Until they could plant a new spotter, the German battalion would resort to blanket shelling rather than targeted shelling.

By the next dawn we had worked our way through our lines and past dug-in regiments of German rifles. In the morning light we gingerly filed through isolated mine fields, now that we knew how to spot a clear path. German soldiers were few and far between. They expected their mine fields to serve as their sentries, so we were well behind the German lines before we had to duck any Panzer Grenadiers.

As we neared the zone north of Carano, Sandy signaled trouble ahead. He had been on left point, off the dirt road, walking on higher ground. We left the farm lane and took to the shelter of berms along the shoulders. Past the curve we found a parked half-track with a four-wheeled gun carriage behind it. A driver sprawled on the front seat of the half-track. In the bed of the truck, a second man sat attentively but quietly at a radio while a third studied a map. Under a canopy of camouflage netting and shrubbery, this detail was just biding time.

Sarge sent Joe and Mouse to skirt the truck and set up a position some hundred yards up the road, and me and Bull to the rear, to watch for any approaching Germans. Sandy and Jersey he stationed a few yards on either side of the road to watch for any sign of life from the parked vehicle and to relay any signals from the forward or rear scouts. Sarge himself went off cross-country on his own recon survey.

An hour later Sarge returned and signaled us in for a report. He had found two more camouflaged half-tracks with guns in tow, again parked on side lanes, and one cluster of support troops and ammo trucks around a bombed-out shell of a former farmhouse.

"There must be a dozen more guns scattered around, waiting for the signal to reconvene and receive firing instructions. They disperse and hide one-by-one. That's how they escape our air recon. This is tougher than I thought. I tried to visualize a brigade moving *en masse* from one location to another, but they seem to spread out in all directions after firing a barrage or two. No wonder our guns can't find them. They sort of melt into the countryside where they wait until time to reassemble in a new location."

"So we take 'em out one at a time," Jersey suggested.

"I don't think we could," Sarge said. "It would probably take a couple of days or more, and after we had knocked out one or two, the Krauts would know something was up and would be searching for us."

"Ambush?" Jersey said.

"When they assemble, they must have more than a hundred men. Too many for us to tackle head on."

"What about mining the roads?"

"If they stick to roads," Sarge said. "But some of them seem to disperse cross-country, and we'd only get two or three at the most."

"There's only one chance, then," Joe said. "Stick to them close enough to pin-point their assembly area before they get set up to fire. Call in our artillery immediately, without waiting to get a bead on them after they fire. They must take longer to assemble and set up than they do to disperse."

"Joe's right," Sarge said. "To set up they have to align their gun positions, dismount their guns, remove the donkey carriage wheels, unhook the tongue and spread it, fasten on recoil absorbers and plant them in the ground, calibrate, load, and wait for the signal to fire. That takes at least fifteen minutes, I bet. Afterwards, it would only take a minute to slip the donkey wheels back under the tongue and hook it back to the half-track, and away they go in a dozen different directions. The support trucks and crews can be moving while the guns are firing. Joe has it. Hit them before they get organized and start firing."

"Makes sense if we can get action from base that fast," Sandy said. "Have we got artillery within four or five miles of here?"

"Ten times what they have. One-oh-fives ought to do it. There's probably fifty or sixty of them just behind the lines." Sarge looked at each of us. "Any other thoughts?" We were silent.

"Okay then, that's what we'll try. Let's pick the most forward gun we can find. I'm assuming they're aiming in the general direction of their next assembly point as they park, since they're all pointed in the same direction. The most forward one should get us to the assembly point early enough to radio Thin Man. Mouse, stick close. We don't want to lose you now."

We moved cross-country to the most forward gun Sarge had discovered. We kept that gun under surveillance while Sandy and Jersey scouted left and right points and returned to report that they had each found another gun, Sandy's being even farther ahead. We moved to that gun, and since further recon found no more near-by guns, we settled down to watch the radio operator. He would spring to attention when he received the assembly message.

As the afternoon crept along, we began to get antsy. Sarge tried to reassure us. "If they're going to get off a four o'clock salvo, the later they are in moving, the closer must be the assembly point. That's good for us. We have a better chance of following them over a short distance." We settled deeper into the scrub brush. I reached into my musette bag and passed out chocolate chip cookies. I shouldn't have brought them. They started me thinking of home again when my mind should have been on survival. I knew we would be creeping into a den of wildcats.

The afternoon sun was halfway through its descent when Sandy, who was hiding closest to the parked truck, signaled back to us to get ready. He heard the static of the radio and the guttural acknowledgment by the German receiver. A moment later, the half-track roared to life and started moving slowly up the dirt lane.

Sarge paused long enough to radio Thin Man and alert him to what we had in mind. Then we started jogging cross-country, crouching to keep from being silhouetted against the horizon.. We had no trouble pacing ourselves parallel to the slow-moving half-track. In half a mile the half-track pulled alongside a parked command car, and the rumbles of other half-tracks approached from all directions.

We retreated to a point of comparative safety and spread out on our bellies, our rifles readied but accompanied by prayers that we wouldn't have to use them.

Sarge studied the area for landmarks. He found the corresponding map and traced the coordinates from west and south off an S-twist in a shallow stream. Mouse sat with his back to Sarge while Sarge put through a blue-streak call to Thin Man, reporting the map number and coordinates in his coded jargon, and noting that they had maybe ten minutes at most before the brigade began to move again.

Through binoculars Sarge counted fourteen guns with scores of men darting around them, like ants crawling over sugar cubes. Ammo trucks dropped forty-pound shells by each gun and scurried off. The half-tracks stayed in position close behind the guns. Gun crews secured recoil arms and took up positions to adjust azimuth and elevation when signaled and then load and clear.

One of the German guns fired first for effect. If they were waiting for a correction report from the spotter Bull had eliminated earlier, they'd have a long wait and the lull would give our guns more time to calibrate their trajectories. But our batteries were evidently all set up and waiting. The German shell had no sooner left the gun than an overhead whoosh from the east came whistling toward us. Our first shell blossomed like a red volcano just behind the command truck.

Sarge called, "Right on. Fire at will." He hung the mike back on the radio and slapped Mouse on the back. "Let's go."

None of us stopped to watch the havoc behind us. The idea was to get as far away from an errant shell as possible.

Before the Germans could react to the first exploratory round, the skies scattered shells over the bivouac like pepper over scrambled eggs. Probably forty or fifty of our one-oh-fives, zeroed in on the reported coordinates, fired in unison. The set-up area erupted in a vast fire-flecked cloud of smoke, dirt, steel, and bodies, and the acrid odor of exploding shells spread across the land. We gasped in awe and before we could catch our breath, a second and a third barrage of pin-pointed artillery fire landed among the smoking ruins.

"Let's get out of here," Jersey gasped.

"No," Sarge aid. "The Major will expect a damage report."

"Do we have to look?"

"It's nothing you haven't seem before, Jersey. Just more of it. Mouse and I could go in, but I'll need you and the team in case any are still alive. I don't want to get shot in the back by some Kraut playing possum. Keep in mind, we can't call in any medics. No time for first-aid even if we have a call for it. End suffering, but remember, we can't handle any prisoners."

Sarge led us around still-smoldering craters, past twisted trucks and gun barrels, between decapitated torsos and severed limbs. Blood was everywhere, and flies had already begun to congregate. The sights of bleeding flesh were accented by the smells of sour cordite, burning bodies, and human feces. We quickened our pace, and Sarge led us back into the fresh air.

Joe assured me that blood had no particular odor, but I swear I smelled blood, along with guts and sulphur. We were on the way home. But I took time out by the side of the road to gag, and gag again, and then finally rid myself of the K ration I had eaten earlier. Still I could not stop, and I gagged even more as my stomach heaved dryly again and again. I found no comfort in knowing I was not the only one of the team gagging.

CHAPTER FOURTEEN

If occupied long enough, foxholes grow into trenches. For two months, our lines and their lines were relatively stationary. There were skirmishes, generated more out of boredom than from strategic planning, and the front would ebb and flow a few yards in one direction or then another, as first one side and then the other would overrun an opposing line, take on a few POWs, and the next day be forced back to its original position. Casualties continued to mount steadily during March and April, but more troops were lost to malaria and trenchfoot than to enemy fire.

The foxholes at first just expanded for personal comfort. Most of the foxholes were in former marshes where the water table was high. The initial innovation was a deep slot in the bottom of the trench where the water would puddle for frequent bailing, leaving a ledge on each side that supposedly kept one's boots out of the water. Then a sitting shelf was added to the side of the foxhole and that was later expanded to provide a sleeping shelf.

One foxhole boasted six rooms, some covered with scrap wood or metal from crates emptied at the supply yards or siding salvaged from shelled farm buildings. Roofed side-rooms were coveted as a means of avoiding the German "butterfly bombs." Foxholes were usually protection enough against fragmentation bombs or surface grenades, but the "butterfly bomb" was a German innovation that clustered a score of small personal bombs and then spread them out just before landing where they frequently fell into hapless foxholes. Digging was a leisure occupation to escape boredom between attacks or bombardments and became a fervent occupation when a suitable piece of crating or tin siding was found that would form a roof over a side chamber.

In short time, foxholes began to join one another, like a connect-the-dots puzzle, for socializing with neighbors between skirmishes or bombardments. By early April they were becoming trenches, not unlike some of the quieter fronts in the earlier world war. Side trenches would provide room for a game of hearts or gin rummy, communal K-ration luncheons, or off-duty night snoozes. When the Third Division was replaced by the Thirty-fourth Division on the front lines, the newcomers brought renewed energy to foxhole digging and expanded the Third's efforts into zigzag trenches sometimes half-a-mile long.

Red Dog occupied these trenches occasionally. With no special assignments, Major House detailed us back to Company D for a week or two at a time, and we would provide temporary relief to our fox-holed company companions. After three days, we would be relieved in turn for a few days rest and then again assigned to usually the same foxholes where we watched German helmets bobbing around a hundred feet on the other side of our barbed wire.

Except for a get-back-in-your-foxhole snipe at some daring German, we had little use for our M-1s. Only once did we use up any real ammunition. In the night we heard scraping noises. Sarge sent up a white flare, illuminating adventurous Germans crawling around our barbed wire with cutters in hand. A German platoon crouched behind them, waiting for a chance to charge through the opened wire. The chance never came. A machine gun to our right cut through the German patrol while we picked off the wire cutters. It was like tipping tin ducks in a shooting gallery.

Early the next morning we were relieved by another platoon, and we crept to the rear while German stretcher bearers, quite unremarked, approached our concertina wire and gathered up the German dead. The Germans would look for a soft spot in some other sector next time.

Back at Antonio's, we were stretched out after a luxurious shower at the now "Setting Sun" bath house. Sarge was sprawled on his bunk, studying a copy of *Stars and Stripes,* when Jersey returned from dockside where he had cadged another copy of *Stars and Stripes* from an incoming trucker driver. Jersey sat at the table where Mouse fiddled with his radio. "Sarge, that's today's paper, isn't it?" Jersey asked.

Sarge glanced at the masthead. "Yeah. Why?"

"I read that this morning before I went for a walk. Then I picked this up." He waved another copy of *Stars and Stripes.* "It's today's, too. But it ain't the same. What's the story in your lower left corner, Sarge?"

Sarge read from the paper:

Pearson Column
Praises Anzio
Ordnance Corps

"Yeah," Jersey said. "That's what I remember. In a recent 'Washington-Merry-Go-Round' column Drew Pearson said the Ordnance boys weren't getting their proper credits for keeping our tanks rolling and our artillery firing. That's nice to hear. But listen to this newspaper. In the same position, this issue says:

President Threatens
Willow Run with
Smith-Connally Act

Jersey held the paper up for all to see. "Same front page. But here the President has to drag out the War Labor Disputes Act for the umpteenth time this year to prevent wildcat strikes by workers back home. And there, we get a pat-on-the-back story. Something's up. Now look on page two, Sarge. What's the picture?"

Sarge held it up. "It's a picture of German POWs being shipped to Africa."

"Yeah," Jersey said, "and here, it's a picture of our old friend, General Patton, now back in England. He's not visiting hospitals anymore. Seems the General has adopted a pit bull named 'William the

Conqueror.' Patton calls him 'Willie.' Now he can 'sic' 'em rather than slap 'em. And what's the story just to right of the picture, Sarge?"

"It's about the NCAA basketball championship. Utah defeated Dartmouth forty-two to forty. What's your story?"

Jersey read from the open page:

No More
Juicy Fruit

'The Wrigley gum company announced that it would manufacture no more chewing gum for the duration. The country's largest chewing gum distributor makes Double-Mint and Juicy Fruit gum, among others, but will suspend production to preserve materials, like chicle, used in gum manufacturing. Chicle, a labor-intensive product of a tropical tree, is grown in tropical climates, including Florida, but is mostly imported from the Yucatan. Shipping restrictions, as well as manpower requirements, make the product scarce. Insoluble plastics used lately in place of chicle have been restricted to war production uses. This adds yet another cherished product to the long list of former comforts no longer available to the American public.'" Jersey tossed the paper onto the radio table. "What's going on? Why the difference."

"Maybe you got the Algiers edition and I have the Naples edition," Sarge said.

"That can't be it. The papers are identical except for those three stories. The driver said it was hot off the press in Naples."

In the silence that followed, Joe finally offered an explanation. "Remember what Major House told us last week? Morale back home is getting as bad as morale here on the front. Fifth Army is sending us teams of correspondents with typewriters and wire recorders to get stories they can send back to our hometowns to help give morale back there a jolt. The same thing's evidently happening on this side. What Sarge has there, probably, is a special edition of *Stars and Stripes* just for us, so we don't get to worrying about food shortages or labor strikes back home and we don't get reminded of General Patton losing his temper with enlisted men. It's still the Naples edition, but modified slightly for shipment to Anzio."

"I'll buy that," Sarge said.

"That makes *Stars and Stripes* a propaganda tool," Jersey said.

"Who ever said it wasn't," Joe said. "Last week I picked up a copy of a German newspaper from one of the POWS. *Fur Die Truppe,* or something like that. *For the Troops,* I think. It was the Kraut equivalent of *Stars and Stripes.* I couldn't read it much, but I figured out that the German soldiers are being told that we're being squeezed to death here and we'll face a Dunkirk-like evacuation in another couple of weeks. Propaganda is for goose *and* gander."

Bull spoke up. "Is a *Willie and Joe* cartoon still in there?"

"Yep," Sarge said. "With bullets whizzing overhead, Willie tells Joe he feels like a fugitive from the law of averages."

"Okay," Bull said. "As long as Bill Mauldin is in there, it doesn't matter what else they put in or leave out."

The radio Mouse was tinkering with crackled into life. We listened to the voice of Bing Crosby, making us all a bit homesick again:

I'll be seeing you in every lovely summer day,
In everything that's light and gay.
I'll always think of you that way.
I'll find you in the morning sun,
And when the night is new,
I'll be looking at the moon,
But I'll be seeing you."

"Talking of propaganda," Mouse said, "guess who I got hold of here."

"Axis Sally," Jersey said.

"Yeah," Mouse said. "Dear old Sally."

The voice of Axis Sally cut in:

"And that is the latest recording of an old favorite, this by our favorite, Der Bingel. We dedicate this to the idle fly-boys of the 459th Bomb Group in Cerignola. We're so sorry you were

forced to stand down this morning. The weather was terrible, wasn't it? We knew your target was to have been the airdrome at Graz, Austria, and we had a fine reception committee waiting for you. Well, better luck next time. You'll be coming back, and we'll have an even warmer reception waiting for you when you fly up this way next time. We'll be seeing you."

"How the hell does she know that?" Jersey said. "She couldn't know what their target was."

"Yes she could," Sarge said. "There are a lot of little ears around. A stupid wisecrack as crews get aboard troop carriers on the way to their bombers could be picked up by anyone. Even your laundry boy could report to some Italian snitch who has a short wave radio."

"You mean our Willie could be a spy?"

"I doubt it. And I don't mean Mauldin's Willie, either. Just watch your tongue."

Sally's voice droned on:

"And now this is for the muddy members of the Sixth Armored Infantry Division trapped in Anzio with so many others. We do wish you would stop trying to break out. We have too many of your pals in our POW camps already. Every time you try to break through, we get another trainload of prisoners up here and we're getting a bit crowded. Just stay where you are. It must have occurred to you by now that you're already in a POW camp. You can't really go anywhere. You're surrounded by barbed wire. And we have guards stationed all around you. Start thinking of going back to where you came from, or be content to wait out the war in your Anzio Prisoner of War camp. This is for you. It's another Bing Crosby recording especially for you. *Don't Fence Me In.* Sorry, but you'll have to accept that. Oh, by the way, if you do go roaming about tonight, remember your password is 'Uncle Ben.'"

The Crosby croon began delivering *Oh, give me land, lots of land under starry skies above; don't fence me in...,* and Mouse asked "Sarge, is she right? Is Uncle Ben our password?"

"I don't know," Sarge said. "We haven't used a password in over a month. But Sally's probably right. She usually is."

"How come she gets the password, and we don't?" Jersey said.

"Someone probably used it," Sarge said, "and a German was within earshot. No great trick."

"And how come she gets all the newest records before we do?"

"Plane from New York to Lisbon," Joe said, "and diplomatic pouch from Lisbon to Berlin. Overnight delivery." And Crosby crooned on: *I want to ride to the ridge where the west commences, and gaze at the moon until I lose my senses; I can't look at hobbles and I can't stand fences; don't fence me in.*

"I wonder if Bing Crosby knows he's part of German propaganda," Jersey mused.

The answer came from a slight figure standing on the bottom step of our entry. "He knows," the newcomer said as he raised his hand to knock on the open door. "May we come in?"

"You're in," Sarge said.

The visitor was obviously a civilian, even though dressed in the Army's olive drabs, a dirty field jacket, and a visored knit cap. He seemed in his forties, but wore no insignia or rank. He was on the short side, somewhat gaunt, and spoke with a mild mid-west accent. Behind him stood a corporal, fresh from a recruitment poster. He wore olive drab wool trousers with a crease, a crisp new field jacket, and mudless polished boots. His sleeve bore his stripes and a Fifteenth Air Force shoulder patch. "Name's Ernie Pyle," the newcomer said. "And this is my keeper, Corporal Ralph Henniger. I'm a reporter for Scripps-Howard. I'm looking for a Sergeant Crafton."

"You found him." Sarge paused, then finally accepted Pyle's extended hand, and shook it quickly. "We don't shake hands much out here. If we know the guy, there's no need. And if we don't know him, we're not sure we want to. Next time we meet, one of us may be just a piece of dead meat and there's no need to begin making friends."

"I think I knew that," Pyle said. "Sorry. Just a civilian habit I carry around with me. Could I meet the rest of the squad. I promise no handshakes."

Sarge ran the roll, mentioning our home towns and pointing us out one-by-one. Pyle nodded at each of us in turn, while the corporal scribbled furiously in a small notebook, evidently recording names and origins. Sarge waved them to folding chairs beside the radio table while he sat back on his cot. "What can we do for you?" he asked.

"Major House said I should look you up for a little background. I don't trust the briefings I get from the brass. House said you had special insights."

"Did Major House fill you in on what we do?"

"Yes. But that's not why I'm here. Maybe you've seen some of my columns."

Sarge hesitated. "Oh, yes, sir," he said. "You wrote that article on Sergeant Eversole of the One-sixty-eighth. I knew Buck. At least I thought I knew Buck. But I learned a lot about him from your column. Quite a guy. Good story. But we wouldn't want a story like that on any of us."

"Understood," Pyle said. "Anyway, I'm leaving Anzio tomorrow. Next stop England. Getting ready for the big jump, I guess. Haven't time for any more in-depth interviews. But I wanted a last-minute perspective. House said you had as good an overview as anyone."

"Nice of him, but I suspect he's just passing the buck. What's your question?"

"Well, for one thing, do you think we're stuck here?"

Sarge looked around at each of us before answering. "No, not really. It gets tougher every day, as the Germans get stronger, but we keep finding soft spots. We just don't follow through yet. But we have too much firepower for 'em. We'll break through to Rome one of these days, but you'll probably be in Berlin before we get to Rome."

"Why are we so bogged down, then?"

Sarge warmed to his subject. "We had the world on a string when we landed. Complete surprise. Hardly a German in sight. We could have cut the main highway between Rome and Naples, taken those hills over there, and set up a perimeter at Rome's doorstep in just a day or two. We didn't, of course. The Krauts set up major attacks three times, and three times we beat 'em back. Again we could have pushed 'em right back through Rome. But we didn't. But I guess we surprised ourselves as well, and we hunkered down to take stock. For weeks we did absolutely nothing, except swap bullets and shells."

"And then?"

"We had them on the run and should have chased them all the way. We could have threatened to cut off their supplies heading south, which might have eased the pressure on the Rapido. But we stopped to lick our wounds. They dug in, brought in more reinforcements. That happened three times. And each time we threw away our advantage. So here we are."

In the pause that followed, we nodded agreement. Pyle waited. When nothing more was forthcoming, he said, "You don't sound bitter about it."

"No need," Sarge said. "That's the way things are. It would be funny, a comedy, if it weren't so deadly."

"Where's the comedy?"

"It's like a Laurel and Hardy movie. What a fine mess you got us into this time. Someday this'll all be just a faint memory."

"And what will you all be doing then?" Pyle asked.

"Well, not shooting people, that's for sure. We'll go home, pick up the pieces. Can't make up for lost time, but it'll be fun building up America. There'll be a lot of houses needed for veterans, and I've got my credentials as a roofer. I'll get a chance to find a decent house of my own, watch my kids grow up and go through high school, maybe even get a chance to go to Syracuse University. I'd like to learn history. Maybe I could become a teacher. That would be a good life. No more depression. No more bread lines or soup kitchens. We know how to build things, now." Sarge turned on his cot. "Jersey, how about you?"

"I'm gonna' own my own gas station. Maybe a string of 'em in Jersey City. Automobiles will be big after the war. Everyone will have one. They'll need gas, and I'll supply it."

"Sandy?"

"I don't know. Nothing, probably."

"You're no help. How about you, Mouse?"

"Back into radio. I suppose my southern accent will keep me out of New York, but there's plenty of opportunity around Virginia and Georgia. Maybe college could ready me for the big broadcasters."

"Joe?"

"I think I'll get a lobster boat. I've often dreamt of life on the water."

"No more teaching?"

"I just as soon not see kids anymore. Memories hurt sometimes more than a Mauser."

"Bull?"

"Back to the ranch, I guess."

Pyle intervened. "Ranch? You from the west? New Mexico, maybe? Anywhere near Albuquerque?"

"Next state over. Navajo land. You from Albuquerque?"

Pyle grinned wryly. "Indiana originally, but we have a house in Albuquerque now. I like the western sands. I plan to travel through the Navajo lands when this war is over. Painted Desert. Petrified Forest. Grand Canyon. All that stuff. Great country."

"And Boots. How about you?"

"College, first. I'm thinking of majoring in political science. I'd like to be a Congressman some day. Maybe I could do something about future war threats. Maybe outlaw foxholes. Or make Generals spend every other day in them."

"Better yet, outlaw mud," Jersey interjected. "Geneva conventions outlaw gas. Get 'em to outlaw mud. Army can't move without mud."

Jersey and I had both been half joking, but Pyle took us seriously. "Veterans in politics. Sounds good. That's what the postwar world is going to need more of," he said.

After a pause, Pyle said, "I see a lot of soldiers who will have a difficult time shaking off the bestiality of war. After all the blood and guts they've seen—or even spilled some themselves—will they be able to go back to the little white cottage with the picket fence, PTA meetings, and eight-to-five routines? After what Major House told me about your methods," Pyle gestured to the sheath of knives on the nearest cot, "it wouldn't surprise me if killing became second nature."

"Not a chance," Sarge said. "We had our share of indoctrination. Why-we-fight, articles of war, the Nazi scourge. We know why we do what we do, and we know how to give it up when the need is gone. In fact, we pray every night for the time when we can give it all up and return to being human."

"I think you'll make it," Pyle said. "Let's hope it's soon. That's why I'm heading to England. The big effort is coming soon. Let's hope it takes the pressure off you and brings all this to a quick end."

"Let's hope," Sarge said.

And then Joe interjected: "After Hitler, we'll still have the Pacific to settle. Maybe after we take Berlin away from the Nazis, we should keep on going and take Moscow away from the Communists."

Sarge turned and spoke sharply. "Don't call for any more bloodshed than we need, Joe. I for one would just as soon leave Russia to the next generation. Maybe the Communists will learn something from this war."

"Yeah," Joe said. "Just what Pyle meant. They're learning mass slaughter, and it doesn't churn their stomachs one bit, not like it churns ours."

"Russia or no," Jersey said, "as soon as we wipe out Hitler, we'll just be transferred to the Pacific to wipe out Tojo. And then, if we live through that, we can talk about wiping out Stalin. We'll be old and grey when we finally hang up our helmets, so it doesn't matter what plans any of us have for after the war."

"That's a bit pessimistic," Pyle said. "I don't think you really believe that. All of you seem to have a hope for the future running through your comments."

"I'll guess you're right," Sarge said. "It just seems, after months here, this thing seems to be creeping on, day after day, without end. Tell us you see an end to this."

"Oh, I do," Pyle said, "and so do you. I read it in every one of you. This will pass if you just keep your sense of humor. Some of the jokes that I hear floating around remind me that this is a citizen army. Bill Mauldin has its measure. As long as *Willie and Joe* can keep poking fun at '90-day wonders,' as long as *Sad Sack* keeps shooting himself in the foot, and as long as *Kilroy* keeps popping up in unlikely places, you'll all get through the worst of this."

Pyle rose from his chair. "Well, I've got a boat to catch. Maybe I'll see you on the road to Berlin, maybe in the Pacific. But I doubt I'll see you in Moscow. Anyway, I really expect to see you back in the West, Especially you, Corporal Wolf. Maybe at the Grand Canyon. Thanks for your time, fellas. Hope I didn't interrupt anything."

"Not a thing, Mister Pyle," Sarge said. "The war could use a few interruptions."

CHAPTER FIFTEEN

Beyond the clamor and confusion of the docks, the rear echelon had assembled itself in three distinct areas that alternately attracted German artillery or German bombers. Least often hit by shells or bombs but nonetheless vulnerable was the "bloody mile" hospital area, where sandbagged wards and quarters were isolated in large green tents marked by large red crosses which seemed to divert bombers but not color-blind artillery.

The second, and next least-targeted, area was "tent city," a square mile of sixteen-foot pyramidal tents that housed reserve battalions awaiting assignment, front line troops resting for five days rotation, and rear echelon workers not able to find billets in vacated villas in Nettuno or Anzio.

Clean-shaven, unmuddied replacements would troop off the landing ships, tank or infantry, and assemble with basic training precision in neat files along the shore road. They would march past the row after row of white crosses and stars that marked the foreboding Anzio cemetery. After two miles, often accompanied by long-range artillery shells bursting beside them, they would settle in at "a tent city." The tents stretched in regimented rows across fields churned into mud flats by thousands of GI boots. Cargo pallets retrieved from supply dumps were pressed into service as duckboard walks between the tents but in time they were almost indistinguishable from the surrounding mud. Orange shell-bursts, white crosses, and black mud screamed: "Welcome to Anzio."

Most often hit by sporadic but daily shellings were the stacks of ammo, rations, clothing, boots, petroleum, and every other supply that an army could conceivably use, filling every vacant lot in town and stretching out over the farmlands wherever a six-by could drive. Fully loaded trucks driving off LSTs at the docks would be directed by MPs to waiting supply points where Quartermaster or Ordnance troops would unload the cargo and stack it neatly in ordered rows like carloads of boards in a large lumber yard. The empty trucks would then scurry back to the LSTs for return to Naples or to outlying Liberty ships for reloading, while six-bys and troop carriers from the beachhead's regiments would arrive at the dumps to reload the materiel for the end users.

This cheek-by-jowl cluster of tents and boxes stretched for a mile in any direction and offered targets for German explosives. Artillery spotters were helpful, but not really required. Any shells lobbed in the general direction of Anzio were certain to hit something. Each block had its own firefighting crew and first-aid station, and they were seldom idle. Shelling was heavier on rainy days when German artillery felt safer from overhead spotters, and the firefighters prayed for sunshine when the big gun batteries would try to hide from patrolling aircraft. And shelling was heavier in the late afternoon when the camouflaged gun batteries hoped they would be shielded by approaching dusk before fighter-bombers could retaliate.

The whistling, rumbling, ear-shattering shells from Anzio Annies—for it was now certain there were *two* large railroad guns out there somewhere—always arrived in late afternoon, regularly and consistently, as if announcing that it was time for supper. A shell from one of guns was called an *Anzio Express* since it sounded like a freight train roaring past.

On clear days the guns avoided observation planes by staying hidden, although occasionally they would get bold enough to fire off one or two shells before ducking back into their holes. On rainy days, free from air observation, they would frequently fire three or four rounds apiece, five minutes apart, before retiring for the day.

On one occasion, during a strong German counterattack a couple of months ago, protected by heavy overcast, the two guns lofted some fifty shells into the beachhead. Then again, in one particularly balmy period, the guns stayed silent for almost three weeks. Major House wanted Red Dog's help in making that silence permanent.

The Major's hand curved across the map as he traced the red line that marked our current front, about seven miles out from Anzio. "We've maintained a front far enough out to keep German medium guns from reaching the beach. For a while they were firing a couple of captured French railway guns. Big ones. Maybe two-forty millimeters. We haven't heard from them lately, and the flyboys claim they found them and took them out. We're also being hit by what we think are three batteries of one-seventies. There were more but you guys helped find some of them, and the Marauders managed to hit a few. But they're highly mobile guns, mounted on four-wheel carriages I understand, and they're hard to hit, as you know. Those one-seventies have a range of maybe eighteen miles, and that's at least four miles more than our one-fifty-five 'Long Toms.' Anyway it's enough to hit the docks from well behind the lines."

Major House moved his hand farther up the map. "And up here somewhere near the hills are some two-ten railroad guns that manage to fire a few rounds and then duck for cover. Most of the shells that we call *Anzio Express* probably come from these guns and not from Anzio Annie. We think these two-tens spend most of their time scuttling along the railroad between Lanuvio and Ciampino, ducking into well-camouflaged side tracks. Our fighter-bombers are continuously looking for them, and a few times they've dropped thousand-pounders close enough to damage them, we think. But the crews are good, and the guns seemed to have quick recovery times. Air photos show the tracks repaired overnight."

Major House moved his hand still farther north and drew an imaginary circle just east of the small town of Ciampino, about three-fourths of the way to Rome. "Now somewhere in here," he said, "Anzio Annie is hiding. Both of them. Maybe together. We received a message from Radio Vittoria that the Italian underground has located them just east of Ciampino on the railroad spur that leads to the old airfield at Frascati. There's nothing else on this line and the line is unused. In some places the tracks disappear entirely. Either the rails have been taken up or they're damn well camouflaged. Somewhere along this line, according to Radio Vittoria, is Annie."

Major House crossed to his desk and picked up a small black box, no larger than a pack of cigarettes. "This is a radio beacon emitter. On a clear day, you plant this under Anzio Annie and one of our Marauders, tuned in to the same frequency, will drop a thousand-pound bomb right on top of it. Can do?"

Sarge took the box from Major House, studied it intently, and passed it to Mouse. "Nothing much to it," Sarge said.

"The assignment or the box?" Major House asked.

"I was thinking of the box. A switch, a timer, and a short antenna. What's inside?"

"A battery and a fixed frequency transmitter. That's all. Just don't turn it on too soon, for the battery won't last too long. About three hours. And the Germans are good at radio detection so they'll probably find it before the battery runs out. So pick a clear day when the fighter-bombers can fly, and get the hell out of the way. Okay?"

"Okay, sir. Understood." Sarge looked around at each of us and found no dissent. "We'll do the best we can."

"Any questions?"

"Yes, sir," Jersey said. "Just how big is this Anzio Annie?"

"From what we know of it, it seems to be about two-eighty millimeters in caliber, bigger than anything I've seen. Remember the big guns on the USS Brooklyn that brought us here? Six inches. We have one eight-inch gun here and a dozen eight-inch howitzers. But our artillery workhorse is the one-fifty-five. That's about six-point-one inches. Annie is eleven inches. Our Long Toms have a range of about fourteen miles. Annie shoots at least thirty-six miles. Her shells probably weigh about a quarter-ton each. Get the picture?"

Jersey whistled softly.

"Sir," Joe said, "if Annie isn't really all that active and the one-seventies and two-tens are doing all the damage, why don't we go after them instead?"

"Well, I hate to say it, but it's a propaganda move primarily. Think of what it would do for morale, both here and back home, if we could announce that Anzio Annie had been destroyed. That's as important as another ammo dump. Maybe more. The whole world has heard of Anzio Annie, and the general view is that the big railroad gun is destroying the beachhead. It isn't, but the perception is what counts."

"Perception is not worth dying for," Joe said.

"Depends on how you measure it. Annie kills some of us every week, almost every day," the Major said.

"Sorry," Joe said, "I wasn't thinking. Let's get going."

"Which way are you going this time?" the Major asked.

Sarge moved over to the map. "That's a long hike. Let's go straight north."

"Up Via Anziate? The Germans are heavily concentrated there."

"Have we retaken Aprilia?" Sarge asked.

"Everyone's calling it 'the Factory' now," Major House said. "And, no, it's still held by the Germans."

"Okay. The Factory. Then, we'll go as close to the Factory as we can get and then cut west cross-country above the Caves and skirt Campoleone." Sarge traced a half-circle to the west of Campoleone. "If we're lucky again, we can tie in with the railroad north of there and follow the tracks right to Ciampino. From there, it's just a matter of finding the spur line back to the east."

The Major nodded. "Need a ride?"

"For the first five miles, I guess. At least as far as we can get on the road to Aprilia. The next twenty miles, we'll have to foot it, overland."

"Okay," the Major said. "Go gather up your gear. Here, don't forget these radio senders. Two of 'em, just for insurance, in case one doesn't work. I'll have a truck pick you up at seventeen hundred."

By sunset we were well on our way to god knew what. We spent the night creeping past scattered German outposts. No action, but we held our breaths through more than one close call. The Germans seemed almost disinterested, pleased that they were well behind the fox-holed lines and content to be beyond our artillery's attention.

We found the first railway, the line that ran from Rome down to Naples, just before dawn, and we decided to risk a daylight cross-country hike to the second railway, the line that seemed to circle the Albano Hills.

We came upon the loop railroad almost twenty miles north of Anzio. Sarge studied his maps and figured we were a good stone's throw above the village of Linovio, which we understood to be a German marshaling area. The town would be home to a number of German lesser commands and probably bristling with sentries. Sarge nixed any idea of our scouting them out since it would raise the odds against our mission. Instead, the Germans would come scouting us.

We turned north along the tracks, looking for a place where we could hide long enough for a few hours sleep. Sandy had been walking point, and inside a mile he signaled us to come ahead.

"Whatcha' got?" Sarge asked as we came up to Sandy kneeling at one side of the tracks. A short side track, well hidden by loose bushes and branches, led off to the side and into an arbor made from camouflage canvas stretched across poles on either side of the siding.

"Welcome to the Sandy Bricker Hotel," Sandy said. "No scenic view, but quiet and isolated. I can't think of a better place for a quick nap. Hidden from any air recon as well as from any artillery spotters hiding in the hills."

We entered the tented side line, and after Sarge posted Joe and me to forward and rear sentry posts, the others sprawled along the sloping banks of the railroad bed. After an hour, Jersey and Mouse replaced us, and Joe and I then enjoyed the luxury of railroad gravel beds. Sleep came quickly and deeply, but not for long.

A distant rumble grew louder and sharper, and we retreated into the side country, looking for natural cover. From a small gully running down from the tracks we watched a donkey engine pull a three-car gun train around the curve and toward our resting site. Just short of the siding, the train stopped and a platoon of Germans scurried over and around a huge railroad gun like ants exploring a damaged ant hill. They traversed the long gun barrel into a southern arc, pointing almost over our heads, while crank-operated slings swung a giant shell and wrapped charges toward the breach. This had to be one of the two-ten guns the Major described.

The German crew worked with choreographed precision, loading the shell, inserting a strange donut-shaped collar, and ramming in two linen-wrapped powder charges. They backed off the gun platform and sought cover as the gun, with ear shattering explosions, launched shell after shell in quick succession toward Anzio, while a German officer stood on the roof of the donkey engine and scanned the skies for nosy pilots.

In less than twenty minutes five shells arched from the gun with very little telltale smoke and virtually no muzzle flash. The officer blew a whistle, and the crew swung the barrel back into travel position. The donkey engine pulled the cars onto the siding beneath the camouflaged tenting and work crews replaced the leafy branches over the exposed side tracks. The gun crew then busied themselves, cleaning and securing the gun and preparing it for their next run up or down the tracks.

"So that's how they do it," Sarge said. "They must have half a dozen sidings like this along the tracks. No wonder our planes can't find them."

"Wish we had bazookas," Jersey said. "Bet we could knock it out."

"And forty troops?" Sarge said. "Not likely. We're after bigger game, anyway."

"What was the round charge they put in just before the powder?" Sandy asked.

"Must be some kind of muzzle flash absorber," Joe said.

"Well, it worked evidently. But we'd better get out of here. They will probably send out perimeter guards, and they'd spot us for sure."

We started moving north parallel to the tracks, and we hadn't covered more than a half a mile before we stumbled into a German patrol, just what we had hoped to avoid. Bent over in a crouch, Sandy was walking forward point when he looked up and found not five feet in front of him the grey-clad back of a German scout. Sandy had no time to attack or retreat when the German turned, stared in surprise, and received three quick blasts from Sandy's M-1. Sandy dropped to the ground and we hurried forward as a fusillade of bullets converged from various points on Sandy's position. We were in our first fire-fight in more than a week.

"Spread out," Sarge called. "Make this fast. The train crew will be coming after us next."

We ran from tree to bush to valley to mound, listening to Mauser fire whining overhead and searching for targets. Sarge's Tommy gun chattered a bit to our right, suggesting Sarge had found some. Bull spotted a rifle barrel protruding from a low bush not thirty feet off and marked it with a well-aimed grenade that scattered chunks of flesh over the bush. Jersey, far to my left, rattled off three quick shots, and a guttural grunt rose from an opposing shrub. A misty figure stepped from behind a scrub tree and was immediately felled by a volley from at least two, maybe three M-1s.

I was on my hands and knees crawling forward. I was scared. What was I going toward? What was I getting into? I had lost sight of Bull on my left, and everyone else in fact. I couldn't go back, which is what I wanted to do. But I reminded myself of Sarge's call that the crew from the train would be on our tail by now, given the guns and grenades which they were certainly close enough to hear. I wondered if I'd freeze again and immediately realized that I couldn't. I—we—had to get out of there, soon, now, as fast as we could, and the only way was over dead Germans.

I half stood and crouched forward, hoping one of our own squad wouldn't appear in my sights, or me in theirs. A figure loomed up before me and I hesitated, not certain if it was us or them, but he raised his rifle with both hands over his head as he rose, and I put two rounds quickly into his chest. As he slumped backwards, I told myself that I was all right, I wouldn't freeze again, that we couldn't take prisoners, that war means death—theirs or mine—and we had to get out of there. I looked around for another target.

Sarge stepped out from behind another tree and called, "Red Dog, ho!" and we gathered from all directions. "All here?" Sarge did a quick survey. "I think we got 'em all, but be alert. Some sniper may still be hiding. Everyone okay?"

"I'm hurt a bit," Sandy said. His rifle dangled from its sling over his right arm as his left hand encircled his right wrist. "One of 'em got me. Clear through."

"Artery?"

"Don't think so. Not enough blood."

"Can you move?"

"Oh, sure, as long as I can hold back the bleeding."

Sarge turned to me. "Boots, grab his rifle and stay close to him. We'll wrap him up when we get clear of here. Let's move. Double time." Sarge led off, racing across mounds and washes, over shrubs and through bushes, and we followed in almost our usual formation. We heard forces moving in behind us. We ran faster.

"How many did we get?" I called to Bull ahead of me.

"How many what?"

"Krauts."

"I figure about a dozen. Normal squad."

"All dead?"

"Better be," Bull said.

And we trotted on in as much silence as our gear and the Italian landscape would permit. Even at a loping pace, we would probably be moving faster than any pursuing German patrol, since they would be watching for an ambush.

We were gasping and breathless, ready to collapse, when Sarge finally led us into a dense, low olive grove and signaled a halt. We collapsed by the closest tree trunk and dropped our rifles. Another step would have been impossible, and Sarge let us rest while he moved back to watch for followers. The train crews had probably found the dead squad members by now and had decided not to pursue the matter—or us—in case their train needed their protection more than we needed following. After half an hour, Sarge moved back from his watch and called Mouse to drop his radio—which he already had—and take over the rear guard. He beckoned me to dress Sandy's wound, which I was on my way to do after having caught my breath.

"Another purple heart, Sandy?" I said, as I sprinkled sulfa powder over his clean wound and wrapped it with clean gauze.

"I'm starting a collection."

"You can stop with this one," I said. "You ever hear of anyone with three purple hearts? The third one can be fatal. Stop with two. Any pain?"

"Some," Sandy said.

"I've got a pill that might help that."

"Will it keep me from running?"

"Might slow you down a bit."

"Forget it. When I need to run, I wanna' be able to run."

I smiled. "As you wish. But I'll stand by in case."

And we slept until the sun was all but extinguished in the western sea. Sarge moved among us, kicking the soles of our boots. "Rise and shine," he said. "Everyone got some breakfast?" He waved a box of Ks.

"It's time for dinner," Jersey said.

"Whatever K you got. Eggs, beans, or hash. They all begin to taste the same."

"You get any sleep, Sarge?"

"Plenty. Joe and Boots took turns on guard, while you lucky souls caught a good three hours sack time. Enough for any growing boy."

"Any idea where we are," Joe asked.

Sarge unfolded a map. "I figure we're a bit east of Albano. Right about here." Sarge fingered his map while we looked over his shoulder. "We should get to the railway yards in Ciampino tonight, find the wye toward Frascati, and begin looking for Annie by first light tomorrow. That's assuming we don't run into any more interruptions."

We downed our canned egg-and-bacon mix and gnawed on cereal bars. Sarge called out, "GI the place. Patrolling Krauts don't have to know we've been here." We dug shallow holes with our "entrenching tools"—army nomenclature for short, folding shovels, M-1 of course—and buried our empty K boxes.

Sandy indicated he was fine, retrieved his rifle, and we filed out of the trees and back along the railroad tracks. Jersey took point, and in the next three hours he signaled three more camouflaged side tracks, one of them holding a big gun train that we had to circle to avoid. The circling took more time than the march, and the first wisp of dawn rose from the east as we found the small marshaling yard on the outskirts of Ciampino.

According to the map, three rail lines ran east from Ciampino. The first we encountered ran into the hills toward Lake Albano. The map indicated that the short line passed Castel Gandolfo, the Pope's summer home away from the Vatican's heat, and ended just east of Albano. The second side line ran a short way through hills to the Fascati airfield, with nothing else along the way. The third track eastward ran around the north edge of the hills and linked up with another line from Rome before branching off again to complete the circle around the hills and right back to where we had started. We hurried along the second single track into the hills, eager to get away from the edge of town before it started to awaken.

The track looked unused. Low shrubs grew thickly and haphazardly along the tracks, some between the ties, suggesting the rails were not maintained. Sarge wondered if the underground Radio Vittoria out of Rome had sent the right information. Joe waved us to a stop while he knelt to examine a few of the plants.

"These have all been planted here," Joe said. "This isn't wild growth. Look. The ground seems freshly dug. At least within the past couple of months. This is camouflage. Someone doesn't want us to know the line is here."

Sarge knelt beside Joe. "Joe's right," Sarge said. "The shadows from these bushes would break up the rail shadows. Hard to detect from the air, I bet. I guess we're close to pay dirt."

Farther along the line the tracks cut through deep, narrow defiles in the hills. Again the shadows from the steep cliffs on either side would make detection from the air difficult, and we could see a few places ahead where camouflaged canvas had been stretched between the cliffs to disguise the rails below. The cuts would make a great shooting gallery. A single machine gun at the far end of the cut could ambush a platoon with ease. Sarge decided we would skirt the hills that had cuts through them.

183

The sun was twelve high when we circled the southern edge of a bisected hill. We walked a narrow dirt lane, looking for a way to cut to our left, back to the railroad line, when we came to a brick drive leading to the north. Grass and weeds growing between the bricks suggested that the drive was seldom used. We turned up the drive flanked by truncated grape vines, passed through an open wrought iron gate that had escaped Italy's salvage drives, and came into a poplar-lined approach to a wide, three-story villa. We split between the sides of the drive and ducked quickly behind the trees when a man in suit and tie and holding a shotgun upright on his hip came out onto the front portico.

"Ahoy there, Yanks," the man called. "Welcome to *Casa di Manfredi.* I say, you are Yanks, aren't you?" The accent was unmistakably British.

Sarge stepped out from behind his tree. "Yanks, yes," Sarge called. "Put the gun away."

The man bent over and laid the gun on the tile floor. "Sorry," he called. "Reflex, I guess. Didn't know what to expect. We don't get many visitors way back here. But come ahead. Please do. Come for tea." He waved us forward.

We kept our rifles trained at the ready as we approached the marble steps leading up to the portico. Sarge climbed the steps quickly, ignored the welcomer's outstretched hand, and peered through the large open doors behind him.

"Alone?" Sarge asked.

"Quite. I've held the house by myself for six years now. The family has moved to Portugal until the end of the war."

"Your family?"

"Oh, no. I'm just the *maggiordomo.* The Manfredi family left the country when Mussolini joined the Axis. They detest Nazis. Any fascists, in fact. They'll come back when the Germans leave, but they've left me in charge. I've been with the family for fourteen years now."

"You're English?" It was more an observation than a question.

"Thoroughly. But my Italian is rather good, and with proper dress I can pass as a *paisano. "*

"The Germans leave you alone?"

"Out of sight, out of mind. They came by here once about a year ago. Scouting for something, I imagine. But we are too far from anything to be of any use except to wineries. I go into town just once a month. The local *polizia* ignore me and I ignore them. And there aren't many Germans around Ciampino. I just tend the vines and store a little wine. May I offer you some?"

Sarge hesitated. "Not now. We've got a job to do. But a cup of tea might be welcomed."

"Well, come in, come in. Do I call you Sergeant? You may call me Ralph, if you wish. Ralph Hennessey in all. But come ahead. I'll put a pot on the stove to boil."

We followed him through rooms with white sheets draped over furniture to a spacious kitchen with a large white table and enough chairs to accommodate a staff of half a dozen or more. In peacetime, the Manfredi family must have lived a cut above the likes of the Camistratas.

Our host busied himself at the wood-burning stove, pouring water from a pail into a large kettle. "You're the first visitors I've entertained in some years, and I must apologize if the refreshments seem austere. I have limited resources here, and the war doesn't help one maintain the proper graces."

We found seats at the table while Sandy stood sentry. We emptied our pockets, and soon the table was littered with K-ration biscuits, chocolate bars, chewing gum, and a few cans of hash. Ralph distributed cups and saucers over the table, his eyes brightening at the array of K-ration leftovers.

"Oh, how pleasant," he said. "We'll have high tea as good as any I've seen of late."

The water boiled, and Ralph threw in a few measures of tea, stirred it slowly, and then moved around the table filling our cups through a small strainer. We had left the chair at the head of the table empty, and Ralph accepted it with a short bow.

"You say you have a job to do. May I be of any service?"

"Not for what we have in mind, Ralph." Sarge said. "Unless you happen to have a cache of explosives."

"Sorry. All I can offer is a few shotgun shells. I'll wager you are looking for some big cannon. Am I right?"

"How did you guess?"

"They shake the windows almost every afternoon about five o'clock. Usually just two or four blasts. Fortunately, they don't fire for very long."

"They shake the windows? You mean they're nearby."

"Practically over my shoulder," Ralph said. "Come. I'll show you." He led us up a winding marble staircase to the second floor, down a long hallway of closed doors to a balcony at the back, and pointed out a tall villa not far behind the Manfredi house, the upper floor visible over the tree tops.

"There you are," he said."That villa is full of Germans who man the guns. The villa is built over a railroad tunnel that passes directly beneath. That's where they hide the guns during the day. They tow them out in the evening, fire a few rounds, then duck back into the tunnel. But I'm afraid the seven of you will have a hard time doing anything about it. There's maybe a hundred German soldiers in the house and in the tunnel. And the guns are bigger than anything you could handle, even if you could get past the guards. Just to give you an idea, the barrel is high as this three-story house. And they travel on massive gun carriages with a dozen steel wheels on each side. I haven't been able to get close to them, but I have watched them a few times from a little hill just to the left of the tunnel. And I shudder when they fire."

"So do a lot of your countrymen at Anzio," Sarge said. "Maybe we can't silence them, but maybe we can set them up so someone else can."

"Dive bombers?" Ralph asked. "That's been tried. Not much success. The bombers never seem to be able to catch them in the open, and they don't seem to know for sure where the guns are hiding. They have blown up a few feet of track a few times, but that's quickly repaired. Further, the dive bombers can't seem to follow the tracks where the line ducks into deep ravines."

"Will you help us?"

"I'll do what I can. What do you want of me?"

"Well, you can show us that hill where you watched them fire. We'd want to study their layout. Can it hide us?"

Ralph hesitated, as if picturing the hill. "I think so. There's plenty of scrub growth all over the hill and a few trees. If you've got binoculars, you'll have a good view. I have a pair I can lend you if you need them. That is, assuming the Germans haven't started posting guards up there since I was there last."

"We'll have to try. And thanks for the binoculars. We've got a couple, but we can always use another pair of eyes."

"There's no point in going now. All you'll see is a lonely guard near the tunnel entrance. If they are going to shoot today, they will drag the big guns out about five o'clock."

"Okay, we'll get some rest, and be ready to go about four. Okay if we spread out in your front room?"

"Be my guest. I'll call you at four."

"I'll be up before that," Sarge said. He led us to a front room and named Jersey and Mouse for first guard shift. "One hour and then wake Joe and Bull. Then Sandy and Boots. Spread out."

Jersey took the back door, Mouse the front, and the rest of us sprawled in a variety of positions among the white cloaked furniture. Bull leaned back against what was evidently an upholstered sofa and stared at the ceiling.

"Go to sleep, Bull," Sarge said.

"Can't," Bull said.

"Look, it's been fifteen, maybe sixteen, hours since we got some sleep. You need it. What's eating at you?"

"Women," Bull said.

"Women? I told you. Put—what's her name?—Alva?—put her out of your mind. She's kaput. Think about big guns."

"I am."

Sarge looked puzzled. Bull wasn't making any sense. Bull read Sarge's expression. "Too many women in my life," Bull said.

He still wasn't making sense. "And too few in ours," Sarge said. "Just what are you talking about, you dumb Indian?"

"Maybe Alva," Bull said. "Maybe Connie. Maybe Axis Sally. Maybe Anzio Annie. All women. All trouble. Too many."

Sarge let out a sigh of exasperation. "Oh, for Pete's sake, Bull, go to sleep." Sarge turned on his side and adjusted his pack beneath his head. He sighed again and mustered up enough courage to let out a final "Kee-rist!"

I knew it was not quite four o'clock when Sarge kicked my boots as he circled the room of sleeping soldiers. "Do what you have to do," he called, "and let's get about it."

Later Ralph came into the front room where we were about organized. He led us around to the back of the villa, through more vineyards, across a wider back road, and onto a small hill among bigger hills. He signaled for quiet and dropped to his hands and knees as we crested a small hill between two smaller hills. Above the hill on our right we could see the tile roof of the large house that straddled Anzio Annie's tunnel.

On the side of the hill we could see a German guard, sitting on sandbags around a machine gun. We could make out a crew of German soldiers clearing loose branches from camouflaged railroad tracks, and we could sight along the tracks to the black yaw of the tunnel. A flood of noises poured from the tunnel—engines stirring to life, guttural commands and responses, cadenced whistle signals, and the squeal of steel wheels on steel rails.

A small diesel-powered engine emerged slowly from the tunnel, pulling a multi-ton rail carriage with a mounted gun. We gasped audibly. We had been briefed on the size of Annie. We were prepared to expect a behemoth. We had watched an almost-as-big two-ten firing shells the day before. But we found it hard to accept Anzio Annie as real. It surpassed our imagination. And we watched in awe as crews hoisted ammo cranes and turned azimuth wheels, loading and elevating the seventy-foot barrel.

Anzio Annie moved a few hundred yards down the track and was followed by a second gun. Again crews went through the loading and preparation drill. Most of us watched the coordinated movements of twenty-man crews, but Sarge, along with Joe and Sandy, scanned the perimeter through binoculars, looking for flaws in the procedures. A short whistle blast sent the crews running down ladders, clearing the gun platform, some taking refuge under the carriage but most scurrying back to the tunnel. And then a second whistle blast, followed by a roar that shivered the land beneath us and echoed through the hills behind us. We didn't hear the shell until it was well on its way, and then the whirring whistle returned to us. As the shell noise faded into the distance, another whistle blast and the second gun fired, again shaking the ground, knocking dead branches from trees, and rattling our eardrums.

Throughout this, a German officer on the opposite bank studied the skies through binoculars, searching for approaching aircraft. His shrill whistle interrupted the second loading. The barrels swung back to parallel the tracks just as the small engines pushed the guns back into the tunnel, the crews scurrying after them, scattering branches over the tracks as they ran.

The noise subsided and we heard the distant drone of planes searching vainly for the firing spot. Unless the planes had been directly above the guns with the ability to look straight down, the surrounding hills and cliffs would have hidden the muzzle flashes and distorted the sound direction. We knew now why Anzio Annie had not been found before.

Sarge rolled over on his back and stared at the sky through half-leafed trees. "Those are two grand dames," he said.

"Dames? You have names for these guns, Sergeant?" Ralph asked.

"We call them both Annie," Sarge said.

"Interesting," Ralph said. "Yanks always seem to give women's names to important things. My father said in the last war it was 'Big Bertha.' The Germans give them men's names. I had a glass of wine one day with a German soldier in a pub in Ciampino, and he said they called the big guns Robert and Leopold. He was drunk and probably said more than he should have said, and he buttoned up after that. Still, I don't see what it hurts for me to know their names."

"Did he say anything about their routines?"

"No. Sorry. But I do not particularly enjoy Nazi company, and I left at first opportunity. I didn't want to attract attention, of course. I doubt if he would have said more, anyway. Just said he worked on the guns every morning."

"We'll have to go in early in the morning," Sarge said. "Surely they sleep. And they probably feel safe, so the guards will be few. We'll duck in before they wake up. We shouldn't need more than ten minutes. In and out. That fast." Obviously Sarge was talking himself into it.

"I guess there's no use asking what you plan to do," Ralph said.

"That's right. Don't ask. What I'd like to do is seal that tunnel for once and for all, but that would take more explosive than we could carry. Probably take more time than we have, too. But we have an alternative."

"Anything I can do?"

"Lead us back to your villa for a few hours' rest. We'll try to sneak in about four in the morning. Before daylight anyway. We probably won't see you again, even if we're successful. Tomorrow morning you listen for airplanes, and if you hear any, get down to the basement. We'll be long gone, if our luck holds."

After a fitful night, we readied our packs and blackened our faces. We crept down the side of the hill from which we had watched the gun movements. We followed the track toward the tunnel. There was only one guard at the tunnel entrance. We could hear two more talking above near the villa, but they seemed unconcerned. And we left the machine-gun nest intact.

Sandy crept up behind the tunnel guard, clapped his hand over the guard's mouth, and drew his stiletto across his throat. Sarge motioned to me and Mouse to carry the body back up the hill. We would take him with us. Better the Germans suspect he was perhaps a deserter than to find his body and know we had been in the vicinity.

Sarge gave Jersey one of the pre-set beacons. The Germans would still be at breakfast or morning chores, and they might not even miss the guard until much later. Meantime our Marauders or Mustangs would have three morning hours to search out and follow the beacons. Sarge motioned Jersey to take the far side of the track and to plant the beacon under the first gun carriage. Sarge would move to the second gun and fasten the beacon to the closest wheels. Sarge stationed Bull on the far side of the track to cover Jersey's back, Joe on his side. Sandy was charged with watching the guards by the villa in case they had a patrol route that brought them our way.

Inside the cave, in addition to the two guns and their engines, were a bunk car and a kitchen-diner. Snoring from the bunk car indicated that some of the gun crews slept in the tunnel and not in the villa. Cooks in the kitchen-diner car were already working under generator lights, preparing breakfast. Their noise was enough to cover the footsteps from GI boots. Sarge didn't move as far as the kitchen car and was in quick retreat in less than twenty seconds. He followed Jersey up the hill and collapsed in an attempt to recover his breath. Maybe it was the exertion of scooting up the hill, but I suspected most of his shortness of breath was pure fear. At least mine was. Sarge recovered his feet, Bull handed me his BAR and slung the dead German over his shoulder, and the seven of us began a double-time retreat cross-country to meet the Lanuvio line we had followed yesterday.

We were in largely uncontested hill country. Sheep grazed peacefully, indifferent to our presence, and farmers stared in unconcerned disbelief at passing soldiers. It was picture-postcard peace, untrammeled by boots and untargeted by guns. We dumped the German in a small cave a half-mile away from his base. He would probably never be found.

Sarge took time out to radio Thin Man of the beacon settings beneath the villa and shrugged when Thin Man responded, "Good work, Red Dog."

Now we had to hope that the radio beacons would not be found. "And," Sarge added, "that the signals would not be swallowed up in the tunnel." We hadn't thought of that. Could the radio signals penetrate the hill? Or bounce out of the tunnel mouth? If not, the whole exercise could have been for naught. And our footfalls seemed heavier, more tired. The sun was well risen when we stopped for a break, estimating we were far enough away from the tunnel to escape detection. Our spirits were not exactly high, and even Jersey skipped his usual banter.

But then, a little after seven o'clock, we saw a formation of Mustangs bank sharply overhead and begin steep dives over our shoulders. We heard the distant thuds of thousand-pound bombs and we pictured them skipping into the tunnel entrance before exploding. At least the Germans might be a long time digging out. We knew that the Mustangs had been specially rigged to fly slower and lower, and the bombs were primed with delayed fuses so they'd bounce before exploding. Red Dog luck and fly-boy skill might just leave a dent in Robert and Leopold.

Two days later, after eluding a dozen German patrols and fighting our way past one road block, leaving four dead Nazis, we broke into the Via Anziate below Aprilia. We left Sandy at a battalion aid station and, driven by visions of Antonio's wine, a shower, a hot meal, and a good night's sleep, probably in that order, trudged happily back to our bunker.

The shelling continued during that two-day march, even as we dragged ourselves back, but the freight-train roar of the Anzio Express seemed to be missing. The larger shells were probably coming from the railroad-mounted two-tens, but they didn't seem as frightening as the bigger shells from the Annies.

Major House waited for the recon photos to come in from the airfields near Naples before saying anything about our mission. With photos and analyses in hand, he hurried over to congratulate us. Everyone seemed to agree that the aerial shots showed extensive damage to the track and tunnel entrance—and presumably to the guns inside. The underground reported that the guns had not been dragged out of their hole. We wouldn't hear from Anzio Annie for quite some time, if ever again.

House also said that since we knew now where the two-tens were hiding, we could go back out and plant radio beacons on them as soon as we rested up. We knew he meant it, but at least he smiled when he said it.

CHAPTER SIXTEEN

For almost four months the extended beachhead varied little from its seven-mile depth and twenty-mile length. The front see-sawed weekly, but no significant land gained by either side was held for more than a few days. The excreta of a war, so concentrated and so intense in an area so confined for so long, accumulated beyond comprehension, wherever we looked in these few square miles, we saw only twisted metal, broken tree trunks, roofless buildings, dead animals, and more often than we thought possible, an overlooked human arm or leg.

Even looking seaward for a refreshing study of pristine waters, we saw only waterbug barges scurrying among anchored Liberty ships and maneuvering cruisers, sprayed by plumes of water raised by splashing shells from the German big guns or errant bombs from German planes.

All day, all night, the smell of cordite, human waste, and death filled the air. The screams of machine gun bullets, passing shells, and agonizing pain echoed between the hills. Senses were continuously assaulted. Sanity was held tenuously.

Almost a sense of relief greeted the Major's suggestion a few days later that we go out again and mark the two-ten railroad guns for dive bombers. We knew now where we were going, how to get there, and what we would find. Planting radio direction signalers might be a challenge, but just to spend some time once again among the greening hills and tumbling brooks would be as good a "rest and relaxation" break as a three-day pass to the Isle of Capri. With packs laden with the new plastic explosive and a half-dozen radio beepers, we left our six-by on the Via Anziate and struck out in the direction of mine fields and patrols.

And we were alone. Where we had crawled past entrenched troops a week ago, we now walked unchallenged past empty foxholes and deserted bunkers. The grounds were littered with loose packs, gas masks, extra clothing, ration boxes, as if a wild and undirected evacuation of the area had been necessitated by a black tornado.

We circled back around Aprilia—the Factory—to the Via Anziate again, expecting to be challenged at any minute by German patrols. Again, there was no perimeter guard. Nearing the road, we heard the steady rumble of trucks and tracked vehicles hurrying north, away from the heavy artillery barrages following them out of the Factory. German soldiers trooped by in nondescript assemblies. Ambulances scooted among and around them. Anything mobile was piled with bodies, wounded, and fortunate riflemen. Was this a full retreat or a sudden regrouping of forces prior to a renewed German assault?

Major House had briefed us on an intended assault up the Via Anziate. It would be an attempt to weaken the German hold on the Gustav line, particularly around Cassino, by threatening to cut off their Route Six supply line from Rome. If we could break through to Route Six, their major escape route would also be cut.

We voiced our displeasure with the plan, and Major House didn't seem too enthusiastic about it anyway. The Germans were heavily entrenched around Via Anziate and we had lost thousands of the British First Division and our Forty-fifth Division in three earlier attempts to get past the Factory. The Major seemed to suggest that the new assault would not be much more effective.

We knelt behind sparse spring foliage and watched the stream of marching camouflaged and grey uniforms and towed howitzers moving erratically and hurriedly back toward Campoleone. We were not thoroughly hidden from the passing parade and even a side glance in our direction would have alerted the passing troops, bringing us at least a fusillade of Mauser fire. But they seemed thoroughly intent on their hasty evacuation of the area.

Sarge motioned to Mouse to bring up the radio. He adjusted dials and switches, and in a voice blanketed by tramping boots and rumbling vehicles he called "Thin Man, this is Red Dog. Come in, Thin Man. Red Dog calling." Three more calls and five minutes later, he received a response.

"Red Dog, this is Thin Man. Over."

"On Via Anziate, north of Aprilia. Mass exodus. German troops and equipment moving north. Advise. Over."

"Hold on, Red Dog. Similar reports from other sectors. Proceed with mission. Will get back to you. Over and out."

Sarge stared at the dead radio. "Headquarters doesn't know what's going on, either," Sarge said. "I think we're on our own. We'd better get out of here." Heavy artillery fire began following the fleeing Germans, then occasionally landing in their midst. The Germans kept hurrying north, more concerned with outrunning the artillery than trying to hide from it. We backed off to the west as waves of fighter planes buzzed the road, strafing the convoys and now driving foot soldiers into the side ditches. This was no place for Red Dog. We scurried westward, looking for a less dangerous route north, hoping to circle around Campoleone.

We were following a dirt farm road when the rumble of a motor vehicle coming up behind us forced us into the side trees. A German staff car with a driver and a junior officer came by and stopped a few feet past us. Driver and officer left the car on either side and walked to the opposite edges of the road, their backs to each other. Simultaneously the noise of splashing water rose from each side of the road, loud enough to cover the approaching footsteps of Sandy and Jersey coming up behind the car and then behind each of the Germans. A quick flash of knives left two more dead Germans in bloody piles beside the road as we congregated at the car and began squeezing the seven us into the small vehicle. Joe took the wheel, with Mouse and Sarge beside him on the front bench.

"You can drive this, Joe?" Sarge asked.

"Of course," Joe said. "Anyone could. It's a Mercedes-Benz. Standard shift. Just don't ask me how to turn on the windshield wipers." Joe waved at an array of unlabeled buttons and switches on the dashboard, turned the ignition switch, and shifted smoothly into what he hoped would be first gear. It was, and we were moving quickly north again, some two miles west of the beleaguered Via Anziate and praying that no scouting Mustang or Lightning fighter would spot a moving staff car to the left of their strafing runs. Red Dog luck held.

We crossed the railroad tracks northwest of Campoleone and headed cross-country to Route Seven and then farther east to find the rail line that circled the Alban hills. One of the heavy gun trains sped past us just as we reached the line. It was heading toward Rome without concern for side lines or camouflage. Given the bright skies now filled with Twelfth Air Force planes, odds were that it wouldn't reach Ciampino. Joe worked his way over the rail and turned so that we bounced along the ties straddling one rail until we reached one of the camouflaged sidings. Sarge had us move the branches and shrubs that hid the side track and we pulled under the canvas and netting to study the map.

Sarge had Mouse set the radio on the hood of the car, called Thin Man again, and this time received a less hectic but still excited response. Sarge gave our map coordinates and reported that the rail guns seem to be fleeing toward Rome.

"Forget the rail guns," Thin Man replied. "All hell's breaking loose. The Polish Second Corps has taken Cassino and the US Second Corps has broken through on Route Seven. The Germans are fleeing the Gustav line. They'll be trying to regroup along the Caesar line, which is just about where you are. Report any sightings of large troop movements. Over."

"Sir, if we can drive due east to Route Five we can trap most of them before they can set up on the Caesar line. We could link up with the British Eighth on the east coast and have most of them trapped. Over."

"Negative, Red Dog. Our orders are to turn north. Take Rome. Over."

"Rome? With all due respect, sir, that's not important. We can take Rome anytime. The Germans are trying to come up on our east. We should be after them, not Rome. Rome will always be there. Fleeing Germans are in disarray. Now's the time to get 'em. Over."

"Agreed, Red Dog. But it's not our call. Give us force reports as requested. The Forty-fifth is heading to Rome. General Clark will be here to go in with them. Over and out."

Sarge sighed and replaced the receiver. "We win by losing again," he muttered to himself. Another three-car gun train sped by, heading north, and not twenty feet from us. The engineer stared at us in amazement as he ran past, but he was out of sight before he could react. A Mustang swept low from the southern sky and followed the train up the tracks. It, too, curved out of sight around the hills but we heard the muffled echoes of twenty-millimeter cannon from the north.

"We going to Rome, Sarge?" Jersey asked.

"Nope," Sarge said. "Remember the old saying: See Rome and die?"

"I thought it was Venice," Joe said.

"Or maybe Paris," Jersey said.

"Whatever it was," Sarge said. "We'll see Rome in a couple of weeks. Right now, we're going to see Route Five."

We left the tracks, turned southeast, and headed cross-country again. Joe maneuvered the Mercedes around sink holes and hillocks, along ravines and gullies, through freshly planted farm fields and scrub forests. In the back, we jiggled and bounced, holding onto the side rails and each other to maintain our balance. After a couple of hours, we were about to suggest that walking would be easier on the kidneys when Joe pointed to the gas gauge and pulled over to a stand of fruit trees.

"Are we carrying a jerry can?" Joe asked. We scrambled out, convinced it would take all seven of us to determine whether a spare gas can was hooked on the back.

Sarge unbuckled the can from the rear bumper, lifted it easily, and shook it. "No more than a gallon or two," he said. He unscrewed the cap and sniffed it. "How far will that get us?"

"On this road," Joe quipped, "not to the next gas station."

"Take ten," Sarge said. He poured the gasoline into the Mercedes tank.

"I'll need twenty," Jersey said.

"For that, make it five," Sarge replied. He spread maps on the hood of the car and studied the surroundings, trying to find our location. "It'll be a long walk back," he said.

We milled around, stretching our legs, welcoming the views of a war-free territory. The trees were whole, not stripped and splintered. The fields were furrowed by plows, not artillery. Pastures were dotted with cows or crowded with sheep. Every farm building we had passed was intact, with glass panes in the windows. The only things missing were people—farm hands, house wives, children. Only seven unkempt, drab GIs populated the pastoral setting. Our presence seemed obscene.

In time Sarge called "Mount up," and we clambered aboard again and set out along a weedy tractor trail alongside a field sprouting early hay. We came to a deep gully running northeast, too deep to cross, and Joe followed the rim, looking for the gully's end. A *Whoomp-WHAM* lifted the right front of the Mercedes and spilled us out onto the field.

"Mortar!" Sarge called. "Cover." And we crawled over the side of the gully and huddled for cover.

"All okay?" Sarge called. We took stock. No one hurt. The spill was worse than the mortar round, but we had no breaks or sprains. "Now, where did that come from?"

Sarge looked east over the far rim of the gully. A straight row of Italian poplar trees ran north to south not too far distant, and a second row of poplars paralleled the first further out. A low hedge row ran between the trees as far as the eye could see in either direction. Sarge could see no movement. "That must be Route Five," he said. Route Five was the most eastern of three trunks that ran south-north toward Rome. With Route Seven and Six being cut by advancing GIs, the Germans would have to swing east from the Gustav line and take Route Five to get to Rome and beyond. Sarge hoped to be able to radio troop movements. "But, first, where's that mortar?"

"Wherever it is," Sandy said, "it'll be searching for us soon. We gotta' get out of here."

"Up or down?" Sarge said, pointing along the short gully. Either direction kept us in mortar range and above the gully put us in rifle range.

"Straight across to those trees," Sandy said. Before Sarge could interrupt, Sandy sprang to the rim of the gully and started across the field toward the poplars. The chatter of a machine gun, along with a score of rifle shots, stitched across his chest. Sandy staggered backward from the force of the bullets and collapsed back into the gully. He lay there staring at the sky.

I scooted over to judge his wounds. Sarge cradled Sandy's head, as blood trickled from his mouth. I unbuttoned his harness and shirt. A line of bullet holes spewed blood from his chest. I looked at Sarge and shook my head. Not a chance, I wanted to say.

"Money belt," Sandy coughed and gurgled. "Four hundred. For Mama. For Anita. Tell her I'm sorry."

"Anita?" Sarge said. "You mean....You? Anita?"

"I . . .I...Panic. She screamed. Sorry. Tell Mama. Sorry." Sandy's head fell to the side.

Sarge closed Sandy's eyes and lowered his head to the ground. I unstrapped Sandy's now-bloody money belt and re-strapped it around my waist. "Can you believe that?" I stammered.

"Yes," Sarge said. He looked back over the rim of the gully. "Bull," he called. "Scoot over here. Bring the BAR." He studied the poplars from behind a small green shrub that grew on the edge of the gully. "Bull," he said, "you see that black spot, that dark hole, about ten feet up in that poplar straight ahead?"

Bull looked through the leaves of another low bush. "Yeah," Bull said

"There's a machine gun up there. I saw the muzzle flash. Don't ask me how they get a machine gun up a tree. Must be well strapped. Anyway, I figure if you put a BAR burst just below that dark spot, you'll hit whoever's behind that gun."

"I guess so," Bull said. He leveled his BAR over the rim of the gully, set it for automatic, and sent a clip of bullets into the tree. The branches shook as a heavy weight fell branch by branch to the ground below. "That's for Sandy," Bull said. A few Mausers responded but there was no machine gun chatter.

A mortar responded too. A *Whoomp-WHAM* echoed from the lower end of the gully. Joe and Mouse yelped in pain as shrapnel tore into them. I started to crawl down to treat their wounds, and a second *Whoomp-WHAM* came from behind me. I turned to watch Sarge and Bull and then Jersey double over.

I heard the whine of airplane engines diving toward the poplar trees and I fancied the clatter of heavy machine guns.

A third *Whoomp-WHAM*, close to where the second shell had landed, splashed blood over me and Mouse, and someone's steel helmet banged against my shoulder. Mouse dropped his radio. He seemed to weave back and forth, held his hand out to me for help, and then fell slowly sideways.

A fourth Whoomp-WHAM seemed to come from the radio itself. I felt a hot poker draw across my forehead just beneath my helmet. I reached for Mouse, as he had reached toward me. And I held his hand. But he wasn't there.

Everything turned red.

I bent down to scratch my leg.

And everything turned black.

Epilogue

Everything was white. I sensed it even with my eyes closed. Cautiously I opened one eye, then the other. I was inside a small white cocoon with a plastic window that looked out on a white world. The ceiling was white. The walls were white. The drapes, the bed sheets, the blankets were white. So was the nurse standing beside my bed.

A nurse. All in white. Not an angel. I wasn't dead. Maybe she was an angel, too, but I knew now I was alive. She pushed aside the windowed-flap of the tent, and stared intently into my eyes.

"You're awake," she said. I didn't want to answer. It had to be obvious to any fool that I was awake. When she received no answer to her implied question, she said, "Hang on. The doctor wants to see you. Stay comfortable." She spooned a bit of crushed ice between my lips. That's the kind of thing angels do. I closed my eyes again. Waking up brought me no comfort.

"Hello, there." A deep voice. "Can you hear me?" I opened my eyes again. Evidently the doctor the nurse had spoken of. He smiled. "Ah, that's better. Can you tell me your name?"

My mouth was dry. I swabbed my tongue back and forth. "Boots," I said.

"You don't need them right now. We'll save them for you. What's your name?"

This wasn't getting anywhere either. "Boots," I repeated, and the doctor just sighed. He leaned forward and directed a small flashlight beam into my eyes. He checked some figures on a clip-board and studied some instruments that seemed to be extensions of me connected with wires, tubes, and straps.

"Wh...where?" I managed to squeak.

"You're in a hospital."

"Wh...where?" I repeated. Why were people so dense these days?

"Naples," the doctor said. "Do you know where Naples is?"

Dense and stupid. It seemed to take all my breath but I muttered, "Italy."

"Good," the doctor said, as if relieved that Naples hadn't been moved to some other country. "There's someone who has been coming by every day to see you. He's waiting outside." The doctor nodded to the nurse, who left the room.

"Every day?" I repeated. "How...how long..."

"Today's June fifth," the doctor said. "Do you remember when you were hit?"

Oh, so that was it. I was hit. When would that have been? I searched my memory. As I recalled we were driving cross-country. When? We had lost familiarity with calendars. Wounded or hale, we treated all days the same, blended together, melding into one long, unending, day-night continuum. The last I remembered was May something. Late May, probably. Thirtieth? Maybe. I couldn't figure.

The nurse returned, followed by a face I recognized. I smiled. "Major," I managed.

"Hello, Holt. I've been waiting for you to wake up. Glad to see you looking so fine. I wanted to say thanks for a job well done."

"How long...have...I been...here...?"

The Major hesitated. "You've been out of it for six days now. We were worried at first, but I knew you'd make it. Do you feel up to talking?"

"Try," I said. "How did I get here?"

"Fighter planes spotted you being belted. They wiped out the firing line and called in medical evacuation teams. The teams got to you within a couple of hours, thank god."

"And I've been here, Doc said, six days? How's the fight?"

"The Germans have all fled north. General Clark is leading the parade into Rome today."

"We took Rome?"

"Yep. Minor street skirmishes, but most Germans had fled."

"Finally," I muttered. "Forty miles in four months. Some *blitzkreig,* huh?"

Major House looked over his shoulder and then lowered his voice. "And the pipe line says it's likely, weather permitting, Eisenhower's going into Europe tomorrow."

"An invasion without Red Dog? Doesn't sound right." I stammered.

"Question, Corporal," he said. "When you were brought in, you were wearing two money belts. Who's is the second one?"

"That's for Mama Camistrata," I managed to stammer out. "From Sandy. Because of Anita. Close the books."

"Oh, so that's it. Sorry to hear about Corporal Bricker. I guess he's paid up in full."

"He's dead, isn't he?" I managed.

"Yes," the Major spoke softly. "Yes, he's dead. I know the family you mean. Annetta and her brother and her son. She does my laundry. I heard Anita sing once. If you'll trust me, I'll see that Annetta gets the money."

"I should take it," I said. "I think Sandy wants me to apologize for him."

"I'll explain for you. You're not going back to Anzio. We were just waiting for you to wake up. You're on the next hospital ship back to the States. They're waiting for you at Walter Reed. They do excellent work with prosthetics."

"Pros...pros..."

The Major cast his eyes down to the foot of my bed. "I'm sorry," he said. "Really. I thought you knew. I'm sorry. It's your left foot. Badly mangled, I'm afraid. By the time the medical team got to you all, you'd lost a lot of blood. We were afraid you wouldn't make it. But you're strong. The foot couldn't make it though. But you'll be fine in no time. Good as new. They do wonders at Reed." Major House picked up a scrap of metal, about the size of his thumb, from the bedside table. "I thought you might want a souvenir. They took this out of your forehead."

Now I became aware of the bandages. One around my head, throbbing heavily. One on my left hand, unfelt. And a big one on what was left of my exposed left leg, tingling sleepily. Tears began to interfere with my vision. Major House hurried to change the subject.

"Incidentally, you're going home a corporal. General Truscott's order. A promotion for each of you, in fact. Red Dog did outstanding work."

"Joe won't appreciate that," I said slowly.

"Corporal Coffey," the Major said, then hastened to amend it, "now Sergeant Coffey, won't object."

"The Joe I know would. Are you saying...?"

The Major shook his head and looked at the doctor, who was standing by with a large syringe. He nodded. "Yes," he said, "Coffey is dead. You might as well know, you are the only survivor. You are Red Dog now, and we'll never use the name again."

I felt the tears burning as images floated through my mind. Sarge. Twangy Jersey. Drawling Mouse. And that "big dumb Indian" Bull. Gone? Gone. Along with Joe. And Sandy, of course. My mouth began to quiver. The doctor moved in and inserted the syringe in a tube leading to my wrist. In a minute I was asleep again. I'd take my time before I woke again. Red Dog's luck was all mine now. I didn't want it.

End

CPSIA information can be obtained at www.ICGtesting.com
Printed in the USA
LVOW07s1713071215

465786LV00003B/509/P

9 781424 171637